BENEATH

THE

MARIGOLDS

EMILY C. WHITSON

BENEATH

THE

MARIGOLDS

CamCat
Books

CamCat Publishing, LLC
Brentwood, Tennessee 37027
camcatpublishing.com

This is a work of fiction. Names, characters, places, and incidents are either products of the author's imagination or are used fictitiously.

Hardcover ISBN 9780744304206
Paperback ISBN 9780744304213
Large-Print Paperback ISBN 9780744304220
eBook ISBN 9780744304237
Audiobook ISBN 9780744304268

Library of Congress Control Number: 2021939006

Cover and book design by Maryann Appel

5   3   1   2   4

For all the Marigolds in my life.
Thank you, today and every day.

PART
1

Prologue

knew too much. On that island, on that godforsaken singles' retreat.
I knew too much.

I ruminated on that thought, chewing it carefully, repeatedly, while Magda, the makeup artist, transformed me into a life-size nightmarish porcelain doll. Ghastly white face, penciled-in eyebrows, blood-red lips. I'd look beautiful from a distance, she had told me, leaving the other part of the sentence unspoken: *up close, it's frightening.* She tsked as she dabbed my damp forehead for the fourth time, her Russian accent thickening with frustration.

"Vhy you sweating so much?"

I worried my voice would come out haggard, so I shrugged, a little too forcefully. Magda shook her head, her pink bob sashaying in the grand all-white bathroom as she muttered something foreign under her breath. My gaze danced across the various makeup brushes on the vanity until it landed on one in particular. I shifted my weight in the silk-cushioned chair, toyed with my watch.

"Magda, what do you want out of this retreat?"

No response.

Did she not hear me, or did she choose not to respond? In the silence, I was able to hear Christina's high-heeled feet outside the bathroom.

Click, clack. Click, clack.

When I first met the host of the singles' retreat, I was in awe of her presence, her unflappable poise. Shoulders back, she walked with a purpose, one foot in front of another, and though she was a couple inches shorter than I was, she seemed larger than life. Her icy eyes, colored only the faintest shade of blue, seemed to hold the secrets of the world—secrets she intended to keep. But I had stumbled upon them just a few short hours before, and I was now afraid her gait represented something more sinister: the march of an executioner.

Click, clack. Click, clack.

Her stride matched the even tick of my watch, and a drop of sweat trickled down my back. Was I being ridiculous? Surely Christina wouldn't hurt me. She had been reasonable with me earlier, hadn't she?

"One meenute," Magda shouted at the retreat's host. She doused my fire-red curls in hairspray one last time before asking me if I was ready to go.

"I just need to use the bathroom." I wheezed through shallow breaths. "I'll be right out."

Magda exaggerated her sigh before shuffling out of the white-marble immurement, closing the doors behind her with a huff. My last remnants of safety and rational thinking left with her.

I shoved the vanity chair underneath the door handle. I grabbed the makeup brush with the flattest head and hurried to the bathroom. I gingerly closed the lid of the toilet and slipped off my heels before tiptoeing on top so I could face the window. After removing the beading, I inserted the head of the makeup brush between the frame and glass. The brush's handle cracked under the pressure, but it was enough to lever the glass out of its mounting. I placed the glass on the floor as gently as I've ever handled any object, trying not to make even the slightest sound, before hoisting myself up and through the window. I jumped into the black night, only partially illuminated by the full moon and the artificial lights of the mansion. I allowed my eyes to adjust.

And then I ran.

The loose branches of the island forest whipped at my cheeks, my limbs, my mouth. The soles of my feet split open from fallen twigs and other debris, but the adrenaline kept the pain at bay. I tripped over something unseen, and my hands broke my fall. Just a few cuts, and a little blood. I couldn't see it, but I could feel it.

I jumped up, forcing myself to keep moving. The near darkness was blinding, so I held my bloody hands up, trying to block my face. The farther I ran, the more similar the trunks of the trees became. How long had I been running? I gauged about a mile. I slowed down to gather my bearings. Behind me, the lights of the mansion brightened the sky, but they were only the size of my palm from that distance.

I heard the hum of a moving car come and go. I must have been near the road. I was about to start moving again when I heard the snap of twigs. Footsteps. I stopped breathing. I swiveled to my left and right, but nothing. I exhaled. It was just my imagination. I continued away from the lights. Away from the retreat.

And then someone stepped toward me: Christina. Her face was partially obscured by darkness, but her pale eyes stood out like fireflies.

"It doesn't have to be like this," she said. Her expression remained a mystery in the darkness.

I turned around, but one of her handlers was blocking that path.

Christina took another step forward, and I jerked away, tripping over the gnarled roots of the forest in the process. My head broke the fall this time, and my ears rang from the pain.

Her handler reached for my left hand, and for a moment, I thought he was going to help me stand. Instead, he twisted my ring finger into an unnatural position. As my bone cracked, my screams reverberated through the woods.

It was showtime.

1: Ann

'm an attorney. A corporate attorney, to be precise—not the kind most often portrayed in books and movies. I don't go to court, and I don't deal with murderers. I close deals—mergers and acquisitions, mostly—behind my desk in the quiet of my office. In layman's terms: I help people buy and sell companies. It's not quite as dramatic as the life of a trial attorney, but it's safe, it pays well, and now that I'm a partner, I can dedicate some of my time to matters closer to my heart. But like a trial attorney—and all good attorneys, really—I spend my day combing through facts.

As such, here are the facts: Reese Marigold has been missing for thirty-one days.

She had been scheduled to arrive in Nashville after a four-week stay at an exclusive singles' retreat. Flight records indicate she boarded her plane as scheduled, and several witnesses recall seeing a woman on the flight who matched Reese's description: midthirties, red hair, about five-four. She was hard to miss: she had donned a bubblegum-pink jumpsuit, keeping the hood up and sunglasses on throughout the flight. I remember seeing this eccentric outfit as I waited for Reese at the airport, but I knew from the body language and gait it wasn't Reese. The police think I could have been mistaken, though, so they asked a few witnesses about this rose-clad woman. Apparently she was as quiet as she was eye-catching, ignoring anyone who spoke to her.

"Again," I huffed in the interview room at the police station, "that's not Reese. Reese can talk to a wall. She's a social butterfly." I threw my hands up in exasperation, but no one in the room seemed to care.

Once the flight landed in Nashville, video footage from airport security shows "Reese" disembarking the plane, collecting her single bag, and heading for ground transportation. She did not make any other stops before getting into the backseat of a beat-up 1992 Ford Festiva. The car was tagless and had tinted windows, so it was impossible to track. A tip led the police to the car three days later near the Riverfront Park, burned to a crisp, ashes littering the ground like confetti. Only the charred remains of a suitcase were inside.

Forensic technicians believe the car was wiped clean before it exploded, although it was difficult to know for certain. Reese's wallet and cell phone were found about thirty feet away, concealed in the overgrown grass.

Her cell-phone history didn't reveal much. There was a missed call from an ex-boyfriend, Luca Ferrari, made two weeks before the retreat started. Reese's relationship with Luca had ended seven years prior, but since Reese was granted an order of protection after Luca attacked her, he was automatically suspect.

To my relief and disappointment, Luca has a rock-solid alibi. He also lives two thousand miles away in Los Angeles—has for six years now.

Police interviewed several other men who had relationships with Reese, but each was occupied during the crucial window of opportunity.

There was one noteworthy text. For the entire duration of the singles' retreat, Reese sent only one message, which was to an unknown number on the last day of her stay. Her radio silence wasn't considered unusual, as the retreat forbids the use of media in an attempt to force participants to focus on "the journey." The message read: *I need to get away. Pick me up at the Nashville airport tomorrow at noon.*

The police contacted the phone carrier of the unregistered phone number, but it was determined to be a burner phone. There were no outgoing calls or messages, no history of any kind, except for the single incoming text from Reese. The burner was discovered with her mobile and wallet in the park.

I found all of this disconcerting, especially her silence toward me. The police didn't share my concern, though, as perhaps she was upset that I hadn't attended the retreat with her. She had, after all, been urging me to go. She had even filled out an application for me, earning me a spot on the island along with her. *We could get engaged at the same time,* she had pleaded. For Reese's sake, I pretended to consider. Of course, I didn't go; that wasn't my thing. So Reese went alone. A hopeless romantic, she was always on a mission to find her next man, her miracle, and her latest obsession was this singles' retreat.

So if things didn't go as planned, if she didn't find love, perhaps she was taking out her frustration on me, police supposed. I told them that was ridiculous. In the ten years I've known Reese, I can count on my two hands the number of times I've seen Reese angry. Afraid, yes. Sad, definitely. But petty? Absolutely not. She would never let my worry fester like this over something like not going on a trip with her.

No, something had to have happened on that island. Something terrible.

Right from the start, I knew the retreat seemed too good to be true. Isolated on its own private island, about a ten-minute plane ride from Honolulu, Last Chance was established with the sole intention of helping people find *true love*. A *soulmate*. Give me a break. I begged the police to investigate, but because the island is outside their jurisdiction, there is only so much they can do without more probable cause.

And besides, they said, Reese wanted to disappear, according to her last text message. She told an employee at the retreat that an associate of hers helped people get out of town. And according to her mom, she ran away countless times in her youth. Before she joined Nashville's most prestigious dance company, she had trouble with drugs and alcohol. Never mind that she had a turbulent childhood, or that she's been sober for twelve years. Never mind that she's helped me, and many others, find solace through Alcoholics Anonymous. Never mind that she was my sponsor in AA for ten years, my closest friend, the only real family I've had since my parents passed. To the police, Reese was flighty–shady.

A drunk.

So the investigation dwindled. Life moved on. But not for me. For the past thirty-one days, I have been swimming in the facts of Reese's disappearance. My mind has been laser-focused on her last movements— primarily on the retreat. I haven't eaten, haven't slept. Twice I've awoken to the sound of an ambulance, after passing out from unbearable chest pain, and twice I've been told I had suffered severe panic attacks.

I only began to breathe semi-normally after I sent in my deposit to Last Chance.

I know something happened on that retreat, and I have every intention of finding out what.

2:Ann

Thirty-three minutes. That's how much time I have before I need to be at the airport. I pace back and forth outside my house as I wait for my friend Honey. The winter wind snakes through the carcasses of trees that line my quiet neighborhood like soldiers. My pulse quickens, too much, so I try to focus on a particular object.

Tick, tick, tick.

My eyes land on my new watch. A Rolex. I normally wouldn't buy something so extravagant, but I had just been promoted, and it reminded me of my mom. She had a similar style: a five-piece link metal bracelet, with three yellow-gold links flanked by a larger stainless-steel link on each side. It wasn't a real Rolex—our family couldn't afford that—but as far as knockoffs go, it was pretty good. She wore this watch on the day she and my father died, otherwise I would have worn hers. But like everything else in the car, the watch was destroyed, blown to bits, never to be recovered. I haven't been sleeping much lately, but when I do, I dream of my mother, rocking back and forth in the chair she loved so much. Just before I wake, she peers down at her left wrist and tells me I'm running out of time.

A car honks, three staccato bleats in quick succession, and I see Honey parked at the curb. She raises her hand in greeting, her five-carat-diamond engagement ring sparkling in contrast to the dull concrete of the winter road. Even with a toddler at home, she is meticulously made-up, not a hair out of place.

"I'm here," she shouts.

I settle into her brand-new Range Rover and inspect my oldest friend. As her name implies, everything about Honey is golden. Honey-blonde curls and honey-colored skin. Even her voice has a warm, mellifluous touch. Honey isn't her given name, but when she was about the age of three, her family decided the nickname was a better fit.

A lot of women don't like Honey. With her magazine-cover face, her family's money, and a propensity to take what she wants, no holds barred, she can be intimidating. None of this stuff ever bothered me, though. She can't help how she looks, she can't choose her family, and I admire the go-getter attitude. I'll admit, sometimes I do need a breather. Like when she got engaged. *That* was a nightmare; we didn't talk for almost a year after that. But as with any old friend, you return to each other because of the comfort of shared history.

Honey could be an asshole, but she was *my* asshole. Her parents died around the same time as mine, and with her older sister out of the picture, we were both in desperate need of some family—even if it was artificial.

"Ann." Honey sighs as she studies me. "You look like you haven't slept in a month."

"I haven't," I mumble.

She reaches in the back of the car for an overstuffed purse, some fancy designer bag that costs more than my car, and pulls out an item. "You're lucky I brought you some under-eye concealer."

"Thanks," I say as she tosses me an expensive-looking container. "Can you please start driving? I don't want to be late."

"All right, all right." She dumps the purse in the backseat and puts the car in drive.

I grip the door handle and the center console. I hate riding in cars. *Hate* it. If I must drive somewhere, I always drive myself. It's one of my ticks. But Honey insisted she take me to the airport. She thinks Reese's disappearance has unraveled me. That's why she came home early from her vacation.

I stare out the window as we traverse the empty Sunday streets. We've taken a back road near the park, and the path is lined with pine trees. Out of habit, I count the trees. *One, two, three.* A bird shrieks in the distance, and I realize Honey isn't speaking. That's unlike her. I study her in the driver's seat, hunched over, hands firmly at ten and two on the steering wheel.

"What's wrong?" I ask.

"Huh?" Honey glances at me before returning her gaze to the road.

"What's wrong? You're too quiet."

"Nothing, just trying to remember how to get there."

I narrow my eyes at her, as if by doing so I can read her mind.

"Okay, okay. Stop looking at me like that." She rolls her neck, pulls back her shoulders. "I'm just worried about you, is all. I know you can take care of yourself, and Reese is probably fine, but in case you are right, and something *did* happen on that island . . . I don't know. It just seems reckless to go there."

"I won't do anything rash. I just want to see the place for myself. Ask a few questions, discreetly."

Honey's shoulders hike up another inch. "Where did Reese even hear about this retreat, again?"

"She got some advertisement in the mail," I say, my mind returning to the fall afternoon when Reese showed me the glossy brochure.

"Look," she had said with bright eyes, "they're even giving away some spots for free in exchange for promotion after the trip. I'm going to fill out an application for both of us."

A couple weeks later, after hours and hours of filling out *very* detailed applications, Reese had secured those too-good-to-be-true spots on the island. One for her, and one for me.

Only, I'm going a month too late. My veins turn to ice at the memory.

"I thought you'd be happy I'm trying to date more," I huff, trying to change the subject.

"I'm not an idiot, Ann. I do want you to date more, but you're not going to Last Chance to be swept off your feet. This is just a ploy for you to do some amateur detective work."

"Don't you want to know what happened to Reese? I thought you liked her." I'm dancing around the subject, I know, but I'm too tired to get into another fight with Honey about going to the retreat. I should have just driven myself.

"I don't *dislike* her." Honey throws up her manicured hands, just for a moment, and I feel my stomach lurch at the sight of the empty steering wheel. "We just don't run in the same circles, is all. I'm not trying to hang out with a bunch of drunks all the time."

I cringe, and I see her do the same in my peripheral vision.

"I'm sorry, you know I didn't mean that."

"It's fine," I lie. I return my eyes to the window, the view outside getting darker.

"Well, you brought your second phone, right? I know they don't allow media during the stay, but I want you to call me if you get into trouble or have any doubts. I checked, and the woman who runs the place did install cell towers on the island. So call me. I mean it. The second you want to leave, I'll fly and come get you myself. Even if it's Christmas Day."

"Thanks, Honey," I mumble, even though there's no way in hell I'd ask her to come get me on Christmas Day. If I'm honest with myself, the timing of the retreat was alluring—the thought of spending the holiday alone, without my parents, without Reese, is almost too much to bear.

"Are you sure you don't want me to pick you up anyway? We aren't using the plane the weekend you're supposed to come back, and it's better than you having to make a pit stop in Hawaii."

"I'm sure." She's trying, but I don't have the energy. I just want her to stop looking at me before—

Something crashes into the right side of Honey's car.

Honey slams on the brakes. We pitch forward. The seat belt cuts into my chest, and I can't breathe. My fingernails dig into the center console and the door handle. After what seems like an eternity, Honey grabs my hand.

"Are you okay?"

I nod. My voice comes out in ragged breaths. "What was that?"

"I don't know."

"Pull over and put on your hazards," I wheeze. "I'll check."

As Honey does so, I unbuckle my seat belt and open the door. I can't stand to be in the car for another second. I tumble outside. The car dings with the door open. My legs are weak; they barely hold me. I lean on my knees and inhale slowly. *I'm okay*, I tell myself. *Just breathe.*

I take a look around. There's a bowling ball-sized dent on the right side of the car. And blood—smears of it on the hood. I search the area for a wounded body, holding my breath for what I find.

Behind us, partially covered by pines, is a tuft of fur.

I exhale. Not a person.

I tiptoe farther into the pines. A deer. I don't want to get closer, but I need to see it.

When I see its caved-in mouth, I realize it's long gone. My stomach drops.

"It's okay, it's just a deer." I say the words, but my heart isn't in it. In the deer's blank eyes, I can't help but see Reese. I'm transfixed by the helpless animal, bile creeping up my throat, when a passing motorcycle breaks my trance.

Honey's now out of her car, cowered behind the hood, frozen.

"Did you hear me? It's just a deer," I repeat. "You're okay."

I can tell her mind is elsewhere. Honey's rarely shell-shocked.

"The deer is okay. Everything is fine."

I go to her side and rub her shoulder. She nods, just the slightest bit. I really need to get to the airport, but I don't want to leave her like this. I check the time to see if I can wait for the police. I hesitate before deciding I'd be cutting it too close.

"Honey, I'm going to call the police, then your husband, then an Uber. Okay?"

At that, her face snaps toward me. "The police? But you said the animal was fine?"

"Yes." I swallow. "But you need the police report for insurance."

Honey assesses the damage of her new Range Rover. "Fuck," she mutters. She rubs her face, takes a sharp inhale. Then, with more emphasis: "Fuck!"

"It's okay," I say as I pull out my phone. "They'll cover it since it's an accident."

"No."

"No, what?"

"No, don't call the police."

My thumb hovers over the dial button. I can't read her expression. "Why?"

"I don't want to be alone, in the dark, waiting for the police. And I don't want *you* to take an Uber to the airport. Insurance will cover it without a police report."

"Maybe, but don't you want to be safe?" I gesture to the dented hood. "You don't even know if it's safe to drive."

She strides to the driver's side and jerks open the door. "It's a small dent, we'll be fine."

I throw my hands up as she slams the door. Faintly, from inside the car, I hear her yell "Let's go!"

Sometimes it seems as if Honey lives in her own world, floating above the rest of us. I try to remember what my dad taught me about checking for car damage. No fuel leaks, no tire damage, no loose parts. From what I can tell, I don't see any safety hazards. Honey honks, and I slap the hood of her car in return, cussing her silently.

"Let me just take pictures of the damage," I mutter, "'cause I know you'll need them later." I snap a few shots with my phone as Honey honks a second time. I've never had a sister, but I imagine their feelings during a fight resemble ours right now.

"You can be so hardheaded," I say as I get in the car. Honey tries to buckle her seatbelt, but she misses. After a few seconds of struggling, she starts to jerk it, but it catches. She lets go, and the buckle cracks against the window. She grips the steering wheel and shakes it before laying on the horn.

"Fuck, fuck, fuck!" She screams in rhythm with the honks. When she finally calms down, she turns toward me. "This is a bad sign, Ann. I don't want you going on that retreat."

I nod. "I know."

She's right, but I can't turn back now. I'm too far gone.

PART

2

3:Reese

Eight Weeks Earlier

loved love.

I'd had far too many, and yet not quite enough lovers in my life when I arrived at Last Chance. Nothing beat the early stages of a new romance: the electrical charge in the air, the stolen glances, the all-consuming thought of *what's next*. The breathtaking first touch. Oh my, I got shivers down my spine just thinking about it.

At thirty-four, you'd think I would have been taken. I was an attractive, loyal woman with an uncontrollable need to please my man, by God. Sadly for me, I had an unfortunate combination of traits that made the settling-down-and-having-babies thing difficult. The first was I had terrible—and I mean *terrible*—taste in men. Slicked-back hair, eyes that rarely leave your breasts, a tendency to say, *Where's that smile?* I usually believed in the best in people, so I was quick to write off red flags as quirks, little eccentricities. (*Ha-ha!* Wasn't that so funny when he grabbed that waitress's behind?) Sure, hindsight is twenty-twenty, but at the time, I never realized how big of a loser each one of them was until the very end. And the irony—the real kick-you-in-the-shin cosmic humor of it all—is that all these men ended up resembling my dad. Unavailable. And like my mom, I chased after them anyway, regardless of the consequences.

The other less-than-favorable trait I possessed was a proclivity to believe a man, the *right* man, would solve all my problems. I know that's not really *en vogue* to admit in this postfeminist, #MeToo era of strong women supporting strong women, but let's get real: What heterosexual woman hasn't daydreamed about finding her Noah Calhoun or Peter Kavinsky? Those stories sell for a reason. Twenty-eight is the average marrying age of women in the United States *for a reason.* (Twenty-six if you live in Tennessee—lucky me!) And any tight-lipped, sexually frustrated woman who tells you they don't need a partner to make them happy is a bold-faced liar.

So when my home life became an untenable minefield, when my dancing wasn't quite up to par, when my affinity for alcohol and drugs became a little too apparent, I would always think, *The right man would make all of this go away.* Or, he'd at least make me happy enough to finally fix the other problems in my life.

And I never lost hope. Once a relationship went up in flames, I only let myself sulk for a day (or two). Just twenty-four hours to watch Nicholas Sparks movies on repeat, eat a pint (or two) of mint-chocolate-chip ice cream, and wear every cosmetic face mask in my possession. And then I'd find a new man.

Or rather, a new version of the same man. Every new beginning was more exciting and hopeful than the last. *This is it,* I would think. *This is the one I've been waiting for. My miracle.*

So attending Last Chance, a singles' retreat on a tropical island teeming with beautiful men was like being a kid in a candy shop. I was a shaken bottle of carbonation just waiting to pop.

That first day was perfect too. Not to sound trite, but a real dream come true. Even after thirteen hours of flying and three stops, I couldn't help but wrap my hands around the gorgeous driver who picked me up at the island airport. (Yes, I had *a driver*. Can you believe it?) I held his face between my palms and planted a big kiss on his pillow lips.

When I pulled back to witness his stunned expression, I realized my mistake. I heard Ann's voice in my head, telling me to *think things through, consider the consequences, maybe get to know the guy before jumping in feetfirst.* She was right. I needed to be smart now that I was here. I was going to find a respectful *and* respectable partner—for real this time. I couldn't go around kissing the first good-looking guy I saw.

"So sorry about that." I giggled nervously as I wiped the lipstick off his mouth. "I'm excited to be here, and I guess I got carried away."

"It's fine." He swallowed as he straightened his jacket. "I'm, uh, Dan. I'll take you to the mansion."

I rolled my window down as soon as I got in the luxury SUV. I had never been to the beach, never been outside of Tennessee, so I took in every sight and sound the island had to offer. The dancing palm trees. The Fruit Loops-colored birds. The intense rays of the sun, which bathed everything in a coat of diamonds. I had had a bad couple of months, but here, today, my luck was going to change. *I* was going to change.

When we stopped for gas, my mouth dropped at the sight of the sea on the other side of the pumps. The water stretched as far as the eye could see, its waves glimmering in the sun like jewels, and all my problems felt so small in comparison.

"I've never seen the ocean before." I was hanging out of the open window like a dog, trying to get as close as I could to this natural wonder.

"Really?" Dan asked with raised eyebrows.

"Would I . . . I mean, would it be okay if I walked to the beach while you're filling up? It's so close?"

"I . . ." He seemed hesitant. "We don't have a lot of time." Something in his demeanor softened when he met my gaze. I probably looked so eager, so desperate for something new and different. "If you go quickly."

I shoved the door open at record speed. "Thank you, thank you, thank you," I cried as I slipped off my sandals. I scurried quickly across the pavement until I felt the sand between my toes. I giggled at the foreign sensation, wriggling my calloused toes in the soft, white grains. All my worries seemed to dissipate with the salt air, so I inhaled deeply, hoping maybe it would heal my internal scars too.

Eventually Dan broke my trance, told me it was time to go. I didn't want to leave, but I had a whole month to enjoy the ocean. Plus, I didn't want to get Dan in trouble.

Driving Dan. That's what Ann would have named him. I sighed as my mind drifted back to my closest friend.

I wished she would've joined me. She was one of those *I-don't-need-no-man* women who acted so tough, with her ugly pantsuits and rigid posture, but I loved her anyway. Because I knew, deep down, she was fragile. And a part of me wanted to do for her what I wish someone had done for me: offer an unconditional friendship, unconditional love. I was going to help her climb the impossibly steep uphill battle of addiction recovery if it killed me. Because helping her was, in a way, helping myself.

I remembered the first time I took her to a party after she stopped drinking. It had taken hours of coaxing, weeks of planning, and still, when I arrived at her house to pick her up, she was in sweatpants.

"I changed my mind," she said, looking at her feet. "I can't do it."

"I know it's hard," I pleaded. And I *did* know. It was like seeing an ex-boyfriend for the first time since a breakup. You tried to chitchat with others, but you couldn't focus on the conversation because *he* was in the corner of your eye, flirting with someone else, having a good time, and, perhaps it's just your imagination, but was he stealing glances at you too?

You swore the whole room was looking at you two, waiting for the inevitable makeup, the inevitable catastrophe, and your skin felt hot from the endless cycle of temptation and perseverance and self-consciousness and anger and grief over what could have been.

But eventually, you learned to sit with the emotions, the unease. The pain became a background noise you learned to ignore.

"You have to start practicing," I pleaded. "It's been a *year*, Ann. It's time."

A film of tears covered Ann's green eyes, and she pushed a leaf around her outside stoop with her foot. I wanted to wrap my arms around her, but I knew she wasn't much of a hugger. I tried to think of something, even something small, that would help Ann feel more in control. Less trapped.

"How about this? You can drive yourself there—just follow me—and that way you can leave whenever you want. Stay five minutes, if that's all you can do."

Ann continued to toy with the leaf before she finally met my gaze.

"Just five minutes?"

"Five minutes. That's all I'm asking. And look," I twisted my hips, allowing the tiny bells on the end of my boho skirt to trill. "I'm wearing bells, so you can't lose me."

Ann laughed then, wiped her cheeks. And we went to the party.

She stayed only five minutes, but it was what she needed. Slowly but surely, she started going out more, staying out later. (And by later, I mean 9:00 p.m.) As long as she had her car, she could go to the most booze-infused party Nashville had to offer. Not that I encouraged attending such parties, of course—there's a difference between living in the world and unnecessary struggle.

Yes, I gave myself a mental pat on the back for that particular guidance. Occasionally, when I set my mind to it, I could give good advice. I felt it in my bones. And in my bones, circulating in my bloodstream, I *knew* a significant other would be the final piece of the puzzle that glued Ann back together again.

She could claim her work fulfilled her, that she was perfectly happy with a flock of girlfriends, but no one could truly be happy without someone to share it with. Perhaps if the retreat went well for me—and why wouldn't it?—that could serve as the push she needed to get her on the island.

"We're here." Dan rolled up my window as we approached the mansion. I reached for my purse on the other side of the car, my tank top tugging up and over my peasant skirt, and I felt Dan's eyes travel to the tattoo on my hip.

"Is that a sponge?" he asked.

I glanced at the orange flower and chuckled. "This? No, no. It's a marigold. That's my last name. I dated a tattoo artist for a bit, and he convinced me this was a good idea one night. He wasn't the best, I'll admit. At tattoo art or being a decent boyfriend."

Dan continued to stare at me, blankly, so I kept talking. I had a bad habit of chattering to fill the silence.

"Anyway, now he helps people get out of town. He's like an unofficial, slightly illegal provider of witness protection. Crazy where the world takes you, huh?"

Dan remained silent, and I cringed. I probably shouldn't have mentioned that. But it was a good reminder of why I was here: I was on a mission to find a new man. The *right* man. Someone who was actually good for me.

"Well, thanks for the ride." I patted him on the shoulder, gave him a quick peck on the cheek, and opened the car door wide for my next adventure.

4:Ann

The mansion at the retreat stops me in my tracks.

The only house I've seen that comes close in size is Honey's childhood home. The structure is similar too, with its gargantuan glass windows and Spanish-style roof. Only in this case, the curved tiles seem to blend into the waves of the ocean behind it. And the marigolds—there must be hundreds of them. Red, orange, and yellow marigolds decorate every inch of the mansion's exterior, drawing me closer, like an uncontrollable magnet.

My heart stops as I think of Reese and her favorite flower. What she must have thought upon her arrival.

I try to wash away the memories by focusing on the chirps and screams of the forest behind me. The eerie absence of cars, human chatter, any sign of civilization. The sun beats down on my skin. Sweat pinpricks my back. I swat at the mosquitoes that buzz in my ear and attack my limbs.

I'm so lost in thought that I almost don't notice the woman. The earth tones of her clothing and peroxide-blonde hair blend in with the warm, neutral color of the fountain that guards the front doors of the mansion. But once I notice her, I don't know how I could ever miss her. Formidable and stately, she stands with as much grandiosity as the house behind her. Even from here, her eyes are shocking and inhuman—the color of ice.

She doesn't budge as I approach. She just watches me, calmly. Waiting.

As I near her, I can better distinguish her other features: unnaturally arched eyebrows, a conspicuously wrinkle-free forehead, pencil-thin lips, and single strip of white on her otherwise blonde head. Not quite attractive, but noticeable—in part due to the diamonds that adorn her wrists, earlobes, and neckline. Once I'm within arm's reach, the woman's lips snake into a smile.

"Hi, Christina," I say.

She studies me for another moment with her colorless eyes before taking my hand.

"Ann, it's so nice to finally meet you. Welcome to paradise." Her voice is husky, masculine. Something about her is familiar, but I can't place it. I run through the few facts I know about her. Lived in California prior to Last Chance. Purchased Phaux Island from the United States four years ago. Ungodly, mysteriously wealthy. Inherited, most likely.

"Have we met before?"

"Well, of course. We met on video chat after you accepted our offer."

I start to protest, but she cuts me off.

"Here." She nudges me slightly, but forcefully, to stand to her right so that we can both face away from the mansion. "That's better. Now you can better enjoy the view."

The lush vegetation in front of me is spellbinding; the forest of palm trees is so thick, you can only see a few feet in front of you, with the exception of the road you take to travel here. But while every inch of the island is mesmerizing, I'm not sure what she's talking about. The forest is no comparison to the mansion that seems to sit on top of the ocean.

"Much better," she repeats as she gazes into the distance, nodding at no one. "I hope your travels were comfortable?"

Comfortable isn't the word I would use, although the retreat does make a strong effort to make the thirteen-hour trip more bearable. There are no direct flights from Nashville to Hawaii, so we had to make a pit stop in Dallas.

My first flight was late, so I had to run through the fourth-busiest airport in the world, trying to avoid the schools of people like a competition-level pinball game.

I barely made the flight to Honolulu, and I was too energized from the obstacle course in the airport to sleep on the plane. There was also a *very* upset baby two rows down. At one point, it got so bad that I shredded my cocktail napkin, stuffed the pieces in my ears, and made a pact with myself to never have children.

Once I landed in Hawaii, I had to rush to the private airport to board the retreat's plane. Since Last Chance is on its own island, there's not a commercial airport, so flying private is the only way to make the final leg of the journey. The plane was small; turbulence was exacerbated. It was like riding a roller coaster that never ended.

When I finally made it to the island, a nervous, fidgety man was waiting for me with a sign and coffee. I went to shake his hand, but my approach startled him.

"Don't," he cried as he threw his hands in the air, his hot coffee raining down on me. I was still wiping my eyes, my skin on fire from the hot liquid, when he grabbed my bags and hightailed it toward the car.

Once inside, he made a point to lock all doors. He kept the windows rolled up, including the one that separated the front seat from the back.

Of course, I'm not going to mention any of this to Christina.

"Very comfortable," I respond. "Thank you for having me."

"Of course. And I would say you lucked out with the weather," she says as she waves her hand to show off the cloudless sky. "But truthfully, the weather is always this nice."

Someone grunts behind me. I feel a tugging at my purse.

I jump.

A small man, no taller than five foot three, stands behind me. His back is curved to an unnatural, convex position. He lifts his massive head so he can examine me, his shaggy brown hair covering most of his face. He shakes his hair out of his eyes, one green and one blue, and he opens his mouth to reveal two very large buck teeth.

"Henry," he says, pointing to himself. "Can I take your bag?" he asks, one hand already gripping my large suitcase, his other reaching up for my purse.

"Hey, I didn't hear you behind me. My name's Ann." I place my right hand in his—the one that's still reaching for my purse—and shift so that my bag is out of his reach. I give him my warmest smile, but he doesn't return it.

His forehead wrinkles, and he rips his hand away.

"I know," he says, lifting his hand toward my bag again. "Can I have your bag?"

"I'm going to hold on to it, if that's all right. I have some, uh, lady things I'd like to hold on to," I lie.

"That's just fine," Christina interjects. "Isn't it, Henry?"

One glance from Christina causes Henry to stoop even lower, his head and shaggy hair hanging.

"Yes, Miss Christina."

She then looks at me. "If you wouldn't mind just handing your phone and any other electronic device to Henry, we'll be sure to store them in a safe place for the rest of the retreat."

"Absolutely."

I've prepared for this. I open my purse to retrieve my work cell phone—my personal cell stored safely out of sight in a concealed pocket.

Although I have almost a thousand contacts on my phone, there are only two I care about while I'm here: Pat Higdon, my firm's former-FBI-turned-private investigator, who I've hired to dig into Reese's disappearance; and Ned Hargrove, my firm's newest associate. Ostensibly, Ned is helping me take care of my clients while I'm gone. In reality, he's my liaison with Pat and is conducting extra research on Last Chance.

It's not forbidden, per se, to ask associates to help with personal matters, but it's also not encouraged. It's not exactly morally sound. But Ned worked in the district attorney's office for almost a decade before transitioning to corporate law. He has invaluable connections and knowledge of Nashville criminal law. Plus, he's so eager. And, I promise myself that I'll recommend a promotion for him as soon as I get back.

I try not let these thoughts take another bite of my conscience as I hand Henry my phone.

"Thanks for understanding," Christina says. "We just want to make sure your full focus is on the journey at hand."

It takes all my effort not to scoff at that word. *Journey.* How ridiculous.

"Henry will bring your suitcase to your room," Christina assures me. "And don't worry about him. His appearance is . . ." She trails off, apparently rethinking her next words. "Henry is trustworthy. Now, before we take a tour and discuss logistics, tell me what you're most looking forward to."

I take a deep breath. I'm not overly sentimental, like Reese, who gushes with emotion in every conversation. I know I can appear standoffish, but it just doesn't come naturally to me. It feels forced, awkward. But I know what she wants to hear, and I need to play the part to prevent arousing suspicion. So I give it my best shot.

"Well, I'm excited to meet some nice men. I've, uh, been a little lonely lately, and it'd be nice to have some companionship."

That's the best you can do, Ann? Really?

"You've had heartbreak in the past." She nods solemnly, her lips taut.

"Uh, yeah. That's right." She must be referring to my boyfriend in college. Reese said she had to detail past relationships in the application process. I wish she had left him out of it.

"But you don't give up easily," she goads. "You believe in true love, and that's why you're here today."

Come on Ann, you can do it. Just say the words.

"Yes, I'm hoping to fall in love and finally find my, uh, *soul mate*." I try my best not to cringe at the term.

"Wonderful." She flashes a wide, toothy grin. With one hand she makes a sweeping gesture, guiding me toward the mansion and the journey. "Let's get started, shall we?"

5: Ann

As Christina leads me toward the glass entrance, two men in all black—one on each side—open the transparent double doors to the house. These beefy men with hardly any neck and baseball-mitt hands tower above us, at around six foot five. I assume they were in the military at some point, with their flattop hairstyles and grave expressions. As I pass a darker-haired man and offer a nod of thanks, I notice a small tattoo below his neck: an eye. It seems to follow me as I step inside the mansion.

"Those are two of our handlers," Christina says, following my gaze. "We have several, to help with all the activities. They also provide security in case anything gets out of hand."

Out of hand? I turn to face her, thinking she may offer a smile or wink—something to indicate she's joking. But there's no smile. No wink. I steal one more glance at the handlers and notice guns in their belts. A shiver crawls down my spine. What do they need guns for? I should have brought my dad's old hunting rifle—any weapon, really.

"So tonight will be the initial meet and greet. You'll be introduced to all the participants—ten men and ten women in total—and start to get a feel for who might be a good match. Tomorrow is your first date, a one-on-one, although you will have some group activities as well, so be thinking about who you'd like to accompany you," she says as she leads me through the front entrance.

A grand Cinderella staircase, with large vases of marigolds on either side, spirals upward to the floor above. The ceiling showcases a massive chandelier dripping with crystals. Six satin-gold tiers, each level getting smaller vertically, hold individual candles—a hundred in total, at least. The candles aren't burning currently, as the glass windows and doors allow natural sunlight to flood the room.

"I like the marigolds," I say as I catch a whiff of their musky odor.

"Oh." Christina's gaze follows mine to the vases on the staircase. "They're not my favorite, but they grow like weeds here. We cut them every day to fill the vases, and they still blossom. Come, let's see the living room."

She guides me toward the plush sitting room behind the staircase. I turn to my left and right to view the symmetrical hallways lined with similarly tall glass windows. The left hallway is dark and ostensibly unused.

"What's down there?" I ask.

"Rooms for the crew," she says matter-of-factly. "There's no need to visit that hallway."

I make a mental note to visit the left hallway.

"How many bedrooms are there?"

"Thirty. One for each participant, and ten for the staff."

"Am I the first, uh, participant?"

"The second to last, actually. Except for one participant, who gets in tomorrow due to a delayed flight, you'll meet everyone tonight." She eyes me up and down, with a hint of disdain. "After you freshen up."

I glance at my coffee-stained tank top, ripped jeans, and ratty tennis shoes. A stark contrast to Christina, who is dressed to the nines: her silk button-down is tucked neatly into her nude pencil skirt, which is complemented by her nude sandals, which seem to blend in with her legs.

"Yeah, I do need a new shirt, don't I?" I laugh.

Christina remains silent, her mouth one fine line.

"So." I change the subject. "Where is everybody?" The mansion is too quiet for me to be one of the last arrivals.

"They're in their rooms, getting ready. Now, this is my favorite," Christina says, as we enter the living room. It's enormous, like the rest of the house, and almost entirely white. White walls, white couches, white rugs. A white Christmas tree with white lights and white ornaments. Without the hardwood floors, gold light fixtures, and wooden coffee tables, the room would be less *House Beautiful* and more mental hospital ward. The only pop of color is the single vase of yellow marigolds on the coffee tables. The room still seems off, and I realize it's because the three massive couches—they could fit twenty people, at least—aren't angled toward a TV. Television, like phones and computers, is forbidden here. It's "distracting," not conducive to the "journey."

Thankfully, the gargantuan kitchen to the left of the room tells me that food—good food, if the size of the kitchen is any indication—*is* a part of the journey. Behind the living room are rows of glass doors, which allow a full view of the infinity pool outside. Christina points to the couches.

"We start the journey in this room, and whenever we all meet together, it's here. This is where you'll meet everyone tonight. But of course," she says, opening the back doors in an elaborate show, "this is the real reason the living room is my favorite."

I take a step outside onto the twenty-foot-deep patio that leads to the pool, and I catch my breath at the view. The infinity pool bleeds into the ocean, creating an expanse of water all around us, the waves of the ocean glistening in the sunlight like diamonds. The patio, with interlocking earth-tone tiles, wraps around the left and right of the house, lengthening in size where the pool ends. A veranda sits to the right of the house; a gazebo, to the left. And marigolds, in all the colors of the sun, dot every available surface.

As we finish touring the backyard—more like a miniature golf course than a backyard—it's impossible not to notice the numerous nooks and crannies. Seating arrangements, perfect for two, populate each niche. Christina occasionally points out a "talking room" where she and I will intermittently discuss my "progress." A stipulation in the contract I had to sign.

As we circle back to the grand staircase to round out the tour, I steal one more glance at the hallway in the shadows.

6: Ann

ifty-five minutes until I need to be dressed and ready downstairs. I let the shower wash over me, ridding me of the travel debris and lingering worry. Adrenaline courses through me, exploding like tiny pop rocks off my chest. *You're fine,* I tell myself. *You're going to be fine, and you're going to find Reese.*

I turn the water off, wipe my eyes, and open the shower door to step into my white-marble bathroom.

I scream.

I stumble, latching on to the nearby towel rack for support. There's a small woman with a pink bowl cut and large, round eyeglasses—rose-rimmed glasses to match her rose-rimmed head—waiting patiently on my vanity stool, with various makeup items scattered around my bathroom sink. I snatch a towel from the rack to cover myself.

"Feel better?" she asks.

"Holy shit." I try to catch my breath and cover my naked body at the same time. I scan my bedroom. Did I leave my door unlocked? That's unlike me. "What are you doing in here?" I cry, when my heart finally returns to a more normal rhythm.

"Ze door vas open, and ve need to start your makeup," she says with a foreign accent. Russian, maybe. "I'm Magda."

Shit. I almost forgot about the makeup. Another stipulation in the retreat's contract is all participants are given makeup and clothes. Two things I don't put a lot of thought toward. I suppress a groan and a nasty remark.

"Ann," I say through gritted teeth. "Let me just put on a T-shirt."

"Be back in here in thirty seconds," she says, tapping her watch. "Ve don't have lot of time."

"Should we set a timer?" I ask, before the rational part of my brain stops me. Magda shoots daggers at me with her eyes. I clear my throat, shift my weight. "Sorry," I mutter. "Sometimes I can be . . . a little cross when I'm tired." *Or stressed,* I add in my head.

She exaggerates a sigh. "Just hurry."

I nod and head into my room. Like the downstairs of the mansion, it's an explosion of white. White walls, white carpet, white furniture. Like someone doused the area in bleach. Atop the Hummer-sized bed is a beautiful, emerald-green gown. I tiptoe closer, careful not to drip on it. I inspect the tag and let out a small gasp. Jesus Christ, it's Hervé Léger. I only know this because it's one of Honey's favorite designers. Are we wearing designer every night?

"Hey," I yell to Magda. "If I mess up this dress, do I have to pay for it? I'm not the most graceful."

"Yes." A woman with wispy, waist-length silver hair slithers into my room. Despite her hair coloring and slender frame, she can't be much older than Christina. Forty at the most.

"Jesus." I clutch the towel I've wrapped around my still-dripping body. "Doesn't anyone knock around here?"

"Don't leesten to Stephanie," Magda calls from the bathroom. "If you spill sometheeng, you spill sometheeng. Accidents happen."

"As your stylist," the woman in front of me says in a clipped tone, "I'll be very upset if there's even a thread loose on that gown. Be careful. Now, let's go. We don't have all night."

I give her an I'll-go-at-my-own-pace glance as I grab some underwear from my suitcase. I turn around, expecting Stephanie to offer some privacy. She doesn't, so like a girl at camp, I pull on my underwear underneath my towel. I'm about to clasp on my strapless bra when Stephanie yanks both my towel and bra out of my hands. For a clothes hanger, she has a surprising amount of strength.

"No bra with this dress."

Shocked, I hold my chest with both arms.

"Bend your head over, and I will wrap."

I flip my hair, and she coils the towel over my damp waves. She reaches for the dress next, unzipping it quickly and nimbly. She holds it up to me and sighs when I remain immobile.

"Turn around then, if you're so embarrassed."

I do as she says, but I keep my breasts covered until the gown has a chance to take over. Despite the curtains that cover the windows, I now have the nagging feeling that someone, somewhere, is watching.

I turn around once she's zipped the back of my dress, and Stephanie smiles for the first time since I've met her.

"Beautiful."

She bends over to pick up the hem of my dress as she shuffles me to the bathroom.

Magda sits on the vanity stool filing her nails, leaning back, her legs crossed on the countertop.

"Finally." She sighs, rolling her eyes. She stands up and points to the stool. I sit, and without a moment to spare, Stephanie and Magda throw a towel over my gown and get to work on their respective tasks. The two make an odd pair: Stephanie is as tall and slender as Magda is short and plump.

While Magda applies the first layer of foundation, Stephanie attempts to slip my feet into nude pumps.

"I can do that." I reach for the shoes, but Stephanie slaps my hand away. Magda clenches my neck, careful not to touch the newly applied mask.

"Stay still," they reply in unison.

I acquiesce and sit back, massaging my neck where Magda tightened her grip.

As Stephanie unwraps my hair and starts the styling process, I analyze myself in the mirror for the first time in twenty-four hours. I must admit the gown looks nice; its color accentuates the green in my eyes.

I'm more attractive than your plain Jane, I'll go ahead and admit that. I don't say that to sound conceited; it's just a fact. I see the way men look at me, and the way their girlfriends look at them. At one point in my life, I took pride in it. It's hard not to relish that kind of attention, to bask in being admired. But after I got sober, once my priorities shifted, it wasn't so advantageous. When you're going to AA meetings, in genuine need of a friend, the last thing you want is to be hit on. Countless times, men at meetings would feign interest in my struggle only to then turn around and ask if I'd like to continue discussing the steps at their place, say, nine o'clock?

I know beautiful women don't garner a lot of sympathy—and they shouldn't—but can you imagine being at your most vulnerable, raw with grief, and at the first spark of hope that you've connected with another person who *might* understand what you're going through, you realize:

Oh wait. They don't give a shit about me. It's one of the reasons I eventually stopped going to AA and relied on Reese to help me stay on the wagon.

Trying to prove myself in the workplace was equally tough. Typically, male associates with the same GPA and the same experience received the benefit of the doubt, the first shot at a deal. Or, on the flip side, I was given a shot over someone more qualified, and I couldn't help but wonder if it was because of the way I looked. So I worked like a maniac to prove myself. And over time, it just became easier to tie my hair back and keep my face bare.

So this new woman in the mirror, with this mask of makeup, I hardly recognize. Or perhaps I do, but it's been so long since I've seen her.

"You like?" Magda asks, after forty-four minutes, three layers of foundation, and what appears to be an entire bag of glitter on my eyes.

"Totally," I lie. I look like a clown. But I'm playing a character here, so I might as well look the part. "Am I ready?"

"You're ready," they say in unison.

I gather my gown, head for the Cinderella staircase, and prepare myself to meet the others. Time to figure out what the hell happened to Reese.

7 : Reese

won't lie: I did not enjoy the dress that first night.

I prefer more billowy clothing: boho skirts, maxi dresses, peasant blouses. Clothing that flows with me, that allows me to easily eat, dance, make love. The fun things in life. But I was vacationing on a tropical island with ten single men, so I could hardly complain about the attire. Even if Christina's insistence on dressing me was odd.

Weirdness and chest constrictions aside, the dress was beautiful. I thought about Ann's friend Honey when I saw it. The gown, like the whole retreat, was very chic. Like her. That woman has never looked unkempt a day in her life. Even though I'm not a huge fan—and that is rare for me, not instantly liking people—she isn't all bad, I guess. She has a soft spot for Ann.

Like me, Honey was always setting Ann up with various men, encouraging her to *get out there and meet someone*. Once, during the one and only *Bachelor* (or maybe it's *The Bachelor?*) viewing at my apartment, we forced Ann to recount every detail of her last date, ribbing her at the same sappy parts. Ann seemed happy then, genuinely happy, and for a moment I could forget Honey's not-so-subtle jabs at my living arrangements and *alternative* lifestyle.

In a way, the retreat reminded me of the reality show. The types of dates, juggling multiple relationships, the goal of engagement at the end.

"Welcome, everyone, to Last Chance: a novel, first-of-its-kind retreat for building successful, long-lasting relationships."

Christina clinked her glass and began her first speech of the retreat on the Cinderella steps, looking down on all the participants in the living room. She was directly under the chandelier, which cast a halo around her white-blonde head and put the rest of us in shadow. She held her champagne glass with a steady, manicured hand.

"My name is Christina, and I'm the owner and hostess of the retreat. This is where we'll reconvene every night at seven p.m. sharp, once the sun goes down, unless otherwise stated. You all have been selected very carefully, based on your compatibility with each other, and over the next thirty days, you'll get to know everyone on both one-on-one and group dates. I'll be here to offer advice, discuss your progress, and encourage fruitful conversations that will prepare you for life outside of paradise."

Blah, blah, blah.

Christina talked quite a bit that first night. I was too busy scoping out the men and women to give her my full attention. Mostly the men. It was amazing how beautiful everyone was. Now, I know I wasn't the best judge, as I thought most things were beautiful, but these participants were objectively attractive.

More than attractive. *Gorgeous.* The kind of beauty that makes the eyes of cartoon characters pop out of their head. The beautiful people you see in magazines. The people who, when they pass by, make you stop and nudge your friend: *Did you see him?*

Maybe that's why Christina droned on. She knew the participants would go crazy over one another, so she upped the anticipation. If that's the case, it worked. The excitement in the room was like the static in the air before lightning strikes. My hair stood on end. My skin buzzed. A soft hum filled my ears.

I had my eye on one man in particular. A man with broad shoulders and shoulder-length shaggy blond hair. His nose seemed to have been broken before, but it gave him an edge. A likeable flaw. Like me, he had seen the dark underbelly of society and come out on top.

He returned my gaze with the same intensity. The same—dare I say it?—twinkle in the eye. But I couldn't get ahead of myself. I needed to stay sharp, rational. I would only pursue him if our personalities and life goals aligned.

"Tonight you will speak to each participant for thirty minutes," Christina continued. I did the math in my head: between ten women and ten men, that was a five-hour night. Not bad, especially since I was told the first night would run until dawn and I likely would be too giddy to sleep anyway.

"We won't use a timer," Christina continued, "So it'll be an un-official round robin of sorts. It's up to you to make sure you've spoken to everyone. At the end of the night, you'll talk to me for about thirty minutes, to let me know how you're doing, and you'll write down your top three choices for your one-on-one date tomorrow. My staff and I will match accordingly. And the bar is open, so help yourselves."

Most people smiled at that. Some whooped, clapped, or raised glasses. Christina let the words sink in, pausing for dramatic emphasis. Then her lips curled to one side, and like Elizabeth Banks in *The Hunger Games,* she declared:

"Let the games begin."

I ended up talking to three other men before meeting the handsome blond. There was a tipsy, very Southern man with a five-o'clock shadow. A tall, gorgeous black man. A smart yet surprisingly sensitive engineer. I don't remember too many details—it was mostly small talk before the blond tapped me on the shoulder.

"Do you want to go outside, maybe go for a walk on the beach?" I asked. I was already missing the sand and the ocean, and I believed I could be more levelheaded with fresh air.

"Of course," he said with a grin. He grabbed my hand, interlocking my fingers in his, and I couldn't help but feel a rush of adrenaline at the touch.

The sun was long gone by that point, so the patio and infinity pool were shrouded in a hazy, golden aura of artificial light. The crickets chirped. The waves lapped in the distance.

"What's your name?" he asked as we neared the spot where the patio met the beach. I took my shoes off before answering, dropping his hand so I could use his shoulder for support. He held the small of my back to steady me.

He smelled of whiskey with traces of aftershave.

"Reese Marigold. You?"

"Lamb Martin."

He held out his hand officially. I took it and went in for my normal kiss-on-the-cheek greeting, but he moved his mouth at the last second, and suddenly my lips were on his. *So much for taking it slow, Reese.*

I jerked back quickly, muttering an apology.

"That's okay." He grinned. "I think I prefer that more than a handshake anyway."

I could feel my cheeks warming. I needed to get back on track. Get to know him, go at a normal pace. Do what Ann would do. We bantered nervously for several minutes, but then we seemed to get a handle on our butterflies, and the conversation deepened.

"So, how does one get a name like Lamb?" I swung his hand as we walked. I loved how the sand molded to my feet, and the lingering warmth of the grains from the day's sunshine.

"Very religious parents. The kind who think chocolate, tank tops, and sex for pleasure are sins." His cheeks were cherry red, and I could feel mine turning a similar color. He was even better-looking up close. "We aren't tight-knit, for obvious reasons."

A man who wasn't close to his crazy family. That, I could relate to.

"What about you?" he asked. "Your parents like candy?"

"Reese's Peanut Butter Cups?" I laughed. "You know, my mom did tell me I was sweet as chocolate, on one of her good days. I think she just liked the sound of Reese. Not a lot of thought went into my birth. It was definitely an accident."

That wasn't the whole truth.

My mother was severely depressed when I arrived. She said it was postpartum, but I think it had more to do with the fact that my dad had just left her, and now she had two unwelcome children with two different, absent fathers, and she couldn't even care for herself. She hadn't thought of a name for me, hadn't thought of any next steps, and so when the nurse asked what she would call me, my mother looked outside at the nurses' station until her eyes found a bag of Reese's Peanut Butter Cups on the counter and decided Reese was a good-enough name. That's how little thought went into the matter.

I couldn't tell Lamb, of course. It was too depressing, and we had just met.

"Sometimes I wish that had been my story," he replied. "There was *too much* planning around my birth. Too many dreams and rules pinned on me. Do you know how hard it is to live up to Bible-belt, born-again

Baptists' expectations? It's like they expect you to be the second coming of Christ."

"Religion wasn't a big part of my childhood," I admitted. Or really any planned social gathering.

"Lucky you."

I nodded, but in actuality, I thought about how nice it'd be to have parents who cared about me that much. I felt my mood shift with each sunken footstep in the sand. I changed the subject, determined to stay positive and bubbling in this short-lived paradise.

"So, what's your story? Why are you on this retreat?"

He chuckled. "How honest are we getting here?"

"As honest as you like."

He seemed to choose his next words carefully, debating how much to say. "Well, to tell you the truth, I have a terrible habit of picking unavailable women. Women who are physically there but emotionally somewhere else. Partners who aren't good for me. So I decided to try something different. At a singles' retreat, everyone agrees the end goal is a stable, long-lasting relationship."

I stopped moving. We had double-backed toward the mansion since our thirty minutes were almost up, but I wasn't ready to go inside yet. Mostly because it was as if this man was inside my head, speaking from my own experiences.

I wondered if he was too good to be true. Could I have chemistry with a man who was actually good for me?

There was a shattering of glass.

Lamb's brows furrowed, and his gaze ping-ponged from me to the noise.

"Should we make sure everything's all right?"

"Probably a good idea."

Just before we reached the patio, Lamb thrust his arm out.

"Wait—it sounded like glass. Put your shoes back on just in case."

"Oh right." I used him once more to steady myself. I slipped my sandals on, my eyes darting from my feet to the handlers swarming near the infinity pool.

"Okay," I muttered as I finished.

When we got closer, we could see the remnants of a broken cocktail glass on the floor. One of the participants was swaying, his shirt untucked. He was the first participant I had talked to that night—Theo. Or Tom, maybe. It started with a *T*. (I really should have paid more attention.) A handler reached for the participant's arm, but Theo-slash-Tom jerked away at his touch.

"Get offa me," he slurred.

All the other participants were staring, and Christina was visibly shaken.

"It's all right, everyone," she said. "Let's focus on the task tonight, and we'll take him to sleep it off."

"He didn't seem that drunk when I talked to him an hour ago," a girl with a pixie cut whispered to a participant in front of me, her arms crossed protectively over her chest. I recall T-something being a little sloshed, but not at this level.

My first instinct was to help him, but the handlers and Christina shooed me away.

"We've got it," one of them yelled.

I didn't know what to do, so I stood there awkwardly. I didn't realize Lamb was still there until he reached for my hand.

"I know our thirty minutes are up, but I don't think anyone is paying attention." He gestured to a seat tucked away in a secluded part of the patio. "Wanna go sit over there and talk?"

I was still thinking about T-something as Lamb shepherded me to the spot he had in mind. "Do you think he'll be okay?" I asked.

"I think he'll be just fine." Lamb's smile was warm and reassuring. "He just needs to lie down." He started massaging the inside of my wrist with his thumb, and my worries started to dissolve again. Something about the salt air, the waves of the ocean, and Lamb's presence were so calming. He inched closer to me, his eyes hooded with longing. I told myself to cut it out, to not do what I always do. But despite my best intentions, I found myself praying he would kiss me. *Really* kiss me.

"I know this is soon," he said, his voice hoarse, "but I feel like I was meant to meet you here. Does that seem silly?"

I shook my head. "No, that doesn't seem silly." My voice was barely above a whisper.

He closed the gap between us, and when his mouth met mine, everything else seemed to slip away. After a few moments, Lamb broke contact and nodded toward the house. I didn't want him to stop.

"C'mon. I know somewhere more private."

I had told myself I wouldn't do anything like this on the first night. I needed to take it slow and all that, but surely our connection was worth an exception? He was kind and stable and interested in a long-lasting relationship. So I followed him, away from the crowd, toward the front hallway—the one to the left when you entered the mansion. It was dark and unoccupied and just big enough for the two of us. Our footsteps became more hurried as we tried—and failed—to open each locked door. Finally, the door at the very end opened—a soft click—and we laughed between kisses as we went inside.

8 : Ann

My heart drums in my ears as I lie in bed, eyes wide open. A sliver of moonlight escapes through drawn curtains, highlighting the closed bedroom door. The down comforter and silk sheets feel like a straitjacket strapping me in place until I'm sure the house is asleep.

At 2:03 a.m. I rise, tiptoeing across the plush white carpet that borders the bed. After what seems like a mile, my bare feet make contact with the cool hardwood. I press my ear to the door, listen for any movement. When there isn't any, I reach for the door handle and turn it gently until opens. The house is dark and still as I creep toward the Cinderella stairs.

Adrenaline propels me forward, keeping me alert despite the long trip and exhausting first night. I was introduced to nine of the men in a round-robin meet-and-greet. Thirty minutes or so for each participant, like a revolving door, trains on a track.

The details were different, but each man was the same—attractive, successful. Put together, for the most part. I had to come up with nicknames to remember them all. There was Richie Rich, an investment banker from New York who oozed hair gel and self-adulation. Doctor Dermot, a neurosurgeon from Houston with sharp angles and a thin scar that bisected his right eyebrow. Peach Pay Patrick, a Californian and one of the principal engineers behind the lucrative mobile payment service Peach Pay.

I caught a second wind with Basketball Blake, who used his thirty minutes to take me to the outside basketball court and *jump over me*—while I was in heels, no less—to dunk the ball. He flashed me the biggest, whitest smile, punctuated by two deep dimples, when I yelped and covered my head with my arms.

After Blake, there was Chef Clay, a reserved, soft-spoken man with cherubic cheeks and blond curls. Guitar Guy, a husky man from Macon, Georgia, who serenaded me with a mediocre rendition of Hank Williams's "Hey, Good Lookin.'" Poker Paul, a professional gambler who showed no facial expression whatsoever. Marketing Matt, a delicate man from Atlanta. I stared at his glistening lips as he discussed his marketing career, and in my run-down state, I asked him if he was wearing makeup. He chuckled and dismissed my comment as a joke, but I was serious: I think I even saw a hint of foundation under his chin.

And then, my night ended with Turnt Teddy. *He* was not put together. More like a big, drunken Teddy Bear. Aided by the open bar, many people became looser as the night progressed, but none as much as Teddy. He went in to embrace me, but since I'm not much of a hugger, or touchy-feely in general, I ducked. He stumbled, toppling over on the floor and spilling his drink all over his untucked, unbuttoned shirt. His glass shattered on the floor, breaking into a hundred tiny pieces. He laughed like a hyena as the handlers escorted him to his room.

It was all so draining, trying to remember everyone while maintaining a plastered smile and combing through every detail in their words and in the surroundings for clues about Reese. And I haven't even met the tenth and final man yet, who couldn't arrive in time due to a delayed flight. Or any of the women, properly, even though they were downstairs with me all night.

And now, instead of recharging my batteries, I'm downstairs once again. Creeping on my toes, stealing furtive glances over my shoulder in the quiet hallway to the left of the mansion entrance. I had tried to investigate the off-limits area earlier, but handlers were everywhere, guarding each room. I wandered toward the restricted section anyway, between my time with Chef Clay and Guitar Guy, inquiring about a bathroom, and a handler shuffled me out quickly—back to the very visible restroom off the foyer.

"Oops, guess I didn't see that." I chuckled.

The handler kept a straight face. "Well, now you know."

So I'm back here now, in the dead of night, trying to find some trace of Reese. It's probably nothing, but something about the area lures me, whispering to take a closer peek. It smells different from the rest of the mansion—musty instead of perfumed. My heart picks up the pace as I approach the first of four doors and turn the knob. To my surprise, it's unlocked. I open the door carefully, slowly, holding my breath. My eyes adjust to the darkness, and I can make out two twin beds. A round child with a bowl cut sleeps on the left, while a gangly teenager occupies the right. My heart goes into overdrive, thrashing against my rib cage like a drummer.

Is Christina hiding children?

No, no. It can't be. Why would she leave the door unlocked? I peer closer, until I realize the children are not children at all.

It's Magda and Stephanie.

I exhale sharply, steadying my heart with a hand on my chest. Just the makeup artist and the stylist. That's all.

I close the door, praying they don't wake. I almost skip the second door when I hear the snores. But then, what if it's a trick? So I check, and sure enough, two twin beds, with a handler in each, their enormous limbs spilling off the edges of the mattresses.

I crack the third door. Just as the light reveals two twin beds and two sleeping handlers, the door hinges squeak. Loudly. The handler on the left—the one with the eye tattoo—sits up.

"What?" he yells.

My feet are frozen. My mouth glued shut.

"Get the watermelon, Jacky boy," he mumbles. His shoulders sink, and he lies back down, his head lolling to the side. The handler to his right wheezes softly, immune to his roommate's sleep-talking. Feeling returns to my legs, breath returns to my ribcage, and I move to the final door.

The rational part of me, the risk-averse part, screams to go back upstairs. *It's just rooms for the crew, like Christina said.* But I have to be absolutely positive. I have to check. So I push open the door at the very end of the hallway.

My heart sinks as I take in the contents of the room.

It's just a closet. A regular, good-for-nothing broom closet.

Great detective work, Ann. You've discovered the cleaning supplies.

I continue to curse myself as I close the door and mentally prepare—finally—for sleep.

And then, a creak in the floorboards behind me. A voice.

"What are you doing?"

My stomach drops.

9: Ann

whip around to face the voice and gasp.

In an instant, I'm back in college, telling a boy with glassy eyes and a lopsided grin to keep the music down. I blink once, twice, three times. It's not him—it can't be.

But the resemblance to my ex is uncanny.

"Are you all right?" My ghost-of-boyfriend-past whispers, his brow crinkling.

"Sorry." I close my eyes and shake off the déjà vu. "You look exactly like someone I know."

"Oh yeah?" He smiles—that same, adorable crooked smile—and my knees buckle. "He better have been damn good-looking then."

I know I should laugh, act normal, but I can't stop staring at him. His grin fades, and he shifts his weight.

"Are you sure you're okay?"

"I, uh," I stammer, my gaze pinballing across the hallway for answers. *Think fast, Ann.* "I think I was sleepwalking. I do that sometimes. I'm not entirely sure where I am right now."

"Well, how about I get you a glass of water, and then we can find your room?"

I nod, and he waves toward the kitchen, leading me with his hand on the small of my back. My skin tingles at his touch, and I say something—anything—to distract myself.

"I'm Ann."

"Nick."

And then it dawns on me.

"Oh, you're the final participant, aren't you? The one whose flight was delayed?"

"That's me," he beams as he ushers me into the kitchen, toward the island and surrounding stools. He pulls out the closest one and gestures for me to sit. I climb up, and the cool metal sends a jolt through me. He takes off his jacket and tosses it on the stool next to mine before heading to the cabinets. The moonlight through the window illuminates Nick's broad shoulders, the sculpted muscles beneath his thin V-neck. I cross my legs and force myself to inspect the room while he fills two glasses with water from the tap.

The kitchen resembles most of the other rooms in the mansion. Enormous, immaculate, with hardwood floors and white-marble countertops. Delicate gold light fixtures hang from the ceiling, and the only pop of color in the sea of white is the single vase of yellow marigolds in the middle of the island.

"So when did you get in?"

"About an hour ago," he says over his shoulder as he turns off the tap. "Christina let me in, and then I spent some time unpacking. Showering."

His fingers brush mine as he hands me a glass of water. I take a sip, hoping to cool the blood that rushes to my face. Then I take another sip, and another, and another, until the glass is drained.

"Here, let me refill that for you," Nick laughs as he takes my glass and returns to the sink.

"Thanks." I blush. "Guess I didn't realize how thirsty I was. You know, you're the first guy who's offered me a glass of water."

All night, I had to bat off dozens of glasses of champagne, wine, liquor—blocking them like tennis shots from a ball machine in overdrive. After a while, I got so fed up that I pulled the bartender aside and asked him if he'd pour me a soda water with lime—a drink that *looked* alcoholic. The bartender's eyes softened, and he cupped my elbow.

"I got you," he said.

I spent the rest of the night nursing that one drink, and I forgot to refill.

"Sounds like the other guys don't stand a chance," Nick says as he leans against the counter, a smile tugging at his lip.

"No, I guess not."

He peers at me for a long while, his deep-set blue eyes boring into mine. I squeeze my legs tighter, avert my gaze.

"You hungry?" he says as he opens the fridge. "Christina said to grab anything."

"Actually, yes. I just remembered we didn't eat dinner." I jerk my head back at the realization, wondering how I could have missed that. With my thoughts consumed with finding Reese, I've been missing a lot lately. The anxiety has also made it hard to digest anything. But no dinner is strange.

Do we skip it every night, or was tonight an oversight? No wonder Turnt Teddy got so tipsy—he was drinking on an empty stomach.

"Looks like we have pizza and salad," Nick says. "What'll it be?"

Neither sounds appetizing. He might as well have said, *Cardboard or cardboard?* But I need food.

"Pizza."

"That's what I was thinking too," Nick says as he extracts a plate of pizza wrapped neatly in cellophane. His eyes keep darting back to me as he removes the plastic wrap, like he's finally solved a riddle.

"What?"

"Nothing," he smiles. "I just have a feeling I'm going to like you."

10:Reese

was so stinking happy before my first one-on-one date. Humming-showtunes, ponytail-swishing, spring-in-my-step happy.

And it was all because of Lamb Martin. Ah, and what a lamb he was, opening doors for me, protecting my poor bare feet from broken glass, always making sure I was comfortable. He was so gentle. But he wasn't gentle in the bedroom. (Or in our case, a broom closet. Ha!) No, in the matter of the birds and the bees, Lamb was like a sailor on leave, pounding the wall, knocking the cleaning supplies left and right. It's hard to find a considerate man who still knows how to properly tend to a woman.

I know, I know. I was supposed to be "good" and "mature" at first. I wasn't supposed to sleep with someone on the first night. But in my defense, I had made sure our personalities and life goals aligned, like I promised myself, so I gave myself a pass. And trust me, it was worth the pass.

As I waited for our first official date to begin, rocking on my heels outside the mansion, I daydreamed about our second encounter. Would we coalesce in a closet again? Or would we move to a more open space, like the beach? Perhaps we'd sneak off into the ocean, where the waves would muffle our cries. The possibilities were endless.

The temperature was perfect that day. Seventy degrees, if I had to guess. I lifted my face to the sun, letting the rays kiss my skin, and I inhaled the salt air that was tinged with traces of fresh flowers. Marigolds, specifically. It was a good omen, I had decided, that the retreat was teeming with my favorite blossom. Lamb bounded outside while I was basking, a Ken-doll smile plastered on his face. He picked me up, twirled me around, and kissed me promptly on the mouth. He tasted like peppermint, and I drank him in like the sun. I was about to kiss him again—a proper kiss—when I noticed Henry lurking at the front door. He was accompanying us on our date that day, a radio to the mansion in hand, just in case we needed something. His multicolored eyes, partially covered by his bangs, were fixed on me. I tried to break the tension.

"Hey, Henry," I said with a smile.

He crossed his arms and remained silent.

I'll admit, his presence was a bit of a buzzkill.

"You ready for our picnic on the beach?" Lamb asked, swinging my arms playfully.

I was *so* ready. What a romantic first date. The picnic was set up about a half mile from the mansion, give or take, so we had some privacy, Henry aside. Christina had offered to have a handler drive us there, but I insisted we walk. How often was I able to stroll on the beach on a first date? Not often—after all, Tennessee is landlocked. I walked barefoot, of course. The sand was warm but not too warm. In this weather, what kind of a lunatic walks on a beach with shoes on?

The answer: Henry.

He stayed a good distance behind us, looking grumpy, picking up his feet like a man stuck in three feet of snow. I tried to ignore him. Ever since I could remember, I was a focus-on-the-positive girl. I don't know if I was overcompensating because there was no happiness in my childhood home, but my theory was: if you act happy, then you will be happy.

Stuff those negative thoughts at the foot of the bed—they can't reach you there!

And anyway, there was simply too much to be excited about. Our walk was brimming with beauty and exotic wildlife. Lamb and I were like children in a zoo, pointing to creatures like our lives depended on it. *Dolphins! Baby turtles! A bird with a banana-sized beak! Oh, wait, watch out for the jellyfish. Yep, don't step there.*

The walk also gave me ample time to learn more about sweet, angelic Lamb. I learned he was a painter (a creative soul, like me). He was from Watercolor, Florida (a fitting birthplace for an artist). He had two older sisters (explained his gentleness). Never been married, but two very serious relationships that came close. (Perfect answer. Perfect match for me.)

Now, I know these types of questions are typically asked *before* sex, but, as I've mentioned, I wasn't a big rule-follower. Plus, I didn't like to answer the same questions—at least not at first. Where is my sister now? *Let's just say she's up north.* Are my parents still together? *Literally never met my dad.* What do you do for work? *Is that our picnic blanket, up ahead?*

Stuff, stuff, stuff to the edge of the bed.

Our picnic blanket—white, of course—was set up in the shade of a palm tree. I was starting to get a little toasty by that point, so that was fine by me. Lamb smoothed the wrinkles out of the blanket, brushing off some windblown sand. He patted the blanket twice, indicating I should sit, and he held my hand as I plopped down. Once I was situated, he sat down too.

"Well, should I see what's inside?" I asked, gesturing to the white wicker picnic basket on the corner of the blanket.

"Yes, please."

As I reached inside, I imagined eating ripe grapes off the vine, sampling various cheeses, a warm baguette that melted in your mouth like butter. It was lunchtime, I had skipped breakfast, and my mouth salivated at the possibilities. But there was only champagne. The surprise must have shown on my face.

"What's wrong?" Lamb asked.

"There's no food in here."

Lamb's eyebrows scrunched in confusion. "Hey, Henry," he called. Henry was still wading through the sand, his scowl deepening with each step. In his defense, his skin had changed from the color of cauliflower to the color of a tomato. "There's no food here."

"You don't eat on dates," Henry called back. "Just drink."

Lamb and I exchanged confused glances.

"Why?" I asked.

"Because," Henry wheezed as he closed the distance between us, kicking sand into our laps and onto the picnic blanket like a red-faced toddler, "Miss Christina wants you to focus on each other, not on food. You can eat when you return to the mansion, in a couple hours."

"We're going to starve by then," Lamb said. (A bit dramatic, I'll admit.)

"Eat a bigger breakfast from now on." Henry shrugged.

"Well, at least we have champagne," Lamb said as he reached for the beverage. He aimed the bottle away from me as he uncorked it, creating a loud *pop* and a small explosion of fizzy liquid that bubbled onto the sand. Lamb laughed at this, and he grabbed a glass to catch some of the champagne.

"Ma dear," he said as he offered it to me.

This was always my least favorite part of first dates—the tricky alcohol situation. Would my date be okay with my refusal of a drink? Would he be insulted? Uncomfortable? Too curious?

"I'm okay." I brushed away the glass with a polite wave. I really wished there had also been a bottle of water in that basket. "Thank you, though."

"C'mon. Don't make me drink alone," Lamb pleaded.

"No, I'm good, but thank you."

"It's already paid for," Henry said. He had started to give us space again, but he returned at this juncture.

"That's not what I'm worried about. I just don't want any."

"I must insist," Henry continued. "It makes the date better. You're more open."

"Trust me, I'm open without it," I laughed. "Alcohol and I don't mix well together. I gave it up more than a decade ago."

I could tell Henry wanted to push the issue further, but Lamb gripped his arm then, a *back-off* look in his eyes. "She doesn't want any, man."

Lamb shot him a look, and Henry stepped away like a dog with his tail between his legs. I remember thinking Lamb handled the situation perfectly. If there was an award for best response to my I-don't-drink announcement, Lamb would have won. Instead of recognizing that something wasn't quite right, I was thinking of all the ways I'd reward him later.

Stuff, stuff, stuff.

11: Ann

The sun dances on my eyelids, turning my black world red. My eyes shutter open—a quick flip of the lids. I check my watch, recently converted to local time: 6:57 a.m. Right on schedule. I watch dust particles twirl in the morning light as I burrow deeper into the soft mattress of the king bed.

My body feels heavy, detached. Like it could sink through the mattress, the floor, all the way to the sand below the mansion. Buried with the island's secrets.

Even though jet lag and the lack of sleep has finally caught up with me, physically at least, my mind still races. Was Reese okay on her first date? What would she be doing at this time? Was that one handler, the one with the eye tattoo, acting suspicious? Did that one crew member stare at me just a *little* too long? What does Christina know, and why does she look so familiar?

And on top of all of that, I can't pinpoint a good nickname for Nick yet. That seems inconsequential in comparison to everything else going on, but it's bothering me. I never have trouble coming up with nicknames. It's a perfectly normal name and a perfectly normal man.

He just rattled me, that's all. I wasn't prepared to meet anyone at that hour, much less someone who resembles an ex-boyfriend.

I don't like to think about my ex-boyfriend. It was the first time—the only time—I was in love. But after meeting Nick, the memories flood my brain like a burst pipe, overwhelming my thoughts as I lie in bed.

I met him, my ex-boyfriend, *the* ex-boyfriend, my senior year of college. I was frantically studying for the LSAT, applying to law school, and researching grad-school loans until my fingers wore my computer keys thin.

He wasn't quite as studious, and that fascinated me. Not at first, of course. It actually drove me crazy, and I told him as much when I banged on his door at 2:00 a.m. to inform him that some of us were trying to study.

"You're studying at two in the morning?" He said with glassy eyes and an adorable, lopsided grin. "What for?"

"Well," I stuttered, taken aback by his Hollywood good looks. "I'm taking the LSAT in a week."

"Smart girl. I wouldn't have expected that from someone who looks . . ." His ears reddened, an infectious and self-conscious laugh erupting from his chest. He turned away from me then and yelled at someone to turn the music down. When he faced me again, he leaned against the door frame and held my gaze a few seconds longer than normal. Likely because he was three sheets to the wind, but alluring all the same.

"Well, thanks," I said, toes curled and chin down.

"Let me know how it goes," he said as I walked off.

I did, eventually, let him know, after several pep talks in front of the mirror and more than one failed attempt to knock on his door. I was hesitant around him, at first, unaccustomed to the strange feeling of lust, but soon enough I couldn't get enough of him. He was just so nice to be around, emanating a warmth that made everyone around him relax. He was naturally happy, and for the first time in my life, I was stupidly happy too. I stopped counting the cracks in the sidewalk every time I walked. I checked to make sure my hair dryer was unplugged only once before leaving the house. I skipped a few classes, not worrying if it'd affect my scholarship. At night, I let my perfect boyfriend *spoon* me while drinking a glass of red wine and watching meaningless TV.

The only issue: I've never been good at moderation. Like a pendulum, I always seem to swing to the extreme ends. A glass of wine with dinner transformed into an entire bottle. Then two bottles. Then shots of hard liquor just to get to sleep. I didn't know what was happening to me, although I knew it wasn't good. My boyfriend started to make comments like *Maybe take it easy for a night* or *How about we just stick to wine?*

I would have had to get sober eventually—let's face it, I'm not the type of person who can have *just one glass*—but my downward spiral was hastened by the death of my parents eleven months later. What could have been a slow burn toward addiction catapulted into a small explosion as I attempted to numb the pain by looking at the bottom of the bottle. The relationship stayed intact, for a few months at least, but it was a ticking time bomb. I don't blame him for leaving me, I really don't. I would have left me too. But to say it made me gun-shy about entering into future relationships would be an understatement.

I eventually learned to date again, with Reese's help. But it took years. I spent the first year out of college getting clean, and the three years after that focusing on law school. I kept my eye on the prize, graduated at the top of my class, and in those three years, I didn't so much as kiss another man. Every time the situation arose, I was met with an onslaught of harrowing memories, the faint aroma of tequila, the taste of bile, and I ran as fast as my legs could take me. Literally. I started running regularly to stay grounded.

But that was a long time ago. Over a decade. I've moved on.

I swing my legs out of bed. Rub the remnants of sleep from my eyes.

From now on, my full focus needs to be on Reese. The interaction with Nick caught me off guard, but now I've processed it, catalogued it, and placed it in the do-not-disturb folder of my mind. No need to linger on the subject.

I throw the covers back and brush my feet across the soft carpet, letting my toes sink in.

I have one hour until I need to be outside for a group yoga session. It's another chance for the participants to get to know one another before our first one-on-one dates. Half the group will proceed with their dates after yoga, while the other half will meet with Christina to discuss their progress, thoughts, and feelings. Then the groups will flip-flop. I'll meet with Christina after my date with Chef Clay. Under normal circumstances, I'd balk at having to discuss my romantic feelings with a total stranger, but I'm actually looking forward to our conversation. She's one of the few people who saw Reese in her final days, and she can offer insight into her mental state and last movements. I can't be too obvious when I ask, of course—I'm here to ostensibly fall in love, and I don't know the extent of Christina's role in Reese's disappearance, if she was involved at all. But Christina also knows Reese and I were close, so it would be just as strange to not inquire about my missing friend. I just need to find a healthy, discreet balance.

I stretch my arms above my head and try to get the blood moving. I need coffee desperately. The retreat staff is serving breakfast downstairs now, but I can't chat with anyone just yet. It's hard enough to wear a mask of normalcy right now, much less to feign giddiness. I take one last deep breath before getting up.

I can do this. I just need to put one foot in front of the other. One day at a time, as they say.

I dig through my purse for my cell phone. There's no one else in the room, but just to be safe, I take it with me to the water closet and shut the door. I text Ned: *Nothing new to report.*

Even though it's only the second day, I still slump at my lack of progress.

I go to check my email. It's been over twenty-four hours since I've touched based with my clients, which is the longest I've been offline since I started at the firm. It feels strange to be so disconnected. I walked around all day feeling exposed, naked. I kept reaching for my "missing limb," instinctively panicking at its absence and then reminding myself it was supposed to be tucked away, out of sight.

As my email loads, I imagine all the fires that have popped up during my time away, bracing myself for the damage, the rush of hysterical emails. *We need to talk ASAP. Urgent matter to discuss immediately. Why aren't you picking up your phone?*

But my inbox is fairly quiet. A few questions here and there, but nothing Ned can't handle. And he did handle it—responding to each and every inquiry within a few hours of receiving it. I sigh with relief, proud of both Ned and my clients for remaining in calm water. I'm about to put my phone away when a FaceTime from Ned comes through.

Damn. I hate FaceTime. Texting is so much easier.

"Hey," I say as I accept the call, a little embarrassed about being in the water closet. Luckily, Ned doesn't seem to mind.

"Well hey there, Ann," he says with a smile as wide as his face. He's in his kitchen making a cup of coffee, the artificial lights creating a halo around his bald head and small kaleidoscopes in his coke-bottle glasses.

"Ned, are you working from home?"

"Yeah, I had a doctor's appointment earlier, and it was easier to stay here. Also . . ." he continues, holding up what looks like the contract for Last Chance, "I had a crazy thought about this retreat, and wanted to share it with you."

My breath catches in my chest. "Okay, shoot."

"Well, I was watching *The Bachelor* with my wife the other night. You know, that reality dating show? The one where one guy picks a wife out of, like, twenty-five women?"

"I'm familiar." I don't watch it, but Reese and Honey enjoy it.

"Okay, so I realized that a lot of these rules in the contract are similar to what people on the show have to do. They can't have phones, they can't wear certain clothes."

I'm about to dismiss this notion as crazy, as there's no mention of cameras in the contract, but then I think about the clothes and makeup. Why else would we have to wear that stuff unless it was for an audience?

"Wouldn't they have to say it's a show?" I ask. As soon I say this, though, I know there are ways around that. I make a mental note to do a quick Google search of Hawaiian recording laws, since Phaux Island would have to abide by the closest state's laws.

"I haven't worked out all the kinks yet," Ned says, "but I do think I'm onto something. I have a buddy from law school who moved out to L.A., does entertainment law out there, and he says some of this language is verbatim what is used on some reality dating shows."

"So, what does this mean?" I try to make sense of this new inform-ation, this debatably insane theory, but my thoughts feel stuck. Like I'm wading through mud in my own brain.

"What if Reese is still on that island, safe and sound, and she's just staying quiet until the show premieres?"

My stomach drops.

Is this right? Could there be a perfectly benign reason Reese vanished?

"But," I add, trying to make pieces from two different puzzles fit. "Why wouldn't Reese just text me and say she was going to stay a bit longer? To vacation?"

Ned purses his lips. "I don't know."

"Why would someone use her license and impersonate her on the plane? That's a misdemeanor in Tennessee."

"I don't know," Ned repeats.

"Why is there a text message from her to a *burner phone* saying she needs to get away?" I can feel my voice rising as the sliver of hope dwindles away. "Why would her phone and the burner be *dumped* at Riverfront Park? Why would she get in a car that then *exploded?* Why—"

"You're right, you're right. It doesn't add up," Ned cuts in, his smile fading for the first time since the beginning of this call.

"I don't think you're wrong," I say, not wanting him to get discouraged so soon. "I think we just need more information. I'll see if I can find any signs of cameras on the island, or any mentions that align with show production." *Not like I know any,* I add silently.

"Sure thing," he says between sips of coffee. "I'm also going to review the public records of Last Chance and Phaux Island again. I can't help feeling like we missed something."

"Thanks, Ned. And any more information on Christina Wellington?"

"Not really." He sighs. "I don't know why Pat and I are having so much trouble. It's like the woman didn't exist until four years ago."

"It's suspicious, for sure."

I hear movement outside my door, and I almost drop my phone in a panic.

"Someone's here. I gotta go," I whisper before hanging up.

I tuck my phone in my bra before exiting the water closet. As I'm coming out, I nearly run into Magda.

"Goddamnit," I scream. I feel my phone slip, but I catch it by pretending to clutch my chest.

"Hey, vatch it," she shouts.

"I'm sorry, but don't you knock?"

"Tventy people. One Magda. No time," she says with flailing arms. She squints at me. "Were you talking to yourself in there?"

Shit. So she heard me. I avoid her gaze and head toward my room. "Yes. You don't talk to yourself when you're getting ready?"

"Vhere are you going?" she calls after me.

"Putting a bra on."

I continue clutching my chest as I hurry to the closet. I check to make sure she doesn't follow me before stowing away my phone.

"Do we really need makeup for yoga anyway?" I shout. "I'm just going to sweat it off."

"Zat's vhy ve use vaterproof mascara."

When I return to the bathroom, she's holding a gold tube. She points the mascara at a set of folded clothes on the counter. "Zees are for you. From Stephanie."

I inspect the thin spandex, unfolding it to reveal black shorts and a small white sports bra with the words 'Last Chance' across the breast. I dig the palms of my hands into my eye sockets at the thought of my chest in a white sports bra becoming transparent with perspiration.

"No. No. Absolutely not. I'm not wearing that."

12:Reese

was still basking in first-date bliss when the second night's cocktail party started. Emotionally, Lamb and I were in tune. Our conversation was natural. We laughed at the same jokes. We even reminisced about similar experiences.

"I used to sign all of those school slips that required parent permission," he admitted. "My parents didn't believe in government education—blasphemy, they said. Obviously, it was against the law to keep me out of school, so I went, but my parents never wanted to hear about it."

I too used to sign my own school slips. By the age of eight, I was washing my own clothes, packing my own lunch, and trekking a mile to and from the bus stop, even in the dead of winter. Not because my family didn't believe in education, but simply because they didn't care. My dad was gone, and my mom was always at some odd "job" or another. Or with her latest boyfriend. Or bailing my sister—technically half sister, on my mom's side—out of jail, again.

"I used to worry that I'd end up like them," he continued, staring absently into his drink. "That crazy was genetic, you know?"

My mouth was too dry to speak, so I nodded, thinking of all the times I found my mom or my sister passed out on the couch, bottle in hand, and I would swear on their grave that I'd never end up like that. (Spoiler: I did. Turns out addiction *is* genetic.)

It was eerie, how alike Lamb and I were. He was like a missing limb, syncing perfectly with my body, recounting past journeys and forgotten steps.

So I didn't mind that he had to talk to other women that second night. I didn't care that Pixie Cut was leaning into him, stroking his knee, her pouty mouth just a few inches from his ear. I knew that Lamb and I had something special, so talking with others and pretending to evaluate our options were just formalities. And besides, I liked getting to know the other participants. I enjoyed meeting new people, from every walk of life, pleased to discover that even the most unsuspecting had an interesting tidbit or two to offer.

The second night wasn't a round-robin style cocktail party, like the first night. It was more of a just-make-sure-to-say-hi-to-everyone kind of deal. It was out on the patio, mostly, near the infinity pool. Stephanie, the stylist, had dressed a lot of the women in sequins, so we shimmered like Christmas lights, the pool lights reflecting off of us in a hundred different ways. Drinks flowed, people got very tipsy. (Except me, obviously.) At one point, a woman with Rapunzel-like braids fell into the pool, and I had to fish her out before the weight of her sequins and her hair drowned her. Even Teddy—I had learned his name by that point—after being dragged to bed the night before for having one too many, was sweating scotch.

It wasn't until the end of the night that I noticed him. Ann's ex-boyfriend. *The* ex-boyfriend. The boyfriend who ruined all other boyfriends. I'm not sure how I could have missed him earlier—I was too caught up in Lamb and Rapunzel and Teddy, I guess. My own silly thoughts. When I saw him, the party seemed to slow down. I was caught in a freeze frame. All movement stopped except for him. He gave me the once-over, raised his glass, and winked at me.

I first heard about Ann's ex about a year into being her sponsor in AA. That's quite a long time to leave out such a crucial piece of your history, but Ann was like that. She didn't offer information willy-nilly. She was like a thousand-petal rose, and each time I peeled back one layer, there would be another, and another, that I'd have to work through. Before I met her, I had been in the program for two years and had two other sponsees, but—let's face it—my work was shabby. Both girls I had sponsored ended up off the wagon within months, and although they tell you not to take it personally, it's impossible not to. You come to care for your sponsees like children, and when they hurt, you hurt. So when I started helping Ann, I was determined to keep her on the straight and narrow. I took her through the Twelve Steps slowly, cautiously. She was like a wild animal, and too much too quickly would scare her off.

Because of all this, she didn't mention her ex for a while, not until we were working on step eight: *Made a list of all persons we had harmed, and became willing to make amends to them all.* I won't sugarcoat it: step eight is a real bummer. Step nine is even worse: *Made direct amends to such people wherever possible, except when to do so would injure them or others.*

No one likes doing these steps, and if you ever hear otherwise, that person is lying. These steps are gut-wrenching—like pouring salt in a wound. But these steps are also essential to recovery. They help you find peace when the shame threatens to consume you.

This is where most people tune out. I get it, I really do: it's like listening to nails on a chalkboard or scratching your eyes out. I expected Ann to run for the hills at this part too. Why make amends when you could do literally *anything* else? But she was resolute, and she stuck with it. She made a painstaking list of everyone who needed an apology, and number one was her ex. Even before her parents died, her drinking had become a problem: she passed out in public places, caused scenes at parties, threw tantrums whenever her boyfriend tried to talk to her about her behavior. She told this to me on the first day of spring—I'll never forget it. We were in the park. The dew was still clinging to the grass, and the sun was just breaking through the clouds.

"I don't know if I can see him again," she had said with shaking hands and red-rimmed eyes. "After everything."

I know they say addicts are weak, but let me tell you: it takes a lot of strength to live with those memories and put one foot in front of the other.

I encouraged her through the process, told her *of course you can see him again.* I helped her rehearse. And when her ex refused to hear her out, I was there for her.

"That's okay," I had cooed when she showed up in my doorway. "That happens sometimes. It's his right to close the door on you. The amends are for you anyway."

I said the words, but I didn't believe them. *Just listen to her. She's trying her best,* I had thought. My heart broke for her, and I would have given anything to take her pain away.

I only met the man once, at a flower shop with Ann. It was about three months after she tried to make amends with him. He was holding hands with a petite blonde, nuzzling her hair, and I remember thinking, *that's the most striking pair I've ever seen.* Especially the man—he had one of those faces you just don't forget. I nudged Ann then, so she could admire the couple with me, but she was already staring in their direction. Her face was white, and she wasn't breathing. She dropped her pot of marigolds, her terra-cotta vase cracking into jagged pieces on the concrete floor, the dirt spilling out like an army of ants. The whole store went quiet, and he inspected Ann then. His lips pinched, his face soured. He recoiled, as if he found Ann disgusting, pitiable, and he shuffled his blonde out of the aisle before she could see anything.

"Don't worry, these marigolds are sturdy." An employee of the flower shop was helping us by then, picking up the pieces of the vase. A tear rolled down my cheek as Ann watched him leave because I finally understood why Ann was the way she was.

I had been resentful of that man ever since, stoking my anger over the years like a fire. Ann thought I didn't get angry often, but I did. I just kept it below the surface, under a lid, until it finally exploded.

My fury toward him was misplaced. But that didn't stop the blood from rushing to my face when I saw him at the retreat. When he had the audacity to *wink* at me. To *raise his glass at me.* My skin prickled. My fists curled. My nails dug into my skin until I drew blood. There's no other way to say it—I was pulsing with rage.

I wasn't proud of what happened next, but I guess it must be told.

I punched him.

13: Ann

'm wearing it.

The small, white sports bra with "Last Chance" across the chest. It's in the contract: wear the clothes or go home. So I'm wearing the clothes. And Ned's theory burrows deeper into my mind. *What if it's all for a show?*

I still don't know what to make of Christina, either. She's too difficult to read. Most of the time, she doesn't even seem real. Her hair is always immaculate, even with the island humidity. Her silk button-downs and pencil skirts are always wrinkle-free. She doesn't have an ounce of spare fat on her. And in a thirty-bedroom mansion with all-white furniture, I have yet to find a spot of grime or a smear of dirt. Even now, on the beach, with the morning sun beating on her back, she hasn't shed a drop of sweat in her spandex.

What is she trying to hide behind that perfect façade?

As the sun ascends three-quarters above the water, the sky transforms from burnt orange to pale yellow to light blue. With the light behind her now, Christina becomes a dark, featureless figure on a yoga mat. Her shadow, three times her size, is a stark contrast to the white sand. Christina sits in a pose she called Sukhasana—her legs crossed, her back upright, her hands resting lightly on her knees. Her eyes appear closed, but it's difficult to tell with the light.

"I invite you to take a cleansing breath," she says with a steady voice. With the soft breeze and the rhythmic crash of the waves in the background, her voice reminds me of one of Reese's meditation guides. But I'm not calm. Not at all. I'm fidgeting, anxious, recounting over and over in my head what I'll ask Christina about Reese.

"In through the nose, out through the mouth," Christina continues.

We, the participants, collectively inhale before letting out a long, guttural exhale. We look like a cult in our spandex uniforms and matching poses. Even without the stress of my current situation, I've never been a big fan of yoga—although Reese tried hard to change my mind. She brought me to dozens of classes, all different types and lengths and instructors, in an attempt to bring me some peace that first year of sobriety.

"Just sit still and soak up the positive energy," she said in our first class, her face to the sky, her red hair piled high on top of her head.

"But I don't like to sit still," I responded as I bounced my knee and stole quick glances around the room. "It stresses me out. If I'm going to take an hour for exercise, I'd prefer to run off my anxiety—pound the pavement until my legs collapse and my head is blank."

"You can get in the same headspace with yoga," she urged, her blueberry eyes wide. "Focus on the positive, and when those negative thoughts bubble up, just pop them like balloons, one by one."

I looked at her like she was crazy.

"Pop, pop, pop." She smiled.

So I tried, again and again. I sat, stood, and lay down in various positions, trying to ignore the stench of a dozen sweaty bodies in an enclosed space that grew more pungent with each minute. I tried to pop the negative thoughts as they arose—the cravings, my parents' absence, my precarious financial situation, my unwanted solitude—but they grew angrier and more violent as the class wore on. The instructor's urges to be grateful, to become one with the earth, to focus on the now made me want to throw things.

"Breathe deeply once more," Christina continues. "I want you to exhale any reservations you may have, any negative experiences that are holding you back from finding true love, your soul mate."

Twenty loud exhales escape into the wind.

"And inhale the possibilities this retreat has to offer, the passion that is yours for the taking. Just reach out and grab it."

I hate this. I hate it so much.

I survey the participants, most of whom are taking this very seriously. A girl with a pixie cut, eyes closed, reaches out in front of her and grabs the air. Next to her, Turnt Teddy also sits with his eyes closed, but he's hunched over. Pale. His breathing is off. Perhaps he fell asleep. Wouldn't be too unusual, considering the night he had before. When his head lolls forward, Basketball Blake elbows him, and Teddy wakes with a start.

In my peripheral vision, I see a couple handlers, all in black despite the sun, guarding the patio doors to the mansion. They're as still as toy soldiers, and I wonder what exactly they're handling. They've got to do more than patrol cocktail parties and yoga sessions. You don't need guns for those activities.

In between the two handlers, half their size, is Henry, the shaggy man who took my bags when I arrived yesterday. With his arms crossed and a wide stance, he surveys the beach, his gaze moving among us like a laser. I return my gaze to the other participants before the laser lands on me.

The few women who aren't closing their eyes—I really need to learn their names today—are staring, gaping, at the newest arrival, Nicknameless Nick. I can feel his gaze boring into my skin, have felt it burning for a few minutes. I glance in his direction, and he smiles at me softly. Offers a quick wink. I avert my eyes and pretend to focus on Christina.

I don't have time for this.

When the session finishes, after Christina has wished us a *glorious* second day on the *journey*, I roll up my mat slowly, hoping it will give one of the other women time to grab Nick. But he's at my side within seconds.

"Let me take that for you." His tanned hand is outstretched, reaching for my yoga mat. He's in front of the sun, light emanating from his body like wings, and I have to shade my eyes with my hand.

"Thanks." I give him the mat, which he tosses over his shoulder like a ragdoll. He helps me stand with his other hand.

"So, are you going on a date now or meeting with Christina first?"

"Date first. Then Christina. I think I'm fourth in line when I get back."

"Same here. Fifth or sixth maybe. I'm going to snag some coffee after my date, if you'd like to join." His smile curves upward and to the left. "I don't know about you, but I can't run on just a few hours of sleep."

"Oh." I look at my feet, disturbing the sand as we march back to the mansion. "I was going to go on a run after, try to get my energy back up." And try to spot anything unusual.

"Wow." His eyebrows lift. "A run. With jet lag. After a yoga session. If I wasn't about to keel over, I'd join you."

"Maybe next time." I shrug.

"Who's your date with?"

"Ch—Clay." I catch myself just before the words *Chef Clay* escape my mouth. I swivel my head to find Clay, but he's gone. He must have already gone inside. "What about you?"

"Trixie."

"Who's that again?"

Nick glances behind him until he spots the woman with the pixie cut. He gives her a slight wave, and Trixie and the woman beside her both blush.

"Interesting name," I say. Pixie Trixie. Too easy.

"Yeah, well, we'll see how it goes." He scratches his cheek as he holds the mansion door open for me. "Hopefully I see you later."

I turn back to face him, to tell him *yeah, maybe*, but the handler with the eye tattoo has already thrown his Popeye arm around Nick's shoulder in a buddy-buddy fashion, leading him toward the kitchen.

The eye follows me as they disappear.

14:Ann

The date with Clay goes . . . well. I guess. I try to concentrate on him during our picnic on the beach, but I keep mentally rehearsing what I'll say to Christina. There's no food, only champagne, so Clay ends up more than a little happy. He repeats the same bits of information: he's a chef, he's from Texas, he found out about the retreat through an advertisement in the mail. That last part piques my curiosity, actually. Every participant I've talked to has gotten a brochure in their mailbox. How were they selected to receive the ad? By looks, background, job? Certainly not by location. And why didn't I receive an ad? What makes me different?

After our date, I run about three miles past the mansion on the beach. Nothing suspicious of note—just forest. I want to run farther, keep checking, but I don't have enough time. I need to shower and let Stephanie humiliate me with her chosen attire before my session with

Christina. And then, finally, it comes. The moment I've been waiting for. Uninterrupted time alone with Christina. A chance to ask questions about Reese that won't seem suspicious or out of place.

I straighten the dress Stephanie deemed appropriate for this occasion and fiddle with my watch before knocking on the door to the talking room. Three quick raps.

"Come in," Christina answers.

I step inside.

The room is small. Not much bigger than an office. Unsurprisingly, the room is all white—white walls, white plush carpet, and two white armchairs facing each other. Unlike the rest of the house, though, there are no windows. No natural light. No dashes of color, however miniscule. There is a single side table—white—next to the empty armchair, and it holds only a box of tissues. Christina sits in the chair opposite me, legs crossed, back straight, hands in her lap. She's as still as a cat, her eyes following me as if I were prey.

"Please," she says, gesturing to the chair in front of her. "Sit."

I do as she says, trying to get comfortable.

"Thank you." When Christina doesn't respond, I continue. "I like the room. It's different from other therapists' offices." No degrees framed on the wall, no desk, no blanket, no personal trinkets. It's colder too, and my post-run sweat makes me shiver.

"Well, I'm not a traditional therapist."

"What do you mean? You follow an experimental school of therapy?"

"No. I mean I didn't study psychology. It's just something I picked up when I started the retreats."

"Oh. What did you study then?"

"I didn't go to college. Wasn't the right fit for me."

Damnit. With a school name or a license, there are public records. I shift in my seat, trying to segue naturally into another personal question.

"What made you interested in running a singles' retreat?"

Christina smiles, like she knows something I don't.

"You remind me of my younger sister," she says with a tilt of the head. "She's always interested in others."

"Well." I catch myself playing with my watch again, and I force myself to stop. "Guess it's just how I learned to make conversation. I'm an open book, though. What about me would you like to know?"

"Let's start with the retreat. Are you comfortable?"

"Very," I lie.

"And you're getting along with the men?"

"Yes, very well."

"Anyone in particular that has caught your eye?" She smiles again, and I rack my memories for her face. I know I've seen it before.

"Um, let's see," I start. I should have practiced this part more. "I liked my date with Clay earlier. He seems like a nice guy. A little shy, but I'm that way too, so I can't point fingers. And he's a chef, which is a very nice skill to have in a partner. I can't cook to save my life, so I need someone to help me around the kitchen." I laugh, a little self-conscious, but Christina doesn't budge. The woman is like a statue.

"What about Nick?" she asks finally, raising her unnaturally arched eyebrows.

"Also seems like a nice guy."

"You two bonded last night, yes? After he woke you from your sleepwalking?"

How did she know that? Did Nick tell her? I must look confused, because she cuts in quickly. "Magda woke up when you opened her door. In the hallway I told you not to visit." I search for signs of anger, but there aren't any. If anything, she appears amused.

"Ah, yes. So sorry about that. Sleepwalking. Now there's a habit I really wish I could break." I'm amazed at how easily the lies are rolling off my tongue. "But yes, Nick was kind enough to get me some water and some food after I came to my senses."

"Between you and me, he's one of my favorites. Definitely one of the more attractive men who have attended this retreat. You would make a striking pair."

"Oh, I don't know." I sigh. I wish she would divulge more of her personal life and fewer thoughts about Nick. "He looks like an exboyfriend. Sort of makes it weird."

"I think that's fate then."

She offers that familiar smile again, and I focus all my energy on acting normal. Better than normal, even. I spend the rest of our time answering questions like Reese or Honey would respond. *Yes, he's very dreamy. He makes my heart race. I can see our lives together at the end of this. I'd be so lucky to end up with a guy like that.* Christina often asks me to rephrase—not unlike an actual therapist—if she doesn't like my first response. *What,* specifically, *do you like about him? Can you repeat his name again, just so I'm clear on who you're referring to?*

I've got to say: I put on a great performance.

But like a spider inching up my spine, Ned's theory won't leave me alone. Is Christina asking me to rephrase just to understand me better, or is it for soundbites? But if it is a show, where are the goddamn cameras? In the walls?

I make another visual sweep of the room, trying to spot discreet hiding places.

Christina clears her throat, and I refocus on her.

"Well, this has been lovely, Ann. I hope you found it beneficial."

"I did. Thank you."

Christina's gaze darts from me to the door, but I remain seated.

"Would you mind if I asked you a couple questions before I go?"

Her eyes narrow, but she nods anyway.

"You know Reese Marigold was my friend, right? She actually wanted me to come here with her." I try not to wince—that last sentence hurts every time I say it. I should have come when she asked me to.

"Ah, yes." She crosses her arms, which is the most movement I've seen from her in the past twenty minutes. "Reese. I was sorry to hear about her disappearance. Has there been any news?"

"No, none." I inch closer to Christina, my butt practically hanging off the edge of the chair. "I was wondering if you could tell me about her time here. Did she find someone? Did she seem happy?"

"Of course," she says. "She didn't connect to anyone in particular. It's unfortunate, but it occasionally happens. She didn't seem too broken up about it, though. She was always in good spirits, and she made a lot of friends."

"Yeah, Reese could befriend just about anyone." My voice cracks, just the tiniest bit, but I recover quickly. "So there wasn't any guy she was particularly interested in?"

"Not that I can recall." Christina flicks her wrist to view her watch. "Well, I hate to end on this note, but I do need to see the next participant if we're going to stay on schedule."

"Of course. Thank you for your time."

As I leave, I stand tall, my shoulders back. A voice screams in my head.

That bitch is lying.

15:Reese

As soon as I smacked that stupid smirk off his stupid face, I realized what I had done. It was like the fury kept my eyes veiled until my fist met his jaw. Then I saw clearly. This wasn't Ann's ex. Ann's ex was back in Nashville, married. I saw his wife, still wearing a wedding band, not two weeks prior while shopping for produce in the grocery store.

"What the hell was that for?" Ann's doppelgänger-ex shouted as he held his face.

"I–I'm so sorry," I stuttered. I was aghast. Yes, I obviously had impulse-control issues, but violence usually wasn't part of my repertoire. "I thought you were someone else."

In my peripheral vision, I saw a couple handlers start to approach me, but Christina stopped them with an outstretched arm. I felt a gentle cup of my elbow. Lamb. He looked at me with wide eyes.

"Reese, what happened? Did he hurt you?"

"Of course not!" The doppelgänger-ex yelled, garnering us even more attention. I could feel eyes on the back of my head.

"I'm so sorry," I repeated. I didn't know what else to say. "I thought you were someone I knew back in Nashville. I realized my mistake as soon as I . . ." I gestured to his cut lip.

"I've literally never been to Nashville. I'm from California. My name is Nick. Nick Keyser."

"Gosh, I'm so sorry. Can I get you some ice? A rag?" I reached for him, but he flinched at my proximity.

"No, I think you've done enough." He lifted his hand from his face, revealing an angry, red splotch of skin. Luckily his nose looked fine. It was just his lip that was bleeding.

I took inventory of my surroundings. The other participants had gathered around us, forming a sort of prurient circle. Gaping mouths, bulging eyes. The ocean waves behind us broke the deafening silence. I inspected Lamb, who was still looking at me with those unbearably wide eyes.

I wanted to disappear.

"I'm going to call it a night," I said.

I didn't wait for a response. I left in a hurry. I could feel eyes following me. The whispers crescendoed as I neared the Cinderella stairs. Lamb bounded after me.

"Reese, wait—"

I couldn't stop. My face was on fire.

"I just need a minute, Lamb." My hands were shaking. I picked up the pace. I stepped on my sequin gown, heard the tear of fabric, the roll of my ankle.

Great, I thought. *Now Stephanie will hate me, too.*

"Reese, slow down. Talk to me."

I didn't stop. I didn't look back.

"Nothing to talk about," I called over my shoulder.

When I reached my room, he grabbed my wrist. Forced me to make eye contact.

"C'mon, Reese. Just slow down. Tell me what happened." He seemed so desperate.

After what seemed like ten minutes, I gave in. "Okay."

I drifted to the hotel-style bed while he shut my bedroom door. I buried my face in one of the pillows, closed my eyes to the scene that had just happened. I needed to block it out, just like all the other better-forgotten memories I kept in lockboxes deep inside my mind. Lamb rubbed my back. Gently, at first, but then more firmly.

"Hey, come on. It wasn't that bad."

"It was worse than bad," I said in a muffled cry. "It was humiliating."

"Okay, it was bad." I felt Lamb's muscles tense. "But it's clear you made a mistake. Just don't do anything like that again, and it'll be all right."

He pried the pillow from my grasp. I stared at the smeared makeup on the fabric.

"Do you want to tell me why you punched a guy you never met?"

"I thought he was my friend's ex." I sighed. "He didn't treat her as well as I would've liked, and I've always resented him for that. I haven't seen him since she told me their story, but I've seen his wife plenty of times around town. I don't know what came over me. It was like seeing him, even after all this time, brought back all this anger I didn't know I had. Like, I never get angry for myself, but maybe I do, and I just store it, and it lies there dormant, simmering, just waiting to burst at the wrong moment." I looked at him with tears in my eyes, pleading. "Does that make sense? That probably doesn't make sense."

"I understand." He rubbed my thumb with his. "I can get angry too."

"I've also . . ." I stared at my hands as I worked up the courage to tell him this next part. "I've also been under some stress lately. Some things happened before I came here that you should probably know about."

"What happened?" His hand roamed to my neck, massaging the skin. But then—and I'm not sure if I imagined this—his grip seemed to tighten.

I grabbed his hand and put it in my lap. His eyes were heavy when they met mine—clouded with lust, or something else, I'm not sure.

A knock came at my door. Christina popped her head in. Two of her handlers were in the shadows.

"Lamb, would you give me a minute with Reese?"

Lamb seemed like he might protest, but something about the look on Christina's face stopped him, and he left the room.

I was in trouble.

16:Ann

repeat the phrase in my head like a mantra as I trudge up the Cinderella stairs, back to my room.

She's lying.

She's lying.

She's lying.

My footfalls become more pronounced with each repetition. It helps to drown out the chatter, splashes of water, and occasional squeals from the infinity pool outside, where the participants who are not on dates or talking with Christina have gathered. Glasses clink, champagne pops, more squeals. I hope these people ate something after their dates.

I don't feel like listening to the same stories over and over again tonight. I tell myself not to turn and look, but I can't help it. The sun is going down, and everything is cloaked in gold. The furniture seems less white, the people less sunburned. A couple kisses on an outside couch—

Basketball Blake and a gorgeous Latino woman. Chef Clay naps in another nook, mouth open and sunglasses on. Nick talks to two women, and both of them laugh and stroke his arm on cue. He must feel my stare, as he glances up at me and smiles. A timid but hopeful smile. I turn away and continue to march up the stairs. Don't have time for that.

When I reach my room, I slam the door and lock it. I sink to my knees, run my hands through the soft carpet, and lie facedown, letting the rug fibers tickle my cheeks. I'm so tired. The jet lag, my late-night activities, the exercise—it's all catching up to me. I run through my conversation with Christina again. There's no way Reese didn't connect to someone in particular. In the ten years I've known her, Reese has always had a boyfriend. Some lasted longer than others, some only lasted a night. Okay, maybe *boyfriend* isn't the right word. Lover? Romantic interest? Regardless of the terminology, Reese has always been linked to *someone.* And she's not quiet about it either.

Once, during a tearful dinner, Reese recounted the details of her latest breakup—a four-year relationship with a sleazy neighbor. The final straw had been that morning, when she found a treasure trove of naked photos of other women in his recent text messages. Reese was a wreck, hiccupping over her uneaten pasta. Our waiter brushed Reese's shoulder, telling her he'd help in any way he could, and she sat bolt upright. Her tears stopped flowing when she realized he had slipped her his number.

The next day, Reese was back to her old self, giddy and drunk with lust.

"I'm in love, I'm in love, I'm in love," she trilled.

She wasn't in love. Of course she wasn't. But she firmly believed it, and she was loyal to that waiter for about two weeks, like she's loyal to all her lovers, until he left her for a younger, bouncier model. Now, I know I'm not painting Reese in the best light; she has her flaws like the rest of us, and her Achilles' heel is her relationship status. She can't stand to be single. Not to sound like every cliché ever written, but I always suspected it had something to do with her family. Her dad left, her mom and sister weren't around. It's only natural, in my opinion at least, to yearn for stability after a home like that.

So that's how I know Christina's lying when she says Reese didn't connect with anyone. Although it would be nice to have some actual, tangible proof. Maybe Ned has figured something out by now. I pick myself off the floor and shuffle to the closet to retrieve my phone. Rummaging in my purse, I find it. No new messages. No emails from Ned, either. Damnit. I'm about to hide my mobile when it vibrates in my hand. The screen lights up and displays Honey's name. I'm not in the mood to discuss, again, how I shouldn't be on this retreat, but then I realize she might have news about Reese.

"Hey, let me call you back in one minute."

I hang up before she has time to respond. I know my door's locked, but Magda must have a key, and I need to be cautious. I nudge the chest of drawers to the right of the entrance, but it's heavier than I anticipated. I try again with gritted teeth, this time putting my back into it, and the chest finally budges, making a horrible moaning noise as it grinds against the hardwood floor. Nails on a chalkboard. I catch my breath once the chest is in its new position and pray no one heard the noise. Then I head to the water closet, close the door, and video-call Honey. I'd prefer a phone call, as it's more efficient, but I know Honey prefers face-to-face interactions.

She answers on the first ring. In a silk nightgown, she's sitting at the marble island in her kitchen with a glass of red wine. It's dark in the room, her hair is curled, and she has on fresh makeup. Her husband is nowhere in sight, which is how I prefer it—she knows better than to call me when he's in the room.

"Are you calling me from the toilet?" she laughs.

"No." I roll my eyes playfully. "Well, yes, I am, but I'm not using it. I can't have my phone at the retreat, you know? So I'm trying not to get caught. What are you doing up? It's—" I check my watch and add five hours to the time. "It's eleven there, right?"

"Yeah, but Kris couldn't sleep. I finally got her to bed, but now I'm wide awake."

I never understood why Honey named her now three-year-old after her older sister. Kris senior was like a stain on Honey's family—something to sweep under the rug and forget about. After she was sent to boarding school at a young age, she found trouble like it was her job. Drugs, shoplifting, cheating. Honey told me they stopped speaking when Kris left for school, after an incident involving her friend Bear, but I've always felt like Honey was holding something back. I can't imagine what it's like to have a poor relationship with my family, but I imagine, under the most atrocious of circumstances, I'd be strong enough to sever ties. For Honey, I don't think it's ever been that simple.

Bear is someone Honey and I don't discuss. It's just too painful. Sometimes, when I'm in that in-between stage of wakefulness and sleep, an image of him will come back to me, unbidden. Hair the color of cedar wood, the biggest dimples punctuating his cheeks. He was a childhood friend when Honey and I were around five. Bear was three years older, and he was technically Kris's friend first, but it was easy to forget the age difference because of his small size. In fact, his stature is what gave him the name Bear. I can't remember his real name. Marc, maybe. It's funny how a single nickname can come to define a person. A complex human simplified into a one-syllable moniker.

When it was nice out, especially in the summer, the four of us would spend hours playing in the creek behind Honey's house, catching crawdads and playacting different characters in various pretend adventures. Bear was my first crush—he was everyone's first crush—so there was usually a fight over who would be his damsel in distress for the day.

I wasn't there the day it happened. It was my mom's birthday. It was the perfect day, just my mom, my dad, and I, the tight elastic band of the birthday hat under my chin, the cake icing coloring my teeth blue. A call interrupted our celebration. I remember how my mom's face transformed as she held the phone to her ear. Her mouth turned down, the smile draining out of her eyes between stolen glances at me.

Bear died in Honey's creek that day. He was with Kris when it happened. Honey had gone inside to gather more supplies for their water adventure, and when she returned, Bear was lying on his back, unmoving, blood staining the water around his head. It was an accident, Kris had said. An unfortunate accident. He slipped and hit his head. Kris left for boarding school the next week, and ever since, I've wondered if there was more to the story than Kris let on.

Tragedy can tether you to someone. Besides love, I think it's the strongest bond there is. Honey and I were chained together from that day forward. Even when our interests diverged, even when we started occupying different social circles, we always found our way back to one another.

"Sometimes I'm convinced that kid is a goblin," Honey says between sips, interrupting my thoughts of the past. "A goblin that tore apart my labia and deepens my crow's-feet on a regular basis."

Honey finishes her wine, twirls the stem of the glass in her fingers, and continues: "So now I'm trying to wind down. Thought I'd give you a call while I drink this glass. Or three."

"Oh," I try to hide my disappointment, but it's too late. "So no news about Reese?"

"No," Honey's eyes droop. "Sorry. I didn't mean to get your hopes up. I was just thinking about you and wondering how you were."

"I'm still alive, if that's what you're wondering." There's an edge to my tone that slips out.

"Come on, Ann," she pleads as she rotates her wedding ring. "You can't blame me for worrying."

"Well, there's nothing to worry about. I haven't found anything tangible yet. Just suspicions."

Honey pours another glass—a heftier amount than normal. I study Honey's face more closely. She's more drunk than I first realized. Stressed.

"Everything okay with you?" I ask.

"Me? Oh, I'm fine. Just . . . we made a business investment, and it's not working out as well as we'd hoped."

"Oh." I'm surprised. I've never heard Honey mention financial troubles. Or any sort of work; Honey never needed a job. I'm proud of her for branching out, trying something new. I've always thought she seemed a bit restless being a stay-at-home mom with two full-time nannies.

"Well, just remember to diversify, and the good will usually outweigh the bad."

"Yeah, little late for that," she huffs. She takes another long sip of her wine, swallows, and sets her empty glass down on the island. She takes a deep breath. "But anyway. Back to you. Why are you suspicious?"

"I think Christina—she's the host of the retreat—is lying about Reese. Christina told me Reese didn't have a connection here."

"And you think she did?"

"Honey, it's Reese. She always had—*has*—a connection." I cringe at my use of the past tense. "You know she can't go longer than forty-eight hours without a new interest."

Honey evades my gaze, runs her palm across the smooth marble. The momentary wave of relief I felt at Honey's interest starts to recede.

I shouldn't have confided in Honey; she thinks what I'm doing is insane. That *I'm* insane.

"You know Reese," I plead. "You *know* she would have fawned over someone. Told everyone about it."

Honey nods, but she still doesn't make eye contact.

"I'm not crazy, Honey. I know something happened here."

"I know." She rubs an eyebrow. "If you find out anything else about Christina or Reese, let me know. I'll pick you up, call the police. Whatever you want."

I know she's placating me, saying the words I want to hear. I can't bear to be the recipient of her pity any longer.

"Honey, I've got to go."

"Wait—"

I hang up. Knock my head against the bathroom wall.

No more confiding in Honey. I can't let her or anyone else make me question myself or hinder my search for my friend. I know something happened here. I just need more information, that's all. I need to keep digging.

I'm not crazy.

I'm not crazy.

I'm not crazy.

I tell myself this repeatedly, like I used to do when I was a child, when I would check the lock three times before I went to sleep. Or when I would check my math problems, three times each.

"I just have to be sure. I just have to be sure," I begged my mother. I cried one night, big fat tears, when she wouldn't let me check the back door for a third and final time. She held me for a while, combing my hair with her hand as I pounded her with my tiny fists.

"I just have to be sure."

17:Ann

need a break. I've been socializing for a few hours now, and the cocktail party is winding down. I've done my part, anyway. Talked to all the men. Well, almost all the men. Not Nick. I've been avoiding him like the plague.

I round the outside of the mansion until I'm out of view. Thankfully, my gown is looser tonight, so I'm able to slide my back down the side of the house. Rest for a minute. The adobe wall feels cool against my head. I knock my head, gently. One, two, three. I close my eyes, try to focus instead on the breeze that rustles the leaves of the forest instead of the hum from the party.

I want a drink, badly. That longing is always there, but it gets louder when I'm upset—like an old friend whispering in my ear: *I can make you feel better. Don't you remember? Just have one. One won't kill you. You can stop after that.* But I can't stop. After a sip, I want five drinks, ten, twenty. Once the booze reaches my head, I disappear, and a different person sets up shop. That person drinks into oblivion, yells at friends, makes a mess.

When I got sober, one of my college friends—a semi-friend, a barely friend—asked me, "Why can't you just have, like, one drink? Just practice moderation."

"Wow, Nancy," I responded. "I've never thought of that before. Thanks for the great advice."

She smiled then, like she had discovered something revolutionary.

Idiot.

I dig my nails into my thighs, but I can't break the skin—my nails are chewed down too much. I don't know who I think I am. I'm not a detective. I don't solve crimes. I've been at this retreat for over twenty-four hours, and all I know is that Christina claims Reese didn't make a connection here.

Leaves crunch, and I turn my head toward the sound. Nick rounds the corner. *Awesome,* I think. *Just what I need.*

"Sorry." Nick stops when he sees me. "I didn't know anyone was back here. You mind if I have a smoke?"

"Go ahead," I respond. What else am I going to say? *No?* I'd look like an asshole.

He slides down the wall. His shoulder brushes mine, and I catch the familiar scent of Old Spice. Another commonality with my ex-boyfriend. He pulls out a packet of cigarettes and a lighter from the inside of his jacket.

"You want one?"

I really shouldn't. It's a gross habit—something I gave up when I quit booze.

But the cigarette, the need for a release, calls to me.

"Sure," I say.

He hands me a cigarette. I hold it like one might hold a bomb. As soon as Nick lights it, I inhale the familiar taste of tobacco, let the smoke fill my lungs. The nicotine hits almost instantaneously, and I feel lighter. The dopamine dances in my brain, and I laugh.

"What?" Nick grins as he exhales a large puff of smoke.

"I haven't had a cigarette since I was in college. Forgot what it felt like."

"You want to wash it down?" He offers me his glass.

Yes, I think. But no. I can't. "No, this is good." I wave the whiskey away.

Nick shrugs and throws back the rest of his drink.

"So what are you hiding from?" he asks when he's finished.

"Oh, I don't know. Just needed a breather, I guess."

"You know it's only day two, right?"

Damn. He's right. My eyes widen. "Yeah." I take a long drag of my cigarette. "So how was your date today?"

"It was okay." He shrugs. "I've already been on a date with Trixie, so I knew it wouldn't lead anywhere."

"Trixie." I chuckle. I can't take it seriously. "That name is for horses."

He laughs too, and we feed off of each other. Soon we're both howling—the type of laughter that can only come from an artificial high. Then something clicks, and I fall silent.

"Wait. What do you mean you've already been on a date with her? Today was the first one-on-one date."

"Well, this is our second go of the retreat. Teddy's too. And Rapunzel's. I can't remember her actual name, but the girl with the braid. Something flowery." He snaps his fingers. "Rhea. I knew it started with an *R*."

I can't believe what I'm hearing. "W-When did you come before?"

"The month before. I took a break between sessions."

So he would have been here with Reese. My eyes feel like they're about to pop out of my head. My arm drops, and the lit end of the cigarette burns my thigh.

"You look like you've seen a ghost," Nick says.

"Sorry." I snap out of it. "It's just my friend was here then too. She's missing now, and the last anyone heard from her was at this retreat."

Nick's eyes pop open.

"Missing? I'm sorry to hear that. What was her name?"

"Reese Marigold. Red hair. Also pretty flowery. Do you remember her?" I search his eyes, praying he recalls something. An emotion crosses his face—something I can't quite put my finger on.

"Yeah," he says after a long inhale of his cigarette. "Yeah, I remember her."

"Did she connect with anyone in particular?"

He nods, exhales the smoke.

"Guy named Lamb Martin."

Lamb Martin. I repeat the name in my head. *Lamb Martin. Lamb Martin.* I knew Christina was lying, I knew it.

"Do you remember where he's from? Anything about him?"

"Actually, yeah. Watercolor, Florida. I remember because he was a painter, and I thought that was a fitting hometown name for an artist."

I notice the use of the past tense. Was that accidental, or a slip? My mind pulsates with the new information. I *need* to find Lamb Martin.

"Do you remember if she seemed happy? Did anything happen that could have upset her?"

Nick averts his eyes. Stubs out his cigarette.

"No. She seemed happy to me."

18:Ann

hardly sleep that night. Every time my eyelids droop, the thought of Lamb Martin creeps into mind, and *bam*—my eyes flip back open like a roller shade. I couldn't call Ned until the morning due to basic human decency, so all I can do is wait. And wait.

And wait. I try every sleeping position imaginable, but they are all equally uncomfortable.

Now it's 4:00 a.m., and if I lie in bed a moment longer, I may burst into flames. Before ferreting out my phone, I shove the chest of drawers in front of the door again, just to be safe. My arms are already sore from yesterday.

Ned answers on the first ring. "Well howdy, Ann," he chirps. "You're up early. How are ya?"

"Good, good." I'm not in the mood for pleasantries, but I inquire about him out of habit.

"*Excellent.* Cindy gave me an early Christmas gift. It's a pilot watch, and it is so awesome."

I suppress a groan. The stories about his wife and his obsession with planes drag on the longest. Ned speaks often and openly about his love of aviation. Instead of storing his car in his garage, he uses the space for an antique plane, which he flies at least once a month. He also proudly displays a robust collection of memorabilia on his desk—mostly miniature models of famous aircraft carriers. If you ask about any of the collectibles, you're in for a twenty-minute story.

"I've been playing with it all day," he continues. "It has all types of cool data: current GPS ground speed, GPS track, distance from waypoints and airports, estimated time en route, bearing, and glide ratio. Oh, and get this: I can build a flight plan and easily upload it to my watch. It's *so cool.*"

"That's awesome, Ned. I can't wait to see it. In other good news, I found some more info on Reese." The segue isn't my smoothest, but I can't contain myself any longer.

"That's great. What is it?"

"Well, apparently, she got close to a guy named Lamb Martin. That's *L-A-M-B*, like the animal. He's from Watercolor, Florida, and he's a painter. Would you be able to track him down, see if he'd be willing to talk to me? He's between thirty and thirty-five, around six-one. When he was here, he had blond, shoulder-length hair, but that could have changed, obviously."

"Sure thing, Ann. I'll do it between meetings today. If I have trouble locating him, can I get Pat involved?"

"Yeah, of course."

"Speaking of the PI, you know the financial documents I mentioned? About the island purchase and the retreat? Well, Pat was able to dig up some less-public records, and we noticed there's a guarantor for both Last Chance and Phaux Island. Someone by the name of Beverly Wellington. I'm assuming she's related to Christina because they share the same last name. A mother, maybe?"

"Christina mentioned a younger sister." The name Beverly rings a bell, but I can't consciously connect it to anything. "I'll see if I can coax the name out of her."

"That'd be helpful, because Pat and I can't find anything on this Beverly woman. There's even less information about her than there is about Christina. With Christina, there are at least records from the past few years. But with Beverly? Zilch. It may be an alias."

"Well, that means she's hiding something, right? So at least we're on the right track."

"That's what I was thinking too."

❧ ❧ ❧

After my call with Ned, I shower. I tidy my room. I surf the web on my phone, although it's difficult without connecting to the Wi-Fi. Through a cursory search, I confirm that Hawaii is a one-party consent state, which means that any recording is fair game if one person agrees to it. So, I guess if this is a show, then any discussion I have with Christina, or any employee at Last Chance, is legally allowed to be recorded and distributed. Which means I need to be even more careful about what I say.

The realization frays at my already shot nerves.

When my watch reads 6:03 a.m., I decide to head downstairs for breakfast. I need food before my one-on-one date, anyway. Christina prefers we don't eat on dates, as it's "distracting," so our meals are relegated to eccentric times: 6:00 a.m., 10:00 a.m., 3:00 p.m., 11:00 p.m. I should have asked Ned about eating on reality shows. Perhaps they don't eat on dates because it messes with the audio. I can't believe I'm still entertaining the theory, but the more I'm here, the more it lines up. The makeup. The dresses. The "discussions" with Christina. But I still can't figure out where they keep the cameras, or why they'd go to all this trouble to keep it a secret. I'd bet there are plenty of people who'd kill to be on a show like this.

The kitchen is quiet, with the exception of the cook, who is in the middle of a culinary concert: drumming pots and pans, sizzling eggs on the stovetop, flipping pancakes. He takes an intermission when I arrive.

"You want four espresso shots?" he says with arched eyebrows. "Four?"

"Yes, four shots." I reply.

"You know that's the equivalent of two and a half cups of coffee, right?"

"In that case, make it five."

I know exactly how much caffeine is in an espresso shot, but his patronizing tone bothers me. *Save the judgment, motherfucker. This is my only vice. With the exception of the solitary cigarette last night, which was a one-time thing.* But I smile innocently, like some dewy-eyed schoolgirl, keeping my cover.

After I receive my lifeline of caffeine, I force myself to stop reviewing the details of Reese's disappearance—a fun habit I've picked up that prevents me from sleeping—and mentally prepare for my one-on-one date with Guitar Guy. I pray he doesn't bring a musical instrument. He's brought his guitar to both cocktail parties now and strummed a second-rate tune each time. I don't think my sleep-deprived headache can handle another one. I wish Christina would have let us choose our second one-on-one dates; I would have selected Nick as my first choice now that I know he was with Reese in her last month. I have so many more questions for him. *Who else did she go on a date with? Was anyone else interested in her? Could she have been stalked by another participant? Did anyone appear suspicious? What did she do on her last day?* I can't ask these questions all at once, not without giving away my ulterior motive in coming here, so I have to space out my interrogation. Nick could be involved in Reese's disappearance, for all I know.

Someone grabs my shoulders. I grip the hot espresso, ready to toss it behind me.

"Boo," Nick whispers in my ear. My shoulders relax, and I lower my mug. *Speak of the devil.*

"Hey." Despite myself, and despite my initial reaction, I smile. An ear-to-ear smile. I need to pull myself together.

He straddles the stool beside me. He can barely contain his excitement.

"You couldn't sleep either, huh?"

"No. I can't say it was my best night's sleep."

"Well." Nick eyes my espresso. "Load up on caffeine. Gotta be ready for our big date."

I tilt my head. *Our date? As in, just you and me?*

"I asked Christina for a favor," he explains. "You and I are gonna get a better view of this island today. You and Guy will get together another time."

"Wha—how?"

"I'll explain later." He stands up and tugs on my hair, which is still drying from my shower. "I recommend a hair tie for today's adventure."

My mouth is still gaping when he leaves.

19: Reese

The talk with Christina was weird. (Truthfully, all our talks were.)

"Let's go to a talking room," she said after Lamb left my room.

I didn't understand why we couldn't just chat in my room, or why there were specific rooms designated just for talking. After the scene I caused downstairs, though, I didn't have the right to protest or ask questions.

"So," Christina said once we were situated. She folded her hands in her lap. "Let's talk about what just happened."

"Christina, I'm so sorry. That was so inappropriate. I understand if I need to leave."

I shut my eyes, ready for the details of my expulsion.

But Christina did something unusual—she grinned. Just for a second.

It was gone as soon as I could register it.

"That won't be necessary. These things happen. Emotions run high on this retreat. I just want to work through your feelings now, to make sure we get to the root of the issue."

"It was a total mistake. I thought he was someone else."

"Perhaps. But that couldn't be all there is to it. The reaction was too primal. Too violent for just that."

I drew in a deep breath.

"Lamb was talking to another woman tonight. They shared an intimate moment—a kiss—just shortly before you attacked Nick."

What? Was that true? No, she must have been mistaken. I shook off the image and refocused.

"No, no. It had nothing to do with Lamb. I thought that guy—"

"Nick," Christina interrupted.

"*Nick.* I thought *Nick* was a friend's ex-boyfriend. He was a jerk to her, and I hadn't seen him since . . . well, since he was a jerk."

She tilted her head and studied me. "This is a safe space, Reese. You can be honest with me."

"I *am* being honest."

"Reese, come on." Christina grinned again. "It was a passionate kiss, and it was right in front of you. You must be disappointed."

Did that actually happen? How did I not see it? I had to talk to Lamb.

"Somehow I missed that. Honestly. But if Lamb kissed another woman tonight, yeah, it would hurt."

This seemed to please her. "You like him. You have a connection."

"I thought so. Maybe . . ." I threw my hands up. "I don't know. Maybe I was wrong."

"Well, let's talk about that. Your connection, and what makes it special."

We went around in circles like this for the next thirty minutes. She would get me to swoon over my relationship with Lamb, bring up this out-of-the-blue kiss with Trixie, make me question my intuition, and recount my attack on Nick. The more agitated I became, the more she encouraged me. It was like she *wanted* me to lose it again. I didn't understand it.

Not at the time.

20:Ann

can't stop bouncing my knee as I wait for Nick on the stoop outside the mansion. I check the time, bite my nails. Magda slapped my wrist three times while she put on my face this morning.

"Stop it," she said. "You vill ruin fingers."

I finally folded my hands under my armpits, which Magda detested equally as much.

"Vhat's wrong vith you?" she snapped. "Now you vill smell."

I'm not excited for the date. Not exactly, not really. More anxious. Yes, that's the right word: *anxious*. I wish Reese were here to calm me down—like she did for my first date after I got sober. I had been clean for about fifteen months at that point, and it was my first year in law school. Another first-year asked me to dinner between classes, and I was caught so off guard—so sleep deprived and mentally exhausted from reading case after case after case—that I said yes.

I wasn't ready to get back on the horse, but Reese was thrilled. Of course she was.

"I think this is just wonderful." She sighed as I paced my ramshackle studio apartment, the only place I could afford on my scholarship. "You're never going to be one hundred percent ready, so you might as well rip the Band-Aid off now before you get too timid over the idea."

"But what do I say when he asks if I want a drink?" I stuttered, barely taking a breath. "I can't just say I'm an alcoholic. That's so morbid and depressing and weird to say to someone you just met. And if I say, 'I'm not drinking tonight,' then he might think I'm not interested, that I'm being rude. Maybe I could say I'm on antibiotics. . . . Yeah. Yeah. That could work. But then what if he thinks I have some sort of gross rash? Or an STD?"

I was tearing up my ratty rug I was pacing so much.

"I got it." She snapped her fingers. "Just say you're pregnant."

"Reese, I'm serious."

My phone went off then—a text from the date. He was taking me to a new winery in town, so I needed to get excited. I flopped face-first onto my bed.

"He's taking me to a winery," I said, my voice muffled by a pillow. "This is terrible."

"Come on," Reese brushed my hair with her fingers. "You're blowing this way out of proportion. Give me your phone."

I handed it to her without meeting her gaze.

"That sounds great," she said as she typed. "I actually don't drink, but the food looks delicious. Can't wait to see you."

"What?" I glanced up then, eyebrows halfway up my forehead.

"It's better this way, trust me. Now he knows in advance, so you don't have to get all awkward and tell him in person. If he asks why, just say it's healthier for you not to. I've tried a hundred different explanations, and that one has *by far* the best results. And eventually, if he earns your trust, then you can tell him your story."

I propped myself on my elbows, mouth downturned.

"There are a lot of things I don't know," she continued. "But I do know dating, and there are plenty of guys out there who don't care if you're sober. Do you believe me?"

"Yeah." I exhaled. "You've slept with half of Nashville."

"Hey." She straightened her posture. "I'm a beautiful, confident woman who enjoys sex. Safe sex. And you should too."

"Reese?" My eyes flitted downward. "I don't know how to have sex sober. I don't know if I . . ." I straightened my duvet. "I don't know if I would be any good at it."

Reese shook her arm, which was adorned in dozens of bangles. She reached for her constant—the bracelet with an orange marigold—and took it off.

"Here," she said as she slipped it on my wrist. "This is my good-luck bracelet. It's scientifically impossible to be bad in bed with this on you."

I tried to respond, to say *thank you*, but a lump blocked my throat.

"Just give it back in the morning." Reese winked.

I reach for my wrist now—bare except for my watch—and feel the sting of the bracelet's absence.

"Hey." Nick grabs my waist and kisses me on the cheek. As he smiles, that adorable lopsided smile, I remind myself that I am anxious, not excited.

"Hey, yourself. Are you going to tell me what we're doing now?"

"Henry, what time is it?" Nick asks over his shoulder. I notice Henry for the first time, hidden in the shadow of the doorway. My shoulders slump. I forgot about the required chaperone on one-on-one dates. Henry's better than the handler who accompanied my time with Clay, but any onlooker makes a conversation difficult. Perhaps they're there as the party needed for recording consent. The realization almost takes my breath away.

"Ten fifty-nine," Henry says as he crosses his arms and leans against the door frame.

"Should be any minute then." Nick grins.

We're hit with a gust of wind and a quick chopping noise. I squint toward the sky to see a helicopter looming above. Nick takes my hand, pulls me toward the fountain for cover. As the helicopter nears the ground, we're enveloped in a vortex of wind, debris, and yellow marigolds.

"Is this for us?" I exclaim.

"It is." He laughs, protecting my face from the flying flowers with his hand.

Once the aircraft lands, a snowy-haired man with aviator glasses and a green jumpsuit emerges from the pilot's seat, like a scene out of *Top Gun*. I snort. My life is one seriously warped cliché right now.

And then I remember something Reese said, after watching one of those dating reality shows. *They always travel by helicopter. Isn't that romantic?*

What did Reese get herself into? What did *I* get into? And why did I not just attend when she wanted me to?

The pilot saunters toward us, introduces himself with a firm handshake, and gestures toward our ride. I can barely hear him over the roar of the rotating blades. Even after I put on my headset, I have to listen carefully to hear the safety protocols.

"You think this is safe?" I scream at Nick, my hair flying, as we finish strapping ourselves into the back of the rotorcraft. Thankfully, Henry is in the front, giving us some semblance of privacy.

Emily C. Whitson

"Why wouldn't it be?"

Oh, there are a few reasons that come to mind, I think as we lurch higher and higher above the mansion. I squeeze my eyes shut, try to settle my stomach and my nerves. After a minute, Nick nudges me.

"Look," he yells, jabbing his tanned index finger at the window. I lean over him to see where he's pointing, and despite myself, I am taken aback by the aerial view. Every aspect of the island appears in technicolor: the blue ocean stands in stark contrast to the dove-white sand, which contrasts again with the dense green vegetation that grows on the mainland. It's all so picturesque, as if someone painted a portrait of the archetypal tropical paradise and saturated each color to its perfect intensity.

And yet the stillness makes me shudder.

"What's that over there?" I point to an enormous structure on the opposite side of the island, the only sign of civilization apart from the mansion and a couple boats off the shore.

"Those are additional rooms for the staff," the pilot shouts. "We don't all fit in the primary building. In front you can see the crops we grow on the island. We have to ship a lot of food and supplies in, but that gets expensive, so we cultivate as much as we can."

I stare at the rows of crops, as small as an ant farm from this distance.

"How far is that from the mansion?" I yell back.

"About thirty miles. The length of the island."

My stomach sinks. I can run long stretches—twelve or thirteen if it's a good day—but I can't run *thirty miles* at once. Somehow, I need to get to that building.

"Hold on, we have a gust of wind coming our way," the pilot announces.

The helicopter teeters, drops quickly, and my insides liquefy. My breath catches in my throat. Nick squeezes my hand, interlocking his fingers in mine. I squeeze back, but only because I'm terrified.

21:Ann

My legs are still wobbly as we make our way to an extravagant tiki hut about ten miles from the mansion, complete with wooden tables, chairs, and a fully stocked bar in the center. The roof is thatched with palm fronds, which is why I didn't notice it from the helicopter. According to the pilot, there are four of these huts scattered on the island—perfect for one-on-one dates. If the open layout is the same, then there's nowhere to hide in any of them. I scan the area all the same.

We take a seat with a view of the ocean. Henry sits on the opposite side of the hut, his face partially obscured by the bar. Only his green eye is visible. A single bartender mans the drinks. He's a strange-looking man with protruding eyes. He looks amphibious with his clown nose and pencil-thin lips. He slithers toward us with two glasses of water.

"My name is Greg," he croaks as he approaches our table. "What can I get you? We have every drink you can think of."

"Scotch on the rocks, thanks," Nick replies.

"Ginger ale would be great," I mutter.

Nick's brow wrinkles as Greg disappears.

"You still feeling queasy?"

"Just a little bit. It'll pass." I need a distraction so I don't vomit. "So, now that we're finally alone and I can hear you, tell me how you managed this last-minute switch of dates."

"I told you." Nick smirks. "I asked Christina for a favor."

"Christina doesn't seem like the type that grants favors," I peer back at him as I take a sip of water.

"Well, I've known her for a while. I know how to ask nicely."

The glass slips out of my hand, cascading water all over the table and my sundress. The liquid is ice cold, and I shoot up as it needles into my lap. Greg rushes over with an armful of cloth napkins. Nick helps him dab the table while I do my best to dry myself off.

"I'm so sorry," I mumble. I notice Henry half standing across the room, determining whether to come over or not. "I guess I'm still feeling a little shaky after the helicopter."

"It's okay," Nick says. "Just a little water." He hands the now sopping-wet napkins back to Greg, nods toward the bar. Greg takes the hint and leaves with the wet mess.

"So, um, how do you know Christina?" I keep my eyes on my lap as I continue to blot.

"She used to work with my parents in L.A. I don't know her super well, I didn't mean to imply that. She just helped them with their wardrobes sometimes."

"She was a stylist?" That would explain her obsession with dressing us.

"Costume consultant on set. My parents are actors." He says it quickly: *myparentsareactors.*

"Oh, yeah? What have they been in? Anything I've heard of?"

Nick stares at his lap, smooths his new napkin.

"Um, yeah. Maybe."

"Well, let's hear it."

"Uh, let's see. My dad was in *Happily Ever After.*"

For a rare moment, I forget about Reese. "I love that movie. I made my parents watch it so many times, they started quoting it when it came on. Who did your dad play?"

I expect him to say a minor, obscure role. He pauses, scratches his head, and utters the main character's name. My jaw drops.

"Wait. So your dad is *Frank* Keyser?"

Nick takes a sip of water, nods sheepishly. I try not to gape, but it's difficult. Frank Keyser is one of the most well-known actors in Hollywood. That guy isn't some run-of-the-mill stage actor—he's a *huge* deal. I used to daydream about him when I was a kid. He was my first celebrity crush.

"Does that mean your mom is Bonnie Ann Tyler?" Another actor. Her split with Frank Keyser dominated headlines fifteen years ago—it was all the tabloids could talk about.

"Yep, that's her." He loosens his collar, watches his ice float in his glass.

"I'm sorry, I don't mean to gawk. It just caught me off guard. So, Christina was in costumes for films? And that's how you met her?"

"Yeah, she was working as an intern on the set of *Happily Ever After.* I was little then—only seven or eight—but I remembered her because her eyes were so noticeable. The color of ice. I feel bad saying this, now that I know her, but she really scared me at first." He chuckles, and I try to keep my next sentence even-keeled.

"Yeah, I could see that."

"I saw her on the set of a few other films as I got older, but she left the industry about seven years ago. Wanted to start this retreat, help people find love and all that. I ran into her at a coffee shop six months back, told her I was looking for a break from Hollywood, and she suggested I come here. And I've gotta say, it's been pretty nice."

I try to breathe normally, sort through this goldmine of new information. With a specific position and time frame, I can get more background on Christina.

"Was her name always Christina Wellington?" I ask.

"I think so." He laughs. "I always just knew her as Christina. Why?" He narrows his eyes. *Shit*. I shouldn't have asked that.

"I did some research on her before I came, and it was hard to find anything. I just wanted to know what I was getting into, staying on a private island for four weeks. It's not exactly easy to leave if I need to."

He shrugs, seems to accept this answer. "That's smart. I probably would have done that if I were you. I said yes and didn't think twice."

Greg arrives with our drinks, and I take a sip, focusing on the fizz of the ginger ale as it trickles into my stomach.

"What was it like, growing up . . . famous?" I ask.

"I don't know." He shrugged. "It seemed normal at the time. I didn't have anything else to compare it to, so I just thought everyone saw their parents on TV more than in real life. For a time, I thought my dad really was a superhero."

He chuckles then, stares off into the distance. He must be referring to his dad's stint on *Two Faces*, a popular television series about a seemingly regular Joe who crunches numbers by day and fights crime at night.

"I used to run around in the cape he wore. It was so heavy—it practically swallowed me—but I just figured if Dad could do it, so could I." His smile disappears. "Then I saw him with an extra between takes, when he thought no one was looking. I wasn't even entirely sure what was happening at the time, but I knew the things he was doing were only supposed to be with Mom. That was a tough day, when I realized my dad and my dad's character were two different people."

He stops his musing and catches my gaze. I must appear sympathetic, as his demeanor shifts. He pulls his shoulders back.

"So, what about you? Were your parents lawyers too?"

I want to reach out to him, graze his arm. But I stay still. "No, no. Mom was an art teacher. Dad was in the lumber business, co-owned a company for a while."

"So what made you decide to become a lawyer?"

Normally I respond with a financial reason: I wanted more opportunities, a more secure lifestyle. Which is partly true. But Nick's transparency and my nausea lower my guard. "Well, speaking of men with two faces . . . my dad's partner forced him out of the business when it hit a downturn. The partner had an attorney in the family, and we couldn't afford one. Not a good one, anyway." I stir my drink, watch the bubbles rise. "I never wanted to be in that position again. Never wanted to feel helpless again."

Before Nick can offer a comforting glance or a pitying note, I change the subject to the more important matter. "Hey." I clear my throat. "I was hoping you could tell me more about Lamb Martin. Did he have a good relationship with Reese?" Out of the corner of my eye, I notice Henry stand and make his way toward us.

"I think so," Nick says. "In the beginning, they were all over each other."

"And that changed?" I try to keep my focus on Nick, but Henry's approach makes it difficult.

As Nick prepares to answer, Henry taps him on the shoulder and darts his eyes toward the exit. "I need to talk to you for a minute."

Nick follows him outside, and my heart hammers in my chest. Could Henry hear us from across the room?

Was he listening through other means? Or was his interruption just a coincidence?

After what seems like ten minutes of my thoughts burrowing deeper and deeper into a rabbit hole, Nick returns, his mouth taut.

"Is everything all right?" I ask.

"Oh yeah. He just wanted a cigarette." He takes a large swig of his drink.

"So, about Lamb and Reese," I continue. "How did their relationship end?"

"I've been thinking." Nick's eyes flick toward Henry, who stubs out his cigarette. "Do you think Reese's disappearance could be due to something . . . closer to home?"

"What?" My voice catches in my throat. "Do you know something?"

Nick clears his throat as Henry walks within earshot.

"Maybe we should talk about something else," he says.

22: Reese

The next morning was a bit of a bummer for me. Not my favorite, no siree. On my group date—a volleyball game on the beach—few of the participants would talk to me. Some would whisper, snigger, steal glances at me, but anytime I tried to break the ice, the men and women would scatter like roaches. Nick was on my group date too, unfortunately. And Trixie. So in addition to bruising my forearms from the couple times I made contact with the ball, putting my highly unathletic nature on full display, and catching Trixie's "accidental" serve in the back of the head, I was also dealing with being the retreat pariah.

I looked for Lamb during lunch, to talk about what had happened the night before, but he was nowhere to be found. Neither was Trixie. I hoped that was a coincidence, but I wasn't so naïve to not connect the dots.

I knew Lamb and I had had something special. We really connected during those first two encounters. Or was it all in my head, as usual?

I was starving, but the thought of eating alone in the kitchen over-powered my stomach.

I went upstairs to my room, closed the door behind me, and fetched my suitcase. From a hidden pocket, I retrieved my ballet slippers. My very first pair, a good-luck charm I brought everywhere. I sank to the floor, staring at them, admiring the worn soles and the silky pink satin.

I came across them by pure chance in elementary school. I was eight. I often stayed late, after class, finding things to do that would be more fun than going home. At home, there was either a screaming match—between my mother and my sister, or my mother's latest boyfriend, or some combination of the three—or the eerie silence of an empty household. Typically, I spent my after-school time in the library. I've always loved stories, getting lost in various adventures. But one day I stumbled across the dance studio. A ballet class. I had never seen that type of dance before, and I was mesmerized. The movements, the dancers, the outfits. It was all so graceful, so elegant, so completely unlike everything I was used to.

An older student caught me watching. She was leaving early or arriv-ing late, I can't remember which, but she startled me when she tapped me on the shoulder.

"Do you dance?" she asked.

I shook my head. "That would cost money, right?"

The girl scrunched her eyebrows. She couldn't be older than ten or eleven. Why would she know about the expense of after-school activities? Unless she lived in a household like mine, where we were conscious of finances right out of the womb.

"I'm not sure," she admitted. She looked sad for me.

"I'm sorry for staring," I said as I turned to leave. "I was just curious."

I was halfway down the hall when she called after me. "Hey, wait!"

I turned around to see her rummaging in her backpack. She pulled out a pair of hand-me-down ballet slippers and held them out to me.

"I have this old pair that doesn't fit me anymore," she said. "I was going to throw them away, but maybe you'd like to have them instead?"

I scowled. "You were really going to throw them away?"

"Honest," she replied. "I'd hate to see them go to waste." (She was very insightful for her age, I must admit. Or perhaps I just like to remember her that way.)

I took her up on her offer, dubiously at first, and then with more appreciation. "Thank you." The shoes felt heavy in my hand, like a treasure. In a rare, out-of-body experience, I realized that my life would never be the same, and I vowed that someday, somehow, I would do something kind for someone else. I would be the girl offering ballet slippers.

After that, dance became the home I never had. I found an after-school class for—and I hate this word—*underprivileged* kids. When I got older and could work part-time, I enrolled in more advanced classes with my hard-earned money. When I was sixteen, I stopped going to school altogether to focus on ballet. It seemed like a good idea at the time, and I didn't have anyone to tell me otherwise.

In fact, it's what got me sober. I'm not sure why I tried drinking in the first place. Perhaps it was pride. *I'm not like my family. What happened to them will never happen to me!* But after my first sip, my first endorphin rush, I knew I was a goner. Alcohol was in the driver's seat, and I was just along for the ride. I remember thinking: *So this is what drinking feels like. I understand now.*

I started missing dance rehearsals. Waking up in strange men's places. Discovering inexplicable bruises. I was so ashamed, after all my years of open disdain toward my mother and sister's addiction, that I wouldn't return home for days, sometimes weeks, at a time. I couldn't stand to see their reaction. I'd imagine them smirking, thinking, *Guess you're not so different from us after all.*

But the final straw that got me to sober up: I slept through a very important ballet audition. A traveling company. My golden ticket out of my lackluster life. Everything I had been working for. I'll never forget the look in my teacher's eye when I saw her afterward.

"If you're smart, Reese," she said. "You'll get help now."

I returned to my part-time waitressing job that night, a sleazy restaurant in an even sleazier part of town. I was wallowing in shame and guilt and indignance. *What does she know? I can control this.* But then a greasy customer I'd never seen before grabbed me between the legs.

"Thought I wouldn't see you after last night," he whispered in my ear. And then he repeated something I had heard uttered to my mother by one of her (many) boyfriends. "You were quite a ride."

I wanted to vomit. I quit on the spot, found the closest AA meeting, and never touched alcohol or drugs again.

I eventually got another shot at ballet, about six months into my sobriety. An audition for the Nashville Dance Company. By some divine intervention, I was offered a job. And just like that, my life had meaning again. Joy. Stability. For twelve years, my life was like that. I danced all day and sometimes all night, and when I performed in front of a crowd, I soaked up every ounce of applause the audience had to offer. I even landed the lead role in my company's biggest production, *A Christmas Bell,* seven seasons in a row.

I went to AA meetings regularly. I tried to get my mom and sister to join me, but nothing I did seemed to work. They weren't bad people—just very, very sick. I started sponsoring other women in the program instead. I met Ann, who became the surrogate sister I *could* save. The type of sister I'd always wanted but never had. I fell in love, multiple times. And through it all, dance was with me, tying together my experiences, good and bad, like charms on a bracelet. Then it all came crashing down, three months prior to the retreat.

I should have seen it coming, but I didn't. When the director asked to speak with me out of the blue, I figured it was to discuss details of *A Christmas Bell*.

I hummed as he closed the door. His office was in the oldest and most decrepit part of the studio. Cobwebs decorated the corners. A light flickered above our heads, highlighting the hundreds of papers stacked haphazardly on the floor, on his desk, and on the single filing cabinet. The most recent photo of the dance company was hanging on the wall, just above the director's head. I was front and center in the group, smiling like a woman who had just won the lottery.

The air reeked of sweat. Nervous sweat.

"Reese, how are you?" His mustache sashayed on his lips as he spoke.

"Fantastic." I smiled as I bounced in my seat. "I'm getting excited about *A Christmas Bell*. It's my absolute favorite time of the year, as you know."

He evaded my gaze, and I knew something was wrong.

"Good, good," he said as he analyzed his tie. "Reese, I'm not quite sure how to say this. But we've decided to give your part to Katherine Phillips."

Katherine was new to the company. Early twenties. Her face was unlined, her ponytail as thick as my bicep, and her metabolism as fast as a racehorse's. She was young, young, young.

"You're just getting a bit . . . old. We would keep you on until the end of this year, but the budget is tight and . . . well, you know how it goes."

The director chuckled nervously, and the floor seemed to open up beneath me. He proceeded to discuss the details of my departure, but I wasn't listening. I had known this day would come eventually—all ballerinas have an early expiration date—but I never let myself think about it too much. I didn't know what I would do without dance.

I didn't tell many people about my layoff. Even Ann. I didn't want to acknowledge it. The longer I kept it a secret, the longer I could continue to live in a fantasy. It was naïve and immature, but I wasn't ready yet.

I had a little bit of savings, but not much. No studios were hiring dance teachers at that time of year. I didn't have any other skills, not even a high-school degree. I tried to get a loan, but banks only give you money if you already have money. I could have asked Ann—should have asked Ann—for help, but I didn't. With ballet gone, she was the one constant remaining in my life. I was supposed to be the one who helped *her*, not the other way around.

So I did something incredibly stupid. I borrowed from Luca, one of my shady exes. Or, technically, I borrowed from some of his friends. I should never have contacted him, but he owed me, and he lived thousands of miles away, in L.A. I knew I'd reached a low point when he and his friends forced me to communicate through a burner phone. I told myself it was just temporary.

But I couldn't find another job in time to pay back the loan. I tried to think of things I could sell, but my only asset was my car. I sold it, gave the money to these guys, and then they wanted more. For their troubles. I didn't have more. I didn't respond to their calls and texts, or even Luca's calls.

Before I could put together a plan, the day before I left for the retreat, I found one of Luca's friends sitting on the front doorstep to my apartment complex. He was twice my size.

"I'm getting the money together," I blurted out before he could ask.

"You're already two days late. Do you know what my boss makes me do to guys who are two days late?"

I shook my head. Whatever it was, I assumed it was bad.

"I break their kneecaps." He stood up, straightened his jacket, and my stomach sank. "My boss is willing to hold off for another day, since you're a friend of Luca's, but only another day."

"I'll have it by tomorrow night, I promise."

I would not have it by then. I would be on a plane to Last Chance. I would also be evicted from my apartment. I hoped, naïvely, that in the month I was gone, Luca's friends would forget about me. I didn't have a job, or a home, or even a car, and they didn't know any of my friends except Luca, so how would they find me? And besides: It was a few hundred dollars. That was nothing to those men, and certainly not enough to start a manhunt.

"You better, or I'll be back, Reese."

He whistled as he strode off, his breath forming small clouds in the cold. I could still hear the tune when I went to sleep each night.

I put my ballet shoes away and went downstairs, to the kitchen, to look for Lamb once more, praying for a miracle.

23:Ann

Back in my room, after my date with Nick, I check my phone for a message from Ned. There isn't one. I check my watch and add five hours: 9:05 p.m. CST. That's not too late to call, right? Plenty of associates work until then, and Ned's a go-getter. I massage my conscience for another minute before dialing. No answer.

"Hey," I say once I reach his voice mail. "It's me. Ann. Just checking in, to see if you found anything on Lamb Martin. I also have some good news: I found out Christina worked on the set of the movie *Happily Ever After* as a stylist or costume designer—an intern, most likely. The movie came out in ninety-two. That should be enough for Pat. If you can, look into Nick Keyser too. The son of the actor Frank Keyser. He's here on the retreat with me."

I hesitate before asking him one more thing that's been bugging me. Then I go for it.

"We also . . . well, we eat at really weird times here, and never on dates. Is that something they do on dating reality shows? Maybe eating messes with the audio? I feel crazy asking, but I can't think of another reason why we can't eat on dates. Okay, I think that's it. Thanks, Ned."

I hang up and take a deep breath. I feel crazy. Absolutely crazy. But the longer I'm here, the more I think maybe Ned is right. This is a TV show. There's Christina's odd fixation on dressing us up. The way she maneuvers us into certain angles. The way she asks us the same question, in different ways, until we give her the answer she's looking for. But I still can't figure out why they don't just tell us? Is it to make the drama more believable? And if it is a show, does that mean Reese is okay? Is she hiding somewhere, waiting for the premiere? But then why would she ditch her phone at Riverfront Park?

My mind is buzzing with all these unanswered questions. My legs itch. I'll go for a run—try to blow off some steam and collect my thoughts.

Twelve minutes later, I'm outside. The sun beats down on me as I pick up the pace on the beach. The sand grabs my feet, holds onto them, but it only makes me run faster. Despite my change in venue, I still can't get my mind to settle. What did Nick mean when he said Reese's disappearance could be closer to home? Was he trying to point me in the right direction, or the wrong one? Or was he simply curious, or trying to be helpful? What did he talk about with Henry? Nick seems sympathetic, with his poor-little-rich-boy story, but maybe it's just an act. Perhaps he's told all the women on the island that story.

What does *closer to home* even *mean*? The police talked to Reese's most recent love interests: a total of six men in the past two years. Three have moved out of the state, and the others have rock-solid alibis. There are other liaisons of Reese, of course—the police could have looked even further into her past, could have interviewed dozens more men. But most don't strike me as particularly harmful. Assholes, maybe. Misogynists and cheaters, most definitely. But harmful? Violent? Not so much. And Reese is rarely one to cut off the relationship—she's loyal until the bitter end—so there isn't a long line of jealous, vengeful ex-boyfriends.

Except for one.

About seven years ago, Reese dated a man by the name of Luca Ferrari. She met him at the restaurant where he worked. She enjoyed her meal so much, she wanted to meet the chef. And then he looked like Luca, which is to say he was gorgeous. Olive complexion, lush brown hair. Obviously great skills in the kitchen. They hit it off right away, but from the beginning, I didn't like him. He was controlling. He texted and called *all* the time, and if she didn't respond right away, he got upset.

"He just worries, that's all," Reese said over coffee one day, as she typed out a message, her phone vibrating with text after text.

The closer it got to Reese's performance in *A Christmas Bell,* the more their relationship seemed to fray. It was like the thought of sharing her with anyone else was too much for Luca to handle.

Luckily I was there when he turned up. From my seat in the audience, I saw Luca saunter toward the stage after her solo. I could tell something was off, so I followed him. Ironically, he and I were able to sneak backstage because everyone—the crew, the audience, the other dancers, even security—was entranced by Reese's performance. It was breathtaking. Transcendent.

She glided like a woman without a skeleton, her limbs moving in ways I didn't think humanly possible.

Despite my best efforts, I couldn't reach Luca in time. Just as Reese exited the stage, Luca grabbed a fistful of her hair and slammed her face into the nearest wall. I remember the blood from her nose oozing onto her pristine white leotard and spotting her tutu.

Security reached Luca before I did, and they were able to escort him out of the building and to the police station before things could get any worse. I filled out an order of protection that night and had it in a judge's hand by the next morning.

Suffice it to say, I've been worried about Luca ever since. Reese *said* she blocked his number, and as far as I know, she hasn't seen him since—although she did lie to me about blocking him, as there was a missed call from him on her phone when the police found it, so I guess she could have lied about seeing him too. I told all of this to the police, when they asked me about suspicious characters.

"Luca Ferrari," I had said. "That's F-E-R-R-A-R-I, like the car. You need to talk to him immediately."

But despite the missed call, they didn't take my suggestion seriously because the relationship had ended seven years prior. But I hounded them and hounded them and hounded them, until they tracked down his current residence just outside of Los Angeles. To my relief and disappointment, he had an airtight alibi.

But, as my legs pound the sand beneath me and sweat pours into my eyes, I still wonder if somehow, some way, Luca had something to do with Reese's disappearance.

24:Ann

run faster, pushing harder against the breeze coming off the ocean. I narrow my eyes, trying to push away lingering concerns. I don't like to think about these facts, but I can't keep ignoring them.

The first is the Nashville Dance Company. Reese had left three months prior to the retreat. After the police informed me of this news, I paid the director of the company a brief visit. A stout man with a seventies-porno moustache, he proved to be entirely unhelpful. He didn't know where she went after leaving his company.

"But I don't understand. Why did she want to leave then, if not for another dance company?" I was dumbfounded. Ballet meant the world to her.

"Well." He looked sheepish. "She didn't want to leave. We had to let her go. She was getting too old. You have to understand, it's just part of the business."

His words felt like a sucker punch to my gut.

Another worrisome item: her apartment. On the day she was supposed to arrive home, I called the landlord to ask if he could check on Reese. I was worried about her, and I hadn't heard from her. He was quiet for a moment, before finally admitting she had been evicted.

Then there's her car. I asked police to look for it, and it turned out to be with an elderly couple who claimed to have bought it from Reese a month prior. They had the papers to prove it, and when describing the woman who dropped the car off, they painted Reese to a tee.

And finally, there's Reese's mom, Lily. Reese's sister was in prison for theft, but the mom—she was still around. The police said they talked to her, and from their conversation, they didn't suspect foul play. I wanted to talk to her myself, though, so I decided to pay her a visit. It took a while to track her down, but Pat was able to get an address from a friend on the police force after a few too many beers.

I drove to Lily's house, a run-down, single-story farmhouse two hours outside of Nashville, making sure to take my father's old handgun. Reese's disappearance was really starting to wear me down at this point, and I wanted to be extra careful. During the car ride, I offered a silent prayer of gratitude for my father's shooting lessons. Our afternoons spent aiming at targets, out in the woods he knew so well.

Lily's house was coming apart at the seams. The windows were boarded up. The wood siding was missing. An enormous hole decorated the rusted metal roof. Plants were overtaking the yard on all sides. Weeds, mostly. No one answered the door for several minutes after I knocked. The house was deathly still, and I wondered for a moment if Pat had received bad information. Or if the police scared Lily off. Just as I was leaving, the door creaked open a slit, and a pair of yellow eyes stared at me from the shadows.

"Whaddya want?" the eyes asked.

"I'm looking for Lily Marigold. I'm a friend of her daughter's."

The door closed then, and I heard shuffling. Whispers. When the door opened again, an older version of Reese greeted me. She was rail-thin, her red hair stringy and unkempt, her ivory skin wrinkled and pocked with abscesses, but she was unmistakably Reese's mother.

"Lily?" I asked.

"Yes. Whaddya want?"

"I'm a friend of Reese's. May I come inside?"

Lily took a step toward me, blocking the entrance. It's amazing Reese was—*is*—as open and lovely as she is, with the family she has.

"I ardy talked to the cops. I dunno where she is."

"You haven't talked to her lately?"

"Not for a year or so. She was trying to get me to go to those damn meetings again."

"Do you have any idea where she would go if she ran off?" It hurt me to consider this course of events, but I was getting desperate, hoping for just a shred of information. "Please, it's important."

Lily peered at me for a minute, sizing me up. After a while, she dropped her shoulders.

"She always liked flowers. Found 'er hidin' at a local garden shop a coupla times. I tried lockin' that girl up, but that girl could pick any locked door. A professional escape artist, that one. So yeah, I found 'er at flower shops. Marigolds were 'er favorite."

My heart sunk thinking of a young Reese—sweet, compassionate Reese—being locked up and forgotten. I knew her childhood was difficult, I knew that. But seeing her mom made the pain and sympathy sharper.

"Okay. Well, if you hear from her, or if you think of anything else, would you mind giving me a call?" I handed her my business card, and Lily stared at it with suspicion. She crumpled it in her fist and nodded.

Her eyes followed me as I headed back toward my car.

"She liked ta dance," Lily called. I leaned on the driver's door and faced her. "She was always dancin' when I found 'er. Never took that damn tutu off."

I could feel a stinging at the back of my eyes, so I just nodded. I waited until I was a mile away before I pulled over to the side of the road and rested my head on the steering wheel. I let the tears fall then. Big, fat tears that pooled in my lap. I hadn't cried in ten years, not since my parents died, and it was like I was making up for lost time.

I cried for a lot of things that day. I cried because Reese was gone, of course, but it was more than that. I cried for her childhood. Her career cut short. Her financial issues. But mostly, I think, I cried because she hadn't told me about any of it. I had thought we were close enough that she would tell me if she was in trouble, but clearly I was wrong.

The secrets hurt. Perhaps that's why I am so focused on the retreat. If something terrible happened to her here, then she hasn't abandoned me. But maybe I am being stupid. Yes, there are signs that point to foul play, but there are also a hell of a lot of signs that point to Reese running. Perhaps she is safe and sound somewhere, trying to get away from her demons, trying to start over. Without me.

25: Reese

The tune Luca's friend hummed was still worming its way into my head as I went downstairs. I opened the door to the kitchen, but as was my luck, it was empty. I must have been up in my room longer than I thought. I was about to turn around, search elsewhere, when a man with dark olive skin in an apron pushed open the swinging door that connected the back of the kitchen to the sitting area.

It took me a minute to realize what I was seeing. It was so out of context, and it had been so long since I'd seen him in the flesh. His dark, curly hair had grown out, and the years had etched new lines onto his face, but it was unmistakably him. Luca.

A lot of thoughts ran through my head at that moment. The first was a memory: the last time I saw him. It was right after I had finished performing my part in *A Christmas Bell.* Luca and I had had a row, right before the show started.

He had thought I was cheating on him (I wasn't), and for whatever reason, my performance set him off. He grabbed my hair and slammed my head into a wall so hard I saw stars. Someone yanked him off of me—another performer, maybe, or security.

He apologized profusely after that (don't they all?), but I didn't stick around to hear it. Ann helped me get an order of protection, and Luca was smart enough to keep his distance after that. His last message to me was that he was moving to L.A. There was a restaurant opening he couldn't pass up, and he decided it was the perfect chance to start over, to work on himself. He said if I ever needed anything, anything at all, he would help me out. I shouldn't have taken him up on the offer, seven years later, but as I've mentioned, I was desperate. And he was so far away. What could he do to me from Los Angeles?

This led me to my second thought, which was that his friends were definitely, absolutely going to find me. I was going to lose a kneecap. Maybe two.

And the third: What were the odds, out of the hundreds of thousands of chefs they could have hired, that they ended up with this one? It was a bit *too* coincidental, right? Had Luca somehow figured out where I was going and tracked me down?

He looked genuinely shocked, though, I'll give him that. "Reese?"

"How . . ." I stammered. "How did you find me?"

"I—I didn't. I got offered a sous-chef job here." He was stock-still, but then he seemed to remember the entirety of the situation. "Shit, Reese, those guys are looking all over for you. They've called me, like, twenty times."

I didn't know how to explain, but I tried.

"You—*they*—didn't tell me they were going to want interest. I sold my car and got evicted from my apartment to pay them back. I can't afford anything extra."

"You sold your car?" His dark eyes softened. "And you moved out? Shit, Reese. I didn't realize it was that bad."

"Why *else* would I contact you?" I yelled, the pitch of my voice increasing. "Why didn't you *warn* me?"

"I didn't think I needed to."

He was right. I should have known. I just didn't have any other options. I rubbed my temples, hoping if I pressed hard enough, the situation might just disappear. Instead, Lamb walked into the kitchen, making my situation even worse.

"Reese? I thought I heard your voice." He seemed to pick up on the tension in the room. "What's going on?"

"Nothing," Luca and I said at the same time.

Lamb didn't seem fully convinced, but after a moment of silence, he gave in.

"Well, okay then. Reese, can I talk to you for a minute?" He gestured outside. "Out there?"

"Uh," I stammered. I didn't know what to do. I wanted to talk to Lamb, but I also needed to convince Luca not to contact his friends.

"Give us five minutes," Luca interrupted. He stepped toward me, and I flinched.

"Reese, come on," Luca said. He looked pained. "I'm not going to hurt you. That was a long time ago."

"What was a long time ago?" Lamb waved his hands in frustration. "What is going on?"

"Nothing, man," Luca took hold of my wrist, and I jerked it out of his grasp.

"I'll talk to you," I pleaded. "Let's just maintain some physical distance while we do so." I gestured to an invisible space between us.

What happened next was sort of a blur. Luca kept reaching for me. I kept pulling away. Lamb kept telling Luca to back off. Luca kept telling

Lamb to back off. And then, before I knew what was happening, Lamb was pulling back his arm, winding it up to make contact with Luca's face, and before he could do so, I caught an elbow square in my eye socket. White-hot pain clouded my vision. I stumbled backward, holding my eye, and right before I fell, I heard Christina rush into the kitchen, other her handlers in tow.

26:Ann

slow my pace as I arrive back at the mansion.

Couples are still socializing on the outdoor patio. I hear laughter, splashing in the pool, and bottles uncorking over the crash of the ocean. I head to the front of the house, hoping to avoid the scene. I'm dripping with sweat, and it glides off of me as I trudge up the steps to my room.

Once inside, I retrieve my phone. My heart stops.

Three missed calls from Ned.

I throw the phone on the bed and heave the dresser in front of the doorway. It seems heavier than normal, and it catches on the carpet. I take a few deep breaths before giving it a final push. I'm melting by the time I make it to the water closet. The sweat messes with my fingerprint, and my phone shudders, remains locked. I try to dry my hand on my shorts, but they're soaked too. Same with my sports bra. I eye the toilet paper and dab my thumb on the top of the roll. My phone unlocks. I call Ned.

"Ann." He answers on the first ring. "I was worried I'd missed you."

"Hey, sorry, I went on a run right after I called. Is everything all right?"

"Uh, maybe. I don't know. I found out a couple things. Are you somewhere you can talk?"

"Yeah, yeah."

"Okay, good. Well, to answer one of your questions: On shows like *The Bachelor*, they don't eat during dates. It does mess with the audio, so they eat off camera."

"Okay." I check my surroundings in the water closet, looking for any hidden cameras. *I can't believe this is my life right now.* "Let's say, for whatever reason, this retreat is being filmed. What does that mean for Reese? Is she safe and sound somewhere, just waiting for the show to premiere? Doesn't explain why the mystery car she got into at the airport would explode and why her wallet and phone were found nearby. And I can't make sense of the bizarre happenings on this retreat."

"Well, maybe—" He pauses. It's unlike him to be quiet. "Maybe we can discuss this in Nashville. I can look into travel arrangements if you'd like."

"Ned, what's wrong?"

"Nothing, nothing." He exhales. "Okay, maybe it's something. I found out more about Lamb Martin."

"That's great news."

"Yeah, I got off the phone with his roommate before you called."

I'm growing impatient. "And?"

Another pause.

"Just spit it out, Ned."

"He never made it home from the retreat."

27:Reese

Sunshine. Birds singing. A breeze off the ocean.

It should have been a beautiful day, but it wasn't. Nowhere near it. I sat on the front stoop of the mansion with an ice pack on my eye, the headache to end all headaches, and Teddy rambling in my ear. After Christina's handlers separated Lamb and Luca, Christina told me my afternoon one-on-one date was canceled. She grabbed an ice pack from the freezer, shoved it at me, and told me to go wait outside while she talked to Lamb and Luca. I hoped I could at least have a few moments alone, but Teddy had found me, plopping down about five inches too close to me. It was 2:15 p.m., and he was still a bit drunk from the night before. I normally had more empathy for people in his situation, but I was in too much pain to think about anyone but myself.

"I jus' don't know why I keep blackin' out," he slurred.

"It's a total mystery," I said. I had heard it all before.

"I mean I only have one, maybe two drinks a night."

I rolled my eyes, an automatic reaction. I regretted the movement immediately—the pain was unbearable.

"Well, I'm glad we're in it together." He sighed. "We're lucky to have each other."

"I've never felt luckier in my life." I flipped the ice pack on my swollen, broken eye and cringed at the few seconds of sunlight. I thought I was going to throw up.

I desperately needed an AA meeting. I hadn't been to one in five days, hadn't spoken to a sponsee in five days. I know AA isn't a cure-all. For some people, it does more harm than good. Ann was one of those people. Meetings tended to make her sullen, depressed, anxious—hearing those bleak stories that were shared over and over again brought her to a dark place. For the longest time, I thought she was just being dramatic, but after one particularly mournful gathering two years into her sobriety, I couldn't get her to lighten up.

I took her to lunch after the meeting because I could tell something was bothering her. "Okay," I had said after watching her plate of food remain untouched.

"Okay, what?" she replied, eyes downcast.

"Okay, you don't have to go to meetings anymore. If they make you sad."

"Really?"

"Really. But promise me three things."

She nodded eagerly.

I held up my index finger. "One, you'll tell me if your cravings get worse."

"Okay, done. No problem."

"Two, you still have to spend time helping others. Volunteer, and when you get to a place where you can afford it, take on pro bono work."

"No problem."

"And three." I sighed and closed my eyes. "Never tell anyone that I, as your sponsor, told you it was okay to forgo AA meetings."

She laughed then, the first time all day. It was a beautiful sound—Ann had one of those laughs that made you laugh. A deep belly chuckle that used every muscle in the body.

"I promise," she said. "I'll make you proud."

And she did. Still sober, eight years later. Just like I had found what worked for me—dance, AA meetings, being a sponsor—she found what worked for her: being a total boss at her job, wearing ugly pantsuits, running a gross amount of miles every week, and telling me I slept around too much.

I didn't know why I was thinking about Ann's life when mine was going up in flames.

Once, someone announced in a meeting—you meet a lot of wannabe philosophers and great ponderers of life in AA—that we tended to zero in on qualities in others that we disliked about ourselves. For example, the speaker *hated* that her mother was *always* fifteen minutes late. But then she realized that she was always fifteen minutes late too. Crazy!

So, maybe Ann's desire to go at it alone rather than ask for support resonated with me on some level.

That's when I remembered another one of my exes—the tattoo artist. I wondered about his new side gig, helping people disappear. I contemplated his clientele, the process. What it might be like to vanish into thin air.

28:Ann

My mouth starts to water—a warm, sweet taste on my tongue. My focus goes in and out, so I close the lid of the toilet and sit down. I focus on the cool ceramic on the backs of my legs.

"Okay," I tell Ned. "Start from the beginning."

"All right, so Lamb was originally supposed to fly from Honolulu to Panama City—that's the closest airport to Watercolor. However, he changed his flight the day before to go to Jackson, Wyoming. He texted his parents and his roommate that he decided to extend his travel plans so he could paint at the Grand Teton National Park. He said he'd be gone a couple of months, and he would turn off his phone for the majority of the trip to focus on his work. He also told his roommate that he would send two months' worth of rent."

"Let me guess," I say, massaging my temple. "No one has heard from him since."

"Nope. Not a word."

"What did the police say?"

"They're not involved."

"What?" I sit up straighter.

"Apparently Lamb goes off the grid a lot. He's an *artist*," Ned emphasizes the word with a hint of disdain, "so he travels most of the year to paint various nature scenes. He's not big on technology, so both his parents and his roommate weren't surprised that they hadn't heard from him. They didn't even bother to call until I begged them."

"What is wrong with these people?" I mutter.

"I don't know. The mom did get a little worried when I told her about the situation with Reese, so she said she would let me know if she hears back. The dad was completely la-te-da about the situation. He told me this was all part of the *creative process* and that Lamb shouldn't be *disturbed* during such a crucial time. Artists," Ned huffs. "I don't understand them. Why do they act so—?"

"What about the roommate?" I interrupt. I need Ned to concentrate.

"Ugh, total stoner. I could hear him inhaling during the entire conversation. He was all, 'Dude, I hardly ever see that guy. It's so chill. He's only here for a couple months out of the year, he pays on time, and he doesn't bother me. It's a sweet setup.' And I was all, 'Dude, this is serious. No one has heard from this man or seen him in close to five weeks, and the woman he was with for a month is missing too. Please, for the love of Pete, call him right now.'"

"Did he?"

"Yeah, but it took a lot of simple words and repetition. He said he'd contact me if he gets a response. I doubt he'll remember with all that Mary Jane clouding his brain, so I'll follow up a few times."

"Thanks, Ned. Did Lamb happen to give his parents or roommate an address?"

"Nope. Just the city. And I did check with the airline, and Lamb—or someone with Lamb's information—boarded the flight to Jackson. I've asked Pat to see if he can get airline footage."

"Surely the FBI will get involved now that there are two missing people?" I know Ned's response before he says it. My shoulders slump.

"Pat said he'd talk to some old colleagues, but without more evidence, it's unlikely they'll investigate. If Lamb were reported missing, that might spur an investigation."

Fuck. I don't want to visit Wyoming.

"Okay, I'll keep digging here."

"And I'll work on finding a complete list of employees for the movie *Happily Ever After.* And look into that Nick Keyser guy. I did a brief search on him when I couldn't reach you, and from what I can tell, he's not too worrisome. Dabbled in acting. Never been in much trouble. I'll go through police records, though. See if I can get an old friend in the Nashville PD to do me a favor."

"Thanks, Ned. I really appreciate all your help. You know that, right? I know this is completely above your pay grade."

"Hey, don't sweat it, Ann. If it was anyone else asking, I might think it was crazy, but you're one of the most levelheaded people I know."

I stare at my feet and keep quiet. Ned's only seen one side of me.

"Heck, it's kind of fun. I feel like Sherlock Holmes. Or Watson, actually. You'd be Sherlock."

I laugh, but it's a half-hearted attempt.

"Ann?"

"Yeah?"

"It could just be a coincidence. Lamb could be painting. And Reese could be with him, safe and sound." I know he's just saying this to make me feel better, to ease my anxiety.

"Maybe." A beat of silence.

"If I don't hear from you for a twenty-four-hour span, Pat and I will take action. I promise. Even if it's Christmas Day."

"Thanks, Ned." Bile creeps up my throat. "I'll talk to you soon."

"Bye, Ann. Be safe."

A minute after I hang up, Ned texts me an image of Lamb. I've started sweating again, so I try to focus on the accompanying message: *Here's a recent photo, just so you have it. His mom took it about a year ago.*

My eyes move to the image.

The picture of Lamb was taken in a studio. He stands next to an easel with a finished painting of the beach—presumably in Watercolor, although the scene is remarkably similar to the one outside my window. The plant life, in particular, is what causes my déjà vu: the palm trees, the taro, the dog tail. The painting is so realistic, it's hard to believe it's not a photograph.

I analyze the artist beside his work, searching for a sign of familiarity, but there isn't one. He's Reese's type, that's for certain: long blond hair, hooded blue eyes, olive skin. His nose is crooked, like it's been broken a few times, but it works for him. I memorize the outline of his face, searching for answers that aren't there.

When I can look at the photo no longer, I put it away.

I lift the lid of the toilet and throw up.

29:Ann

After Ned's call, I'm more certain than ever that something happened to Reese on this retreat. She *didn't* run away. She couldn't have. But I need more information to prove it. I need evidence. I need to talk to someone else who was here with Reese at the retreat.

My eyes scan the cocktail party for Rhea, the participant with Rapunzel-length hair. Tonight, the theme for our attire is basically no attire at all, which only exacerbates my anxiety.

And my lingering nausea. One woman—she goes by Princess, I swear to God—even comes out in a robe and lingerie, holding two pieces of fabric that I guess pass as gowns.

"I didn't know which one to wear," she giggles as she displays the dresses in front of her. "So I thought I'd let the men decide."

I roll my eyes as several men and even a few women let out cheers and catcalls.

My own gown barely covers my breasts, and as if that isn't enough, it also dips much too far down my backside. If I am being recorded, then I will absolutely be fired by at least one of my clients.

I remind myself that this will all be worth it if I can find Reese.

After a few minutes, I finally spot Rhea outside. She's on the patio, a few feet from the bartender and the infinity pool, talking to Chef Clay. They've been spending more and more time together; I could tell Clay was interested in her even on our date. They fit together as a couple. Both golden, glowing, and quiet. They remind me of baby deer, with their big eyes and child-like innocence. If I didn't know any better, I'd think they popped right out of a cartoon storybook.

"Rhea, right?" I try to approach her naturally, but she still looks startled.

"Yes," she says, hand to chest. She has a breathy, eloquent voice. A voice of old Hollywood. "My apologies, I didn't see you there."

I don't know how that's possible—her eyes take up half her face.

"I'm sorry. I didn't mean to scare you. Would you mind if I talked to you for a minute?" I peer at Clay. "If that's okay with you." He shrugs.

"Absolutely," she says. "Where would you like to talk?"

"How about over there?" I point to a quiet spot just outside the patio, where we're still visible from the mansion but more difficult to overhear. She nods, and we start for the beach. It's darker, away from the artificial lights of the patio, but the wedge of moonlight offers a soft white glow. We both take off our heels so we can walk on the sand, still warm from the sunset. Mosquitos prick at my neck, and I swat at them unsuccessfully.

"I like your dress," I say, gesturing toward her lavender gown with puffy sleeves and a corset. I don't actually like it, but it's too bizarre not to mention—an eccentricity that stays on the tip of your tongue until you spit it out.

"Thanks." She brushes her knee-length hair over her shoulder so I can have a better view. "It's the strangest thing–Stephanie, the stylist, always gives me purple dresses. I don't mind. Purple is my favorite color, and she makes me look like a princess, but it's a bit odd, right?"

"Yes, it is." I can't wait to get off this island. "I'm Ann, by the way."

"I know. You're the one Nick likes."

"Oh, I don't know about that."

"No, it's true. All the girls have noticed. A few are bent out of shape about it. He doesn't give anyone else the time of day, and I would know–this is my second retreat with him."

I peer at Nick on the patio, talking lackadaisically to two women. He must feel my gaze, as he glances back at me and offers a small smile. I feel a mosquito bite the back of my neck, and I slap the skin.

"You know, that's actually what I wanted to talk to you about."

"Oh?"

"One of my good friends was at the last retreat you attended. Reese Marigold. Do you remember her?"

"Yes, of course. I didn't know her well, but I liked her. She helped fish me out of the pool one night when I had one too many glasses of bubbly." She giggles and points to her champagne flute. "Now I limit myself to one."

"Smart," I nod. "I'm glad you liked Reese."

"Oh, she was lovely. I could tell she was a romantic, like me. We both thought this experience was a dream come true. So much so that I came back for a second round." She laughs.

"Did you not connect with anyone at the last retreat?"

"Not particularly. There were a few who caught my attention, but I didn't find that soul mate I was yearning for. That true love, you know?"

"Sure." I don't. In my opinion, soul mates are a thing of fiction. An idea generated by Hallmark and Hollywood executives. Even if you find someone you like, they'll leave you. Or you'll fuck it up. It's just the way the world works.

"So I pleaded with Christina to let me come back, and she agreed. But only if I promised to keep searching for that special someone at *any* cost. I told her 'easy, peasy.' Finding a husband before thirty-two is my priority. I mean, what else would I be doing?"

"Nothing. That's definitely the most important thing."

"So how's Reese doing?"

"Well." I clear my throat. "She's actually gone missing. No one has heard from her since the retreat."

Somehow, Rhea's eyes get even bigger. She clasps her heart. "My goodness. That's terrible."

"Yeah, it is. I was wondering how she seemed on the retreat. Nick said she spent most of her time with a guy named Lamb?"

A flicker of realization crosses Rhea's face, and she pauses.

"Yes," she responds. "Yes, she did spend time with him."

"And?" I can tell she's holding back.

"Well, okay, I don't want to spread rumors, but I overheard Magda saying she had to cover up bruises on Reese. And then, I didn't see what happened, but Lamb came back one day with . . ."

Rhea stops.

"Yes?"

"Well, with blood on his knuckles. It was on his shirt too. He said it was a nosebleed, but now . . . I don't know."

"Oh my God," I whisper. "Do you think—" Now the words catch in my throat. "Do you think he hit her?"

"I—I don't know. I didn't like him much, but I never actually saw any violence. It could just be a coincidence."

"How did Reese seem when she left the island? Did she seem scared?"

"Well, that's the thing. I didn't think anything of it at the time, but now . . . well, she didn't leave with the group. She and Lamb both left early. Christina said things didn't work out between them, and they were ready to go after that."

"But Reese boarded her scheduled plane home. She didn't take an earlier flight."

"I–" Rhea raises her shoulders. "I don't know. Maybe she hung out in Hawaii for a few days." Rhea glances toward the patio, where two of the handlers are whispering. The larger one heads our way. His legs slice through the sand like tree trunks. I only have time for one more question.

"Do you remember if you saw Reese *after* you saw Lamb with all the blood?"

The handler is now within earshot. He's rapidly approaching.

"I can't be sure." Rhea wrings her wrist. "I don't think so, though."

The handler reaches us.

"Girls, would you mind coming back to the patio? We just want to make sure we can keep an eye on everyone."

"Of course." Rhea nods. "We'll follow you."

The handler narrows his eyes. He turns back to the mansion, but he glances over his shoulder to make sure we're behind him. When he's not looking, Rhea grabs my wrist.

"Talk to Trixie," she whispers. "She was involved with Lamb too."

30:Ann

n the restroom, I splash cool water on my face. I need a minute alone before I talk to Trixie. I knew there was a possibility that Reese might be . . . deceased, but it was always some vague what-if. Now, that thought is becoming more of a possibility. My stomach turns.

There's no use in melting down just yet, not without more answers. I still have hope.

Trixie is near the bar, with Nick, Richie Rich, and an impossibly small woman whose name escapes me. Sally, maybe. Small Sally, that's it. Trixie is sitting on Rich's lap on a couch, while the other two circle around them. Rich's hand snakes up Trixie's thigh through the slit in her gown that nearly reaches her pelvis. His tar-black hair, curled at the ends from an excess of oil, drips onto Trixie's arm.

I didn't like Rich right from the get-go—he's cocky, patronizing, entitled. After he discussed his investment-banking job with me for forty-five minutes, the longest forty-five minutes of my life, he bragged about sneaking cocaine onto the island.

"I've got a little—" he brushed his nostril and gestured toward the mansion, "if you really want to get the party going."

"I'm an addict, so I think I'll pass," I said.

That effectively ended our relationship.

As I reach the group, Nick beams.

"I was wondering when you were going to come talk to me," he says as he touches the small of my back. I kiss him on the cheek as he pulls me forward.

"Actually, I was hoping I could talk to Trixie."

Nick's face drops. There's a hush among the group, exchanged glances. Rich pulls his hand out of Trixie's dress. She sneers. I instantly dislike her.

"Sure, let's chat," she says with a wad of gum and a Southern California accent. "Let me just refill my drink."

She slithers toward the bar, hands the bartender her glass, and bends forward enough to reveal her cleavage. I try not to stare, but she's popping out of her dress—it's a size too small in the bust. It's like watching a train wreck.

"And what can I get you?" The bartender asks me.

Wine. I want wine.

"Ice water would be great," I say.

"Lame." Trixie rolls her eyes. "So, what did you want to talk about?"

We take our drinks, and I lead her to a vacant spot on the patio, near the infinity pool. Trixie pops her hip out and stares at me expectantly, the highlighted ends of her hair glinting in the moonlight. Most women can't pull off such a short haircut, but Trixie has the cheekbones, the attitude, and the body to do it. With her neck bare, she is fleshier, more naked, more seductive.

"Well, this might sound strange, but I was hoping you could tell me more about Reese Marigold. She was at the retreat a few weeks ago. Rhea and Nick both said you were here too?"

"Yeah, I knew her. Didn't care for her much. It's hard to meet someone who's both easy and living in a fairy tale. I mean, the woman wouldn't cuss, but she would spread her legs within thirty minutes of meeting a guy."

My ears are on fire, so I rest the cool glass against them.

"She was definitely eccentric," I say.

"Why do you ask?"

"Well, she's my friend, and she's gone missing."

"Yikes," she says with a grin. "Sorry about that."

I think about hitting her. I refrain.

"I heard she was seeing a guy you were involved with too. Lamb Martin?"

"Yeah, Lamb and I used to sneak off together when Reese wasn't looking. Although she was such a moron, I could kiss him right in front of her and she wouldn't notice."

"But you didn't leave here with Lamb?" I should stop there, but I can't help it. "Otherwise, you wouldn't be back for a second round."

"No." She narrows her eyes. "Our relationship was more physical. I couldn't live off a poor painter's salary."

She's lying. Trying to save face. I don't know for certain, but I have a feeling that's what's really happening below the surface.

"So why did Lamb leave?"

"I don't know," she says as she inspects her nails. "I had moved on at that point, so I didn't pay him as much attention at the end."

More lies. Why is she lying?

"Is that it?" She sighs.

"Just one more question. Was Lamb ever violent with you?"

"I mean, he sometimes choked me in bed, but I'm into that sort of stuff. I wouldn't be surprised if he hit Reese, though."

"Why?" I clench my fist.

"'Cause *she* was fucking violent. It was probably their thing."

"I don't believe that. Reese would never hit anyone."

"Ha." She brays—an unfortunate neigh of a laugh. "Nick would disagree. She practically tore his face off right here on the patio. In front of everyone. If you don't believe me, ask him yourself."

I glower at Nick, who is still talking, half-heartedly, to Sally and Rich. Is that true? Why would he keep that from me?

"Well, I've gotta go," Trixie says. She glances back and forth between me and Nick. "You should too, if you're smart."

As she walks away, I step on the hem of her dress. Her ankles roll, and she falls face-first into the pool. When she emerges, thrashing angrily, fits of laughter erupt from the other participants.

"Sorry about that," I mutter as I walk by.

31: Reese

"Reese, can I talk to you?" Lamb appeared on the mansion's front door step. His hands were in his pockets, his head hung low. I had been searching for him all day, desperate to talk about the night before, but now that he was here, it was hard to form words.

"Y-Yeah, come sit down." I gestured to the spot on the stoop next to Teddy. He was in the middle of the space, while I was on the left, so Lamb had no choice but to sandwich Teddy between us.

"Hey man, what's up?" Teddy chirped.

"I've been better, Teddy." There was an awkward pause, so Lamb was more direct. "Do you mind if I have a minute with Reese? Alone?"

It took a moment, but finally Teddy read the room. "Oh yeah, man. Of course."

He sauntered inside. Once the door clicked shut, Lamb reached for the ice pack on my eye. "Do you mind?"

I shook my head. I watched as his eyes grew wide at the sight of my swollen face.

"Reese, I'm so sorry. I didn't realize you were that close behind me."

"I know. I shouldn't have tried to get in the middle of it."

Lamb shifted his weight. "I shouldn't have lost my temper like that. It's unacceptable."

I flexed my bruised knuckles from hitting Nick earlier. (On a side note, no one tells you how much it hurts to hit someone. Like, it *really* hurts.)

"I can't really point fingers." I said. "Literally."

Lamb gingerly wrapped my injured fist in his. "I guess we're two peas in a pod then."

"No more hitting?" I asked.

"No more hitting," he agreed. "No more violence."

After a moment of silence, my hand in his, he continued. "So, what's the deal with you guys anyway?"

I sighed and rotated the ice pack on my eye, debating how much to say. I decided to give him a short, glossy version of our relationship, leaving out the part where Luca's friends were threatening to break my kneecaps if I didn't pay them interest on a loan. After I finished running through the story, Lamb still seemed shocked by the assault, so I guess I didn't do too good a job at glossing.

"Reese, that's terrible. He can't be here if he's violent."

That was good logic, but I didn't want to antagonize Luca and give him a reason to disclose my location to his friends. "It was a long time ago, and he's apologized. Everyone deserves a second chance. Besides, there are a million people around, so I don't think he'll try anything here. I can lock my door at night."

Lamb didn't look convinced, but he dropped it for the moment. I took a deep breath and plucked up the courage to bring up the topic I really wanted to discuss.

"Did you kiss Trixie?" I asked.

Lamb's eyebrows raised in shock. "What? No. Why would you think that?"

"Christina said you did."

"What?" His voice raised. "Why would she say that?"

"I don't know, but she seemed pretty sure." I shrugged. I looked at my feet. "It's okay if you did. I know we're not dating or anything. I was just surprised, 'cause . . . I don't know. I thought we had something."

I flinched. I sounded so stupid. I was glad the ice pack covered my profile, but Lamb started to remove it again. He was delicate with it, like a surgeon. He put his hands on my cheeks, careful not to touch my injury, and he turned my face so I would look at him.

"We do have something. Something really special." He wasn't blinking. "I don't want to do anything to jeopardize that."

He leaned toward me, hesitantly. I didn't back away, so he leaned in further until his lips met mine. It was a soft kiss, just what I needed. I don't know if I fully believed him, but I wanted to. More than anything.

32:Ann

((| 'm not sure what she said to you, but I'm betting she deserved it."
Nick laughs as he catches me escaping the vicinity of the infinity
pool. My skin feels wet. I want to get inside, escape the humidity.
All night I've felt as if I've been swaddled in a warm, wet blanket. Nick
touches my wrist when I don't respond.

"Do you have a second to catch up?" he presses.

"Yes," I say. "Yes, I do. Let's start with why you lied to me."

His face contorts. "What are you talking about?"

"Reese didn't attack you?" By his expression, I can tell Trixie was
telling the truth. "You said she was happy, no problems. That doesn't
sound happy to me."

Nick pauses, exchanges a glance with a nearby handler. I have the
distinct feeling that I'm being watched.

Played.

"Do you think I'm an idiot?" I say as I point to the handler. "I can see you looking at each other."

"No," he sighs. "No, I don't think you're an idiot. Not at all. Will you just listen to me? I'll explain."

He walks to the periphery of the backyard of the mansion, pulls a pack of cigarettes from his sport coat. I cross my arms, tap my feet on the lanai. My need for answers outweighs my pride, so I follow.

When we're alone, out of earshot, he hands me a cigarette. I only think about refusing for a split second. *This* will be my last one, I tell myself.

"I didn't lie," he says as he lowers the flame to the butt of my cigarette. My hands are shaking, so he holds them steady. "I just didn't tell you everything. Reese did seem happy, from what I saw, apart from that night."

"Why would you not tell me she attacked you? That's a pretty fucking important detail." I take a deep drag, praying for the dopamine rush to hit me quickly.

"Because I thought it would embarrass you."

"Embarrass me? Why would that embarrass me?"

"Because she thought I was your ex-boyfriend. It took me a while to put it together that you were the Ann she was talking about—I thought your name was just a coincidence, your reaction to me that first night was a coincidence, until you mentioned you were friends with Reese. That's when I put two and two together." He exhales, a cloud of smoke distorting his image.

"Oh" is all I can muster. Before I can stop it, a portion of my rage directs at Reese. I admire her loyalty, her unwavering friendship, but sometimes she can be so unbelievably stupid.

"You want to tell me about him?"

"Not really."

"What?" He snickers. "So *you* can keep secrets, but *I* can't?"

My mouth tightens. He's right. And I need him on my side. I need him for information. I'll spit it out quickly.

"He was the first guy I really cared about, and the relationship sort of imploded. It was a rough breakup. Happens to everyone. I'm not sure why Reese made such a big deal about it."

"Why'd it implode?"

I take a long drag, let the smoke fill my lungs until it pushes everything else out.

"I developed a drinking problem, and then my parents died in a car accident."

He purses his lips, nods solemnly. "That's rough. I'm sorry."

"Yeah." I laugh—a small giggle, then I cut it off. "Sorry, sometimes I do that when I feel uncomfortable. I think it's the nicotine."

"So where's the guy now?"

I start to chuckle uncontrollably. I hold my stomach as the muscles tighten.

"He's married to my best friend."

33:Ann

ick doesn't laugh. Not even a flicker of a smile. "How did that happen?"

"I'll need another cigarette for that story."

He hands me one, lights it. As I breathe in, I organize my thoughts. It's been nine years since I discovered Honey's affair, but the memories still take the wind out of me. I flick ash from the butt of the cigarette onto the patio. I desperately want a drink. I'd kill for just one, repercussion-free sip.

"Actually, it's not even much of a story. My friend Honey started dating him after we broke up. I found out a year later, which is when she claims the relationship started, but I've always wondered if they got together sooner. She says they both tried to ignore the mutual attraction, but they fell in love. It was inescapable."

I think back on the moment I discovered they were seeing each other. It was a brutally cold day in Nashville, a day where the wind cracks your skin open. Reese wanted to get some flowers, to have a little summer in the middle of winter, so we went to a boutique garden center near her apartment. I'd never been to the place before—it was nowhere near where I lived, or where Honey lived. Which is maybe why Honey chose to shop there; she thought I'd never see her.

Honey and I had grown distant since my relationship with him started. This was partially because I was consumed by him. I didn't have time for anything, or anyone, else. I was like a statue that had been brought to life. I saw and felt the world in ways I had never experienced, and I never wanted to go back to the way things were. I remember watching him sleep one morning, the daylight creeping in around the edges of my curtain. He was so peaceful, so beautiful. I remember thinking, *So this is it. This is what it feels like to be in love.*

But Honey and I also grew apart because she didn't like my new drinking habits. She didn't even recognize me, she said.

"Honey, I'm just having some fun," I argued. "I never have fun. Or take breaks. I'm always studying or working or worrying about something. Why can't you just be happy for me?"

"I am happy for you," she pleaded. "But I know you, Ann. You can't do anything halfway. I'm just worried, that's all. But if you're happy, I'm happy."

"I am fucking happy," I screamed and slammed the door in her face.

I started ignoring her calls. I was burning with rage at her callousness, at her hypocrisy. I had stood on the sidelines for years as Honey went through a string of relationships, always telling me that I'd find someone someday. And now that that someday had come, Honey couldn't stand not to be the center of attention. I noticed how she studied my ex, how she peered at him with longing, how she gazed at our embraces with envy.

It made me want to tear her hair out.

But subconsciously, I was angry because she was right. I was spiraling toward a place of no return. I could feel my wings melting as I got closer and closer to the sun, and I didn't have the humility—not at that time, at least—to ask for help. Like everything else in my life, I thought I could fix my problem with hard work and sheer force of will. Besides, I couldn't have a problem. Not me. Not Ann, the model student and child. I was a normal person with a normal life and a normal family. And the more I failed to turn things around, the more I drank and the angrier I became.

And then one morning, I woke up in a soaking-wet bed, no recollection of the night before. I was disgusted. I was disgusting. The shame burned my skin, little flames biting at my neck. I noticed my boyfriend, sleeping on the floor. How many times had I apologized? A hundred? A thousand? Every morning, I promised to be better. And every night, I was worse than the day before.

I wrote a note telling him I'd buy him a new mattress, again, and then I grabbed my purse and left. It wasn't until I reached the nearest gas station, with bare feet and tear-stained cheeks, that I realized I'd left my phone in his room. I made a call on a pay phone, digging for the few coins I had remaining in my purse. When I finally found enough change among the cocktail of drugs, I called my parents. I asked them to come and get me. I was in trouble, I told them. I needed them. They told me to stay right there, they would come straight away. They were so good to me, and I cried harder, because I didn't deserve their kindness.

But they never came. Some teenager was texting and driving. On the highway no less. My parents tried to avoid her car, I was told, but it was an overcorrection, and their car flipped. Not once, not twice, but three times. They died instantly.

It was the most beautiful spring day, not a cloud in sight, and I remember thinking that something so terrible couldn't possibly happen on a day like that.

So when I saw Honey in that nursery a year later, her arm around my ex's waist, slap-happy smiles across their faces, I felt it was a punishment I had earned.

"And you're still friends?" Nick asks. "And her name is Honey?"

An expression crosses his face, one I can't put my finger on.

"Yeah," I swallow. "Yeah. It was hard at first, but after my parents died, Honey was the closest thing to family I had left. I couldn't afford to lose anyone else."

Nick taps out his cigarette in an attempt to hide his disbelief.

"So, if you and Honey are still friends, why did Reese act like she hadn't seen me—or, rather, your ex-boyfriend—in a decade?"

"I don't think she has." I try to remember if there's an encounter I'm overlooking. Honestly, I haven't even seen him much since the wedding. He's sort of a don't ask, don't tell thing between Honey and me.

"She rarely sees Honey," I continue. "They don't like each other much. Different crowds, different interests. It is weird that Reese would get so angry about something that happened so long ago. She was having a rough go of it before the retreat, so maybe her own stress tipped her over the edge."

I remember my conversation with the sweaty dance director, the encounter with Reese's mother, and I shiver. Nick rubs his chin before speaking.

"Well, it sounds like Reese is a loyal friend."

"She is," I whisper, so quietly it's almost inaudible.

Nick takes my hand, massages my thumb. His gaze is so intense it makes me uncomfortable.

"I'm sorry, Ann. About everything."

I give a terse smile, a quick bob of the head. If I speak, I know my voice will break. He leans forward then, and because of the nicotine, or the lack of sleep, or the uncomfortable memories, I let him kiss me.

Perhaps I understand Reese's romances more than I thought I did.

34: Reese

The next week came and went with relative ease, thank goodness. No physical altercations, no blood, no drama. The bruises on my eye and fist started to fade, and with Magda's help, I hid the lingering discoloration with makeup. At cocktail parties and between dates, some of the other participants started to talk to me again. They were hesitant, after everything, but with time, their apprehension faded. That's the thing about time—it can dull just about anything. One of these days, I'd look back on this period of my life and laugh. Wasn't the host of that retreat just so strange? Wasn't it just so funny when I got in the middle of a fight and got a black eye? Ha-ha! Oh, good times.

Nick was also embroiled in his own drama, so that helped take the spotlight off me. He was interested in two different women—or, more accurately, they were both interested in him—and he couldn't decide which one he should seriously pursue. Now, I know I'm a bit biased due to his doppelgänger status, but to me, he was your typical want-what-you-can't-have guy. As soon as one of his love interests' attention waned, his attention was piqued. It seemed very unfair. He seemed very unfair. But it was like watching a car accident; you couldn't not look. It dominated the chatter among participants. Conversations typically went something like this:

"Can you believe how Nick is acting?"

"Such an asshole."

"You can't have your cake and eat it too. That's not how it works."

"I just feel bad for the women. They are being played."

"I want one of them to grow a backbone and move on."

Christina was not immune to this attraction. Where the action went, she followed. You'd think she would have invested most of her time in couples that were doing well, as that was her retreat's supposed mission, but that wasn't the case. Not at all. In fact, she seemed almost annoyed if you had no problems to discuss. During one of our talks, which I came to dread more and more with each session, she wouldn't let me leave until I shared something negative about Lamb.

"So, Lamb," she had said. "Tell me how that's going."

"Much better," I said. It had been seven days since the clash with Luca, and Lamb had been excessively gentle with me. Every touch felt like a whisper, a piece of silk. And when we were together, he only had eyes for me; he barely acknowledged anyone else. On the surface, everything was great.

But, deep down, I still wondered about Trixie. Plus, I hadn't seen Luca since his fight with Lamb, and with every passing day, I grew more and more anxious that he had talked to his friends. I jumped at the slightest sound, wondering if it was them, coming to find me.

Of course, I wasn't going to tell Christina any of this.

"No more fights?" she prodded.

"Nope, none. It's been smooth sailing."

"What about his dates with other women? Does that bother you?"

"I understand it's part of the process—"

"Journey," she interrupted. Just like everything else—our attire, our food, our dates—she was very specific about words we could use. The word "process" was a no-no.

"Excuse me," I corrected myself. "I understand other dates are part of the journey, so I've made peace with it." That was a lie. I was not cool with the other dates, but it was in the contract that we had a one-on-one date with every participant before getting more serious with one. Lamb was diligent about reassuring me before and after each date, telling me it was just a formality, that he only had eyes for me. The concern still nagged at me, though, worming its way into my thoughts and mood.

"But what about his dates with Trixie? He seems interested, does he not?"

I sighed, telling myself she was just trying to get a rise out of me. I don't know why she did that, but she did. She was a very, very odd woman.

"He says he's not. He says you kept pairing them up despite his wishes."

"Is that what he tells you?" she asked.

"Yes."

"And you believe him?"

"Yes," I repeated, but with less confidence.

After our session, I gave myself a mental pep talk. *Don't let the strange woman get to you,* I thought. *She's just interested in some drama. Things between you and Lamb have been great. Perfect, even. No need to worry about something that doesn't exist.*

I repeated these musings to myself as I walked down the long corridor to my room. The talk with Christina and the endless yo-yo between creeping doubt and self-reassurance was making me tired. I fantasized about the lushness of my bed and the temptation to sleep the rest of the afternoon away. I didn't normally take naps. In fact, I didn't sleep much at all—I could usually get by on five hours of sleep or so. I never wanted to miss out on the sunshine, the action, the promise of a new day. There was always something to do and someone to talk to. But the long nights and early mornings were getting to me.

My daydream about sleep was interrupted when someone snatched my wrist and pulled me into the closest room. I took in the surroundings. The room was a replica of mine: white bed with a white carpet, white armchairs, and a white-marble bathroom. Another participant's room, surely.

Then I registered the person who seized me: Luca. His nose was still swollen from Lamb's punch. His eye socket was a sickly yellow. The cut on his lip and the bridge of his nose were still visible.

"Luca, w-what are you doing?" I stammered. I needed to talk to him, but I was still afraid to be alone with the guy.

"Shh," he said as he put his finger to his lips and closed the bedroom door. "We need to talk."

My heart felt like it would explode out of my chest. I could scream if I needed to. Someone would hear me before something happened. He seemed to read my mind, as he walked to the bed and sat on the edge.

"I'll sit over here if it'll make you feel better."

My heart rate did seem to slow with the distance. That gave me a running start if I needed one.

"Did you . . ." I faltered. "I mean, did you tell your friends where I am?"

"What?" He seemed to have completely forgotten about that very important detail. "No, no. I shouldn't have gotten you involved with them in the first place. They think you skipped town, and since it isn't a lot of money, I think they've stopped looking."

I didn't realize I had been holding my breath. "Thank you, Luca." I sighed. The tension I'd been holding in my shoulders seemed to ease a little.

"No, there's something else I need to tell you." He eyed the door. "But I'm still afraid someone can hear us from here."

Yes, I thought. That's a good thing.

"Let's go in the bathroom. We can turn the faucets on." He raised his hands. "I promise I won't hurt you."

I shook my head.

"Please? I could get in a lot of trouble for sharing this." He took a step forward, and I moved backward. I felt the door handle on my back, and I wrapped my hand around it.

He looked desperate. "Reese, you're making this more difficult than it needs to be. I really have changed. I went to a therapist, anger management sessions. I'm not the same guy you dated."

I shook my head again, gripped the door handle tighter. He dropped his shoulders and lowered his voice. "Ok. fine. Look, there's something you don't know about your relationship with Lamb."

"What?" I tried to sound casual, but of course this piqued my interest.

"It's not . . ." His eyes darted around frantically. "It's not real."

My stomach sank. Luca wasn't the most reliable source, but it was too coincidental for both he and Christina to say the same thing. "So . . . you're saying . . . all this stuff he's been telling me . . . us having something special. It's not true?"

"Exactly."

35: Ann

That night, I dream of Reese.

The dream starts on Phaux Island's beach. I'm walking alone. Despite the humidity and the heat, I'm not sweating; I'm not even warm. I feel empty and cold. I eventually wade into the ocean, drawn by some unseen force into the water. *Just let me drown*, I think. *Just make it stop.* But my reflection in the water gives me pause, waking me from my trance. My eyes—my mother's green eyes—are gone, hidden behind a veil of black.

There is another woman in the water's reflection, lying supine on the beach. When I turn around, I see that the woman is Reese. She wears a tattered white sundress, the shreds of which are blowing in the breeze. Her eyes are closed, her skin pale, her red hair dirty and tangled. She is motionless. She must be dead. I'm afraid to get closer, but I know I have to. When I'm within an arm's reach, she wakes, violently—her eyelids shuttering open like the lens of a camera. Her eyes are as black as coal. No pupil, no iris, no color. Just like mine. I jump back in terror. She cocks her head at me and sits up on her elbows, her black eyes following me. I crab-walk backward, trying to get away as fast as I can.

"How's it going to end?" Reese asks. Her voice is faded, distant. Like an echo.

I'm too afraid to respond, so I keep crawling farther and farther away from her. I pause when I feel someone's legs against my back. I jump at the touch. Scream. It's my mother, but she is long past dead, her skin hanging off her bones like sheets on a clothesline. She points at her wrist, to the watch she loved so much.

"Time is ticking," she announces.

I wake with a gasp, drenched in sweat. I throw the sheets off and sit up with a start. My hair is sticking to my neck.

It was just a nightmare, I reassure myself. *Just a nightmare.*

Once I catch my breath, I realize I feel hungover. Between the nightmare, my vulnerability with Nick, and my sleepless nights worrying about Reese, I'm left feeling hollow. I can still smell the smoke from the cigarettes on my hands, in my hair, on my clothes. It makes my head spin. I take the empty glass by my bed and head to the bathroom, where I fill my cup once, twice, three times with tap water. I drink like there's no tomorrow.

After a long shower where I rub my skin raw, I head downstairs to the kitchen. I'm normally the first one there, so I'm startled to see Nick with multiple glasses and plates of food.

"Good morning," he chirps.

"Morning," I say as I take a seat across from him. "Are you hungry?"

"No, some of this is for you," he smiles as he slides a mug toward me. "I got you espresso—four shots, right?"

I nod as I take the cup.

"I notice you also like to put ice in your espresso, which is sort of strange, but I got you a cup anyway."

"It's normally too hot," I murmur.

"And, finally," he continues, "I got you a bagel. I know you normally skip breakfast, but I've got to admit, I'm a little worried about all that caffeine on your empty stomach. So I figure some bread can soak up the acid."

"Thank you." I feel a flush creep up my neck. "That's very observant of you."

"Anything for my girl," he says with a wink. The phrase echoes in my head: *my girl.* The words, the gesture, the secrets, the kiss—it's all too much. It feels wrong.

"So, are you excited for your date today?" he continues.

"Uh, yes," I stammer. "Yeah, it'll be interesting."

With all the excitement of last night, I completely forgot about my date with Teddy. I requested time with him so I could inquire about Reese, and I figured he'd be more coherent during the day. I also asked if we could hike the northern part of the island, as I want to get a closer look at the house for the crew that was pointed out to me by the pilot. I can't run the distance, so a one-on-one date is the only way I can think to investigate. To my surprise, I was granted both wishes. If Christina were trying to hide something there, surely she wouldn't approve, right? Of course, she did allow me to come on the retreat knowing my background and connection to Reese. So if something did happen on the island, she's either incredibly stupid or incredibly arrogant. Or I'm on the wrong track altogether.

No, no. I can't think like that.

"What do you think about Teddy?" Nick asks.

"Truthfully, I don't know that much about him. He seems okay, I guess. Maybe a bit of a mess," I admit as I tear off a piece of bagel. Before

I put it in my mouth, my stomach turns. I force myself to eat anyway–if I lose any more weight, I'm going to start having health issues.

"He does like to party," Nick agrees. His smile fades, and he studies me while I chew. "Just be careful, okay?"

"Why? Do you know something about him?"

"No, no. Nothing like that. He's just been getting a little more out of hand lately."

I scan his face for nonverbal clues, hidden meanings. Like I'd read a client, I search for subtle shifts in speech, evasions, lies. But he maintains eye contact and an even tone. He appears to be telling the truth, so I take his words at face value.

"I'll be careful," I promise.

❧ ❧ ❧

Back in my room, safely hidden in the water closet, I take out my phone. I'm hoping for a text from Ned. There are still so many loose ends that need to be investigated. What's Nick's background? Who is Christina's guarantor, Beverly Wellington? Is this Beverly aware of the island's happenings, or is she more of a silent investor? Is she even a real person? Is there proof that Christina worked on the set of *Happily Ever After*? If so, did she go by Christina Wellington? And most important, is there an update on Lamb? Has he been located? I would follow up on all these questions myself, but I don't have the resources at the moment. I tried using my phone's internet, but it's been spotty ever since I researched Hawaiian recording laws.

To my disappointment, there's nothing from Ned. So I text him my daily update. I proceed to filter through my email, to see if there's an urgent notice from a client, and my heart stops when I see a message from one of the founding partners from the previous day.

The subject reads *Inappropriate use of company resources.*
My finger trembles as I click on the message.

Time sent: 3:06 p.m., December 23, 2018.

*Message: Ann, It has come to our attention that you've been
using one of the new associates, Ned Hargrove, to investigate
the disappearance of your friend, Reese Marigold. I don't need
to tell you that the use of his time on your personal affairs is
highly unprofessional and against company policy. The other
partners and I will discuss an appropriate course of action, and
we will schedule a meeting after the holiday break to discuss
next steps with you. Be on the lookout for a meeting date and
time.*

My palms have become so sweaty, and my hands so shaky, that my
phone slips through my fingers and lands with a thud on the bathroom
floor. I see it crack, the breaks in the glass crawling up the screen like
vines. My entire body feels hot. The room starts to spin, and for the
second time in two days, I throw up.

When I'm finished, I rest my head on the lid of the toilet and laugh.

36: Reese

After my encounter with Luca, I was too riled up to take a nap. My pulse was pounding in my ears. A flush crept up my neck. I needed to cool down, get some water. I had almost made it to the kitchen when I heard a familiar voice coming from the hallway for the crew. Lamb.

I followed the sound. Why would he be in a crew member's room? Did Christina move their talk there? If so, maybe I could eavesdrop, hear what he said about me. But just as I neared the hallway, I heard another voice, higher-pitched. Trixie.

"Keep your voice down," Lamb whispered. "Someone might hear us."

A smacking sound. Lips on lips.

"Who, like Reese?" Trixie giggled between kisses.

"Yes, like Reese. I mean it, I don't want her to know about this."

And then, moaning. Trixie's moans. Lamb's moans.

I don't know how long I stood there at the door. A minute? Two minutes? Ten minutes? It seemed like an hour. I tried to make sense of the situation, but it was like I was paralyzed, the neurons in my brain in a freeze frame. Perhaps my body was generating some sort of defense mechanism, as if it knew that if I fully comprehended the situation right then and there, I would have broken. Or maybe I was already broken, and that's why these men kept searching elsewhere for the missing pieces. But, isn't everyone a little broken? Just a tiny bit? What was it about me that wasn't enough for someone?

My body snapped out of it before my brain did. I backed away from the door like it was lava on my fingertips, and I found myself wandering outside. The patio was strewn with statuesque, semi-starved bodies, like a magazine cover. Or a graveyard. The sky was bubblegum pink, with cotton-candy clouds. I found myself taking off my shoes. Without stopping to talk to anyone or listen to the chatter, I descended into the water. I went in methodically, using the pool steps. The cold water took my breath away, but somehow I still felt numb. I watched my sundress billow around me like jellyfish, and I couldn't help but think it was a beautiful sight. I thought about staying under, just for a second, but the burning in my lungs brought me back up for air.

When I emerged, gasping, I discovered Rhea sitting on the edge of the pool, her feet dangling in the water. Her golden hair fell in rivulets onto the lanai, and her enormous eyes were glossy. She looked like a very sad, very beautiful Barbie doll.

"Are you all right?" she asked.

I waded to where she was sitting and put my elbows on the tile. I brushed the hair out of my face, the water out of my eyes, and tried to focus on what she was saying. Was I all right? Again, my body responded before my brain did, and the words were out of my mouth before I could make sure they were coherent. They were, I think.

"Just needed to cool off."

"I know what you mean. It can get hot in those dresses."

"Yeah." I noticed there were bags under her eyes, and her face was swollen. The sight was enough to jump-start the gears in my brain. I couldn't think about what happened with Lamb, but I could think about talking to Rhea. "What about you? You seem a little . . . bummed."

"Oh," she waved. "I'm fine. Just feeling a little blue."

"Well," I said as I got up and out of the pool. "Tell me about it." I sat next to her, but not so close as to get her wet.

"It's just . . . well, I haven't really connected with anyone here. I'm starting to feel like I'll never find my person."

"Just because he's not here doesn't mean he isn't out there," I said reflexively. Up until then, this had always been my mantra: your dream man is just one date away.

"But I'm thirty-two," she whispered. "I'm . . . old. If it doesn't happen now, I don't think it will ever happen."

"Hey, I'm thirty-four, and I don't feel a day over twenty-five." This wasn't entirely true, but I was trying to help a sister in need.

"But you have someone. Lamb worships you."

I laughed, loudly. It escaped my mouth before I could catch it. I could feel the dam that was holding my feelings back starting to splinter, and I held my chest in an attempt to stop the imminent flood.

"Sorry," I said after I composed myself. "I, um, have a tickle in my throat."

"I think I'll be alone for the rest of my life." Rhea sighed.

If I had a dollar for every time I'd heard that declaration—usually from women—I'd be a rich, rich lady. I repeated a different mantra, this time Ann's:

"Maybe there are other ways for us to feel fulfilled."

37:Ann

This part of the island can only be described as a jungle—the vegetation is rougher, denser, and more tangled than the forest of palm trees that surrounds the mansion. The gnarled roots on the ground are like a thick web that traps us at every turn. I stare at the dappled sunlight through the canopy of trees, little pockets of white in an overgrowth of green, but I'm having trouble concentrating, like I have for the past two hours. I keep thinking about the email from the firm's founding partner and the potential repercussions.

Hopefully, I'll just receive a slap on the wrist, but I'm aware they might terminate me.

Jesus Christ. I could be fired.

The thought makes me feel faint. I love this job. It makes me feel powerful. So much of my life is out of my control, but this, this is the one aspect of my life that feels stable.

And yet I willingly lied to my partners. I used company resources for non-work-related activities. I took advantage of a new and vulnerable associate. My actions were completely inappropriate. I knew it was wrong, and I did it anyway. I worked twelve-hour days for seven years so I could be the youngest female in the firm's history to make partner, and now I've just flushed all that hard work down the toilet. In a matter of weeks. Gone.

I lean against the trunk of the nearest tree and try to slow my breathing. I feel a panic attack coming on.

"Can we stop for a minute?" I ask Teddy.

"Yes, thank God," he says as he deflates, wiping sweat from his ashen face. "I thought you'd never ask. Henry—wait up, we need to stop."

Henry has been ten steps ahead of us the entire hike. He isn't ambling along as he normally does; he's walking quickly now.

At Teddy's request, Henry groans and throws his hands in the air. "We're almost to the crops and livestock. You're the one who requested this, Ann."

"I know, I know. Just one minute."

Teddy plops onto a fallen tree trunk, panting heavily.

The sight triggers an old memory. An afternoon in the woods with my father, listing the names of the trees. Oak. Pine. Spruce. Before he lost his lumber business, he would quiz me on the different parts of the forest, ensuring I had a good understanding of nature. If I did well, and even if I didn't, we would conclude the day at my favorite place, Dragon Park. It's named for its 150-foot-long serpent sculpture, complete with various steps and nooks for climbing.

That was, and still is, the primary attraction. But I wanted to spend my time on the merry-go-round. It wasn't just any carousel either—it was this new, big-kid merry-go-round. Painted the color of cherries, the ride was visible from a mile away. My father and I would spend hours on it. Even after he passed, I'd return to that spot, inhaling the scent of pine trees. I'd pray for a chance to start over, my feet hanging listlessly from a metal swing.

I need a distraction.

"So, Teddy, tell me more about yourself," I say. "Where are you from?"

"Los Angeles," he wheezes.

"Don't tell me: your parents are famous actors."

"What?"

"Nick's from L.A., too. His dad is Frank Keyser."

"Really?" Teddy's eyelids disappear. "That's awesome. I knew he lived in Hollywood, but he never told me what his parents did. I wonder if he'd let me meet them. . . . Do the other participants know about this?"

Shit. I probably shouldn't have said that.

"Uh, you know what? Let's actually keep that between us. I don't know if he wants that out there." When he starts to protest, I continue. "So, your parents. What do they do if they're not in show business?"

His eyes roam the area, like he has to really think about the answer.

"Accountants," he says finally. "They own a small firm together. I started working for them after college."

"Well, that's cool."

"Not really. That's why I drink."

I laugh, and Teddy offers a coy smile. I push myself off the trunk of the tree and perch on the log next to him. Woodpeckers drill in the distance. A bird shrieks. Mosquitoes hum in my ears.

"Henry, do you have any bug spray?" I ask.

Henry is still in the same spot, hands on hips. "No, but there is a can at the house. We can get it if we keep moving." He shows us his wrist and points to his watch.

"Okay, we're coming, don't worry. Why don't you join us while we catch our breath?"

Henry taps his foot, crosses his arms. Finally, he gives in and joins us. "Just fifteen minutes, though," he grumbles.

"We can sync our watches," I say as I tap my wrist.

He rolls his eyes at my sarcasm. I continue anyway. "Your turn, Henry. What's your story? How did you end up here?"

Henry bends down to tie his shoes. "I was trying to get a job as a waiter," he mutters as he tightens his laces. "Miss Christina, she was eating at the restaurant when the manager threw me and my résumé out the door. She helped me pick up the copies, said she would give me some work, if I wanted. She was starting this retreat, and she needed help putting it on—organizing the activities, making sure the guests were comfortable, keeping an eye on things. She offered me more money than I'd ever make as a waiter."

"That was really kind of her."

Henry meets my gaze. He doesn't blink. "Not everybody understands Miss Christina's ways, but I do. She's the smartest person I ever met. She knows what she's doing."

"I'm sure she does," I nod. Then something clicks. "This restaurant. Was it in L.A.?"

"Yep," Henry says. "Sure was."

"That's a bit odd, right?" I prod. "That so many people here are from the same city?"

Ned's damn reality-show theory comes back to me. It's looking more and more accurate. I sit up straighter, making sure my cleavage is TV appropriate.

"Not really." Henry rolls his eyes again. "Miss Christina is from L.A. She just started the retreat. It makes sense that friends of friends would be the first participants."

"Is that how you learned about the retreat?" I ask Teddy. The words 'through a friend of Christina's' are halfway out of my mouth when I notice Teddy has become paler. He's sweating profusely, drops of perspiration streaming down his face.

"Whoa, Teddy, are you okay? Here, drink some water." I reach for my water bottle, but it's empty. I check his canteen, but it's out too. I peer at Henry. "Henry, do you have water?"

He shakes his head.

"Shit. Okay, Teddy, let's take your shirt off. Maybe you're just getting too hot."

I reach for his top, now completely drenched, and pull upward. Teddy sways gently.

"Teddy, I need you to lift your arms up, okay? Henry, can you help me?"

Henry comes toward us, but he seems unconcerned. He yanks Teddy's arms above his head, and I'm able to get the clothing off. Teddy still looks faint. His eyes droop.

"Why don't you lie down? On your back."

He slumps onto the jungle floor, leaves crunching and twigs snapping beneath him. I lift his legs and place them on the nearest log.

"Henry, do you have any food with you?"

"No, but there's some at the house. We only have a half mile left."

"Why don't you go get some—something sugary—and bring it back to us? Water, too."

"Okay," he huffs.

I turn my attention back to Teddy. He's not sweating quite as much, and some color has returned to his cheeks. I wipe some of the perspiration from his forehead with a towel I brought.

"I'm okay," he says. "Just a little hungover."

"How much did you drink last night?"

"Just two or three scotches." I give him a skeptical look. "I swear. That's all I remember. I don't know what happens to me here. It's like . . . it's like . . . ah, forget it."

"It's like what?" My curiosity is piqued.

"It makes me sound crazy."

"Just tell me."

"It's like . . ." He blinks rapidly. "It's like they're slipping me something."

"Slipping you something? Like drugs?"

Eyes wide, he nods.

38: Ann

An hour later, we're touring the crops on the far end of the island on a tractor. The meticulous organization is a drastic departure from the wild nature of the jungle: rows of sugarcane, sweet potatoes, yams, and taro line the land as far as the eye can see. As we travel farther away from the jungle and toward the sea, the second mansion on the island becomes visible. It's just a speck at first, but slowly, gradually, it transforms into a gargantuan development, towering over the crops like a larger-than-life minister preaching to a congregation. Various fruit trees—orange, banana, mango, papaya—stand sentinel to the left of the mansion. On the right, a barn for the livestock.

The mansion is similar in design to the participants' mansion: Spanish-style roof tiles, stuccoed walls, earth tones. The only difference is the lack of glass. There are no windows, there is no transparency, and the front door is just one massive piece of wood.

"So, as I've mentioned," Henry yells over the roar of the tractor engine, his mess of dirt-brown hair flapping in the wind, "we try to raise as much food as we can on the island because it's expensive to ship things."

As Henry continues to explain farming to us in a lazy, annoyed manner, I study Teddy. He seems better now. More color in his face, less sweating. But he appears completely spent—his shoulders are hunched, his eyes droop.

I've been chewing on his admission that he thinks he might be drugged, but I can't make sense of it. If Christina were slipping him something, why would she drug only him? Was it some form of cruel entertainment? And if Teddy had these thoughts, why would he come back to the retreat a second time? I posited these questions to Teddy back in the jungle, but he didn't offer any helpful insight. He just kept shaking his head, saying, "I don't know. I don't know." And eventually, with a twinge of fear: "Just forget it. I don't know why I said that."

Nevertheless, I decide it would be a good idea to watch Teddy's drinking tonight. I should be more careful about what I ingest too. Instead of getting water from the bartender or the cook, I'll fill my glass with tap water.

As we near the barn, the smell of manure and rotten eggs floods my nostrils. It's hard to breathe. When Henry turns off the tractor and gestures for us to get down, the lack of wind makes the aroma even more overwhelming. Teddy bends over, hands on knees.

"Oh my God, it smells like shit," he says. "I think I'm going to throw up."

"Fine." Henry sighs. He points to the crops adjacent to the housing. "Just walk that way, and we'll find you after I give Ann the tour."

I want to join Teddy, but I need to see what's inside that barn. I need to have a good layout of the entire island so I can discover potential hiding places. Whether it's Christina or Reese or someone else who's doing the hiding, I have yet to determine.

Inside the barn, the window slits provide only spotlights of visibility. It's dark, dank. Eerie. Flies are everywhere. The large fans on the front and back entrance creak and moan with every cycle.

"I'm not sure why you wanted to see this," Henry says as he leads me down the center aisle, flanked by stalls of cows on each side. "It's just a bunch of stupid animals that get slaughtered after they're done milking."

I cringe at his words.

Most of the cows are unbothered by our presence, but one acts as if she's waiting for me. She's all white—no spots like the others—and she's smaller. Her head sticks out of her cage, her big brown eyes following me as I trail behind Henry. I stop when I reach her. Tags pierce her ears. Fleas swarm her face, her mouth, her eyes.

She seems so sad, so alone, and I have the strongest urge to open her cage and release her.

"What are you doing?" Henry asks when he realizes I'm not behind him.

"Just getting a closer look."

The cow's eyes don't leave me. Despite the smell and the fleas, I rub the tuft of hair on the top of her head. It's softer than I thought. Her eyes close, and her tail swings from left to right.

"Well, we need to keep moving. We're already behind because of Teddy."

I do as he says, but my eyes stay on the white cow as we exit the barn.

Outside, dozens of pigs and chickens roam small plots of land separated by pens. The chickens are loud—clucking, flapping, screaming. Their beady eyes dart every which way. They look deranged.

"And here are the pigs and chickens." Henry says. "Now let's get going."

"Wait, that's it?" I analyze the small barn and its surroundings, disappointed. There's not nearly enough space to hide something. Or someone.

"Yep. Now come on. Teddy's probably passed out in the field right now."

"What about the house? Can we see what's inside there?"

"Absolutely not. That's for the crew. It's off limits."

I scan the house as I follow Henry, searching for answers. I need to get inside.

Teddy isn't visible when we return. We call his name, but there's no answer.

"Goddamnit," Henry mutters, stomping his good foot. "I don't have time for this. You keep looking for him. I need to go pull the car around and get you back to the mansion."

"Okay, will do." I peer at the sky and offer a tacit thank-you. I haven't had much time alone with Teddy, and I still need to ask him about Reese.

I run down the aisle between the rows of sugarcane, yelling Teddy's name. Eventually he calls back.

"Over here."

I hurry toward his voice, taking a shortcut through the sugarcane. The grass is tall—I'd guess between ten and thirteen feet—and I can't see more than an arm's reach in front of me. The plants whip my face, my limbs, my torso. But I keep running, running, running, until I collide with Teddy, knocking us both to the ground. He laughs, brushes the dirt off himself, and helps me stand. It's the most energy I've seen from him all day.

"Where were you?" I ask as I take his hand. "Henry is not pleased."

He grins. "I have to show you something. This way."

He makes his way back through the sugarcane, and I follow. Now's my chance.

"Hey Teddy," I call as I whack the grass from my face.

"Yeah?"

"Did you know Reese Marigold when you were here last time?"

He continues to elbow his way through the plants, breaking the stalks at the root and squashing the ground beneath. This was stupid. I should have confronted him when I could see his facial expressions.

"I did, yeah," he says eventually.

"How did she seem when she was here? Was she happy?"

"Uh, she wasn't particularly happy when I was here. But I left early, so things could have changed after I was gone."

"Why wasn't she happy?"

"Well, this guy she was seeing, Lamb, had hit her, so she had a pretty nasty black eye."

My chest tightens. So it is true: Lamb hit Reese.

"That's terrible. Surely someone did something about it?" Please, God, tell me someone beat him senseless, kicked him off the island, did something after that.

"Well, not really. It was an accident. Lamb was in a fight with some ex-boyfriend of Reese's, she tried to pull him off, and she caught an elbow in the eye."

"Wait. Ex-boyfriend? You mean like an ex-boyfriend on the retreat? Someone else she was seeing?"

"No, no. An ex-boyfriend from before."

I stop. The stalk of a sugarcane snaps against my cheek, its leaves whispering in my ears.

"What was this ex-boyfriend's name, Teddy? Do you remember?"

He turns to face me, his lips contorted.

"Teddy, it's very important that you remember his name."

"I–I can't remember exactly." He scratches his head. "Oh–it was a car's name. Italian. Lamborghini or Maserati or something."

"Was it Ferrari? Luca Ferrari?"

"That's it," he exclaims. He takes my hand. My legs move, but I can't feel them. "Come on, we're almost there."

"Wait, Teddy. What happened to Luca? Was he a participant here?"

"Uh, no. He was part of the crew. A cook, I think."

"Did he remain on the island after the fight?" My heart is jackhammering inside my rib cage as I try to keep up with Teddy, my sweaty palm loosening from his grip. A cut piece of stalk catches my forearm, slicing the skin open and drawing blood.

"Yeah, I'm pretty sure he stayed. Oh, here we are."

We emerge out of the sugarcane into an open field. Before us are hundreds of marigolds—red, orange, yellow. They aren't separated into rows or aisles like the crops. They are wild, unruly. The sight is beautiful. Breathtaking. I want to wade into the foliage and collapse.

Teddy breaks off an orange blossom and hands it to me.

"For you, my lady."

I take it, studying the red thumbprint on the stem. I notice Teddy's thumb is bleeding. A drop of blood escapes his skin and falls to the ground, staining the soil.

39 : Reese

R hea wasn't super-pleased at the thought that just maybe, just maybe, she didn't need some guy to make her happy. Her eyes darkened.

"I think you're wrong," she said.

I shrugged. "Maybe."

I was not in the right mindset to ponder the meaning of life. I wanted to get out of the conversation, but I wasn't sure how. As if Christina could read my mind, she entered the patio, four handlers in tow, clinking a champagne glass with a knife.

"Everyone, can I have a moment?"

The area fell silent. Christina's facial features were downturned, and her eyes were dull.

"I just want to make a quick announcement before tonight's cocktail party. It saddens me to say Teddy is recusing himself from the rest of the retreat. Some personal matters have come up, and he needs to attend to them right away. He needs to leave in a hurry, so he wanted me to tell you all good-bye, and good luck."

I looked around at the participants to gauge their reaction. Despite the news, there was a palpable excitement in the air. When Christina turned to leave, an unreadable expression on her face, I turned to Rhea. She wasn't immune to the schadenfreude.

"What do you think that means?" she said with wide eyes.

"I don't know," I said. "Would you excuse me? I'm going to see if I can find him."

"Okay, tell me what you find," she yelled after me.

I grabbed a towel from the stack kept near the patio doors. I dried myself off as best as I could, but I was still too wet to enter the house. I made a move anyway.

I wasn't sure exactly what I was going to say if I found Teddy, but I knew I had to see him. A part of me thought he might be trying to get clean—I found him passed out, again, by the pool at eleven that morning. Three hours later, he was positively sloshed, barely able to form words. If he was leaving to get help, I wanted to give him my number—just in case he ever needed to talk to someone—and perhaps a few words of encouragement.

I made my way upstairs. My dress was still wet, dripping onto the hardwood with each step. I knew Teddy was on the second floor some-where, so I checked each door until I found him. He was in front of an overflowing suitcase.

"Teddy?"

He jumped at my voice. When he saw me, he backed up until he was touching his belongings. He blocked the bag with his hands. He seemed completely with it. How had he sobered up that fast?

"You must be feeling better," I said.

"I do, yes. I got some food and some water." His voice was steady. No slur.

"So I hear you're leaving us?"

"Yeah. Hate to leave in a hurry, but it's something of an emergency."

"I hope everything is okay," I prod.

"Oh yeah, just some family stuff."

"I see. Well, if you ever need someone to talk to, connect with me on Facebook or something. I'd love to keep in touch."

"Sure, will do."

He seemed to want me to leave, so I took the hint. I was about to head to my room, get out of those wet clothes, when something on top of his bed, next to his suitcase, caught my eye.

It looked like a check. Difficult to see from a distance, so it was hard to be certain.

He followed my gaze and quickly stuffed the item in his pocket.

"Is that all?" he asked. He looked frenzied, almost frightened, so I lowered my head and left.

40: Ann

My hands are trembling. I clench and unclench the leather seats of the SUV as we head back to the mansion. Teddy is saying something, but it's distant. I can't hear him over the pounding in my ears. I can't believe Luca has been on the island this entire time, right under my nose.

"Ann." Teddy touches my forearm. "We're here. I was saying I had a great time with you today."

"Oh." I notice the car has stopped in front of the mansion and Henry is exiting the vehicle. My eyes follow him as he goes to the trunk to retrieve some of the items we took on our hike. "Yeah, same here."

"Do you want to take a swim before dinner?" Teddy pleads with raised eyebrows.

"You go on ahead. I'm going to grab some coffee."

"Suit yourself." He looks dejected, but he leaves it alone.

Inside, the house is quiet. When I peer out through the glass doors to the patio, I notice Christina is down on the beach talking to three of her handlers. They're having a meeting of some sort. Everyone seems serious.

Now's my chance.

I hurry to the kitchen. Nick is sitting at the marble island, drinking water and staring off into space. Why is he always . . . just . . . around?

"Well look who it is." He beams. "How was your date?"

"Good, good. Do you know where the cooks hang out when they're not here?"

"Uh, I assume back there." He points to a closed door next to the participants' entrance. It blends in smoothly with the wall—it's completely white, even the handle. If you weren't looking closely, you'd miss it.

41: Ann

throw open the door to the back kitchen. It slams against the wall, and the thud reverberates throughout the room like a wrecking ball.

Luca is the only one in the room. He's in an apron, cleaning the stovetop. When he sees me, he lowers his head, closes his eyes, and mumbles "shit" under his breath. I stride toward him and use the momentum to push him against the refrigerator. His smell—sharp cheddar and coffee—fills my nostrils. I grab fistfuls of his shirt and shake him.

"What did you do to her?" I yell.

"Nothing, I swear."

"Whoa, whoa," Nick says. His eyes are frantic. He pulls me off of Luca and gets between us. "What is going on? How do you know this guy?"

"He's Reese's shitty ex-boyfriend. Reese was granted an order of protection after Luca attacked her at one of her performances. After he smashed her head into a wall, he yanked her by the hair and dragged her across the floor."

"Is this true?" Nick asks Luca.

"Yes, yes, it's true." Luca looks sheepish, but I'm not buying it. "I made a horrible, horrible mistake. But it was seven years ago, and I've apologized about a hundred times."

"Sorry, buddy," I say. "That's not how it works. You don't get to act like a crazy person, apologize, and then go back to normal like nothing happened."

"Speak for yourself," he exclaims as I continue to rail against Nick, my arms flailing in every direction. Nick grips both my arms firmly and holds them at my sides.

"Just calm down," Nick says. "Let's talk this out."

"Don't you dare tell me to calm down," I scream.

"I'm sorry, I'm sorry," Nick coos. "Bad choice of words. Let's just hear what he has to say before hitting him. We'll get more information that way."

"Hey, what the fu—" Luca asks just as Nick turns to him, grips his neck, and slams his head into the refrigerator. Luca's eyes roll back into his head, and for a second I'm afraid he's really hurt. "And you're going to stay here and answer her questions, okay?"

Luca rubs the back of his head and nods. I stop wriggling.

"Fine," I say to Nick. To Luca: "Tell me what you did with Reese."

"Nothing. I swear to God. I didn't even know she was going to be here."

"That's bullshit," I say. "So Lamb just hit you for no reason then?"

"No. Well, yes. He hit me when he learned about the order of protection. The fucker broke my nose. I couldn't see straight for a week. I'm not saying I didn't deserve it, but I've changed since then."

I stare more closely at his nose. It seems fine, but it has been about five weeks.

I tap my foot, cross my arms. "So I'm just supposed to believe that Reese's abusive ex-boyfriend shows up a mere few weeks before she disappears, and it's a total coincidence?"

"Abusive is pushing it," he says. "It was one time."

Nick and I give him a look, and he puts his hands up in defense. "Look, there's nothin' I can say that'll change your mind, but that's the truth. I saw her that one day, that was it. The rest of the retreat I stayed out of her hair."

I'm about to protest when I hear Christina's deep voice behind me.

"Ann, I need to talk to you."

She's between two handlers, and her eyes are the size of small slits. I don't know how she found me so quickly. She was outside, all the way down on the beach, and there was no one near the kitchen, aside from Nick, when I entered. I want to tell her to fuck off, that I'm in the middle of something important, but I doubt that will end well, not with her enormous bodyguards by her side.

"Fine," I say through gritted teeth.

Christina turns on her heels, and I can tell our conversation won't be pleasant.

"I'm not finished with you," I mutter to Luca as Christina exits the room. I'm almost out the door when Luca calls after me.

"She was upset about Lamb. If you find him, I'll bet he has answers."

"I'm working on it," I mutter under my breath.

42: Ann

"Sit down," Christina says as we enter the talking room, alone.

I close the door behind me and take the seat opposite her. My temples throb. My blood boils. I squeeze the arms of the chair until my nails tear the fabric.

"Why is Reese's ex-boyfriend here?" I ask.

"Luca? He's one of my cooks. I had no idea he was connected to Reese until she arrived."

"So you know their history then?"

"She told me as much when she discovered he was here."

"And you didn't think to do anything about it?" I'm shouting now, but I don't care. "Maybe, I don't know, fire him?"

"He's a great worker," she says evenly. "He never gave me a reason to doubt him. I believe everyone deserves a second chance. I would think you, of all people, would understand that."

"What's that supposed to mean?"

She sinks back in her chair. For the first time, I realize there's a sadness there, under the surface, behind all the polish.

"I don't know," she sighs. "Everyone on this retreat has failed in some way to develop a healthy, successful relationship. My job is to give them another opportunity before it's too late."

"Too late, as in reaching the age of thirty-five?" I scoff.

"More or less," she says. "After thirty-five, it's harder to have children, so your chances of having a family dwindle. If you're still single at thirty-five, no prior marriage, it starts to become distasteful. People take pity on you. They whisper behind your back. They believe there must be something inherently wrong with you." She sounds like she's rehearsing a speech, and then she seems to ad-lib. "Trust me, I would know."

I'm not sure how to respond to that, so I mutter under my breath: "This is so fucked up."

"We can agree to disagree." She smooths the hem of her skirt. "The fact of the matter is, Ann, that you are staying at my place, attending my retreat, and while you do, you will abide by my rules. If you don't like them, you can leave. But I can't have you interrogating the participants. Threatening my staff. Sneaking around the house and looking for clues. I put up with your behavior at first because of your . . . let's call them special circumstances. But now, I'm fed up. You're making a mockery of my business."

"Why didn't you tell me about Lamb?" I say.

"What?" She seems to break, just for a second. But perhaps I'm just imagining that. "What about him?"

"You said Reese didn't connect with anyone here, and I've heard from several others that she did."

Christina sighs, closes her eyes, and rubs her temples.

"Reese didn't leave engaged or in a committed relationship. I don't consider that a 'connection.' Just a fling."

"But you lied to me. Why?"

"I didn't lie. I just told you—we have different definitions of the word *connection*."

"Is it because something happened to him? He's missing too, but I'm sure you already knew—"

Christina puts her hand up. "Enough. I'm tired, Ann. So very, very tired."

Her head is lowered at an angle that highlights the dark circles under her eyes. Without the intense lights in this room, I don't think I would have ever noticed.

"I don't ever want to hear Reese's name again," she continues. "If you're only here to follow some trail of nonexistent breadcrumbs, then I can arrange for you to go home. As soon as today. There are a lot of people who actually want to be here to fulfill a dream, and if you don't believe in that dream, then there's no point continuing this journey."

My heart pounds in my throat. I take a deep breath, try to think rationally. I could continue to be stubborn, but then I would leave the retreat empty-handed. I've come this far, and the answers are this close—I can feel them at my fingertips, just within my grasp. If I could reach a bit further, then I would hold something tangible. But I can't do that if I'm not on this island.

So I nod. A tacit surrender. A white flag.

"Do you want to go home, Ann?" she clarifies.

"No," I whisper, so soft it's barely audible. "I don't want to go home."

"Okay, then." She exhales. "No more mention of Reese while you're here. Is that clear?"

I nod again. "Clear," I mumble.

"Now, is there anything else you'd like to discuss. Perhaps your budding romance with Nick?"

I swallow, try to formulate an appropriate answer. I don't want to play this game anymore, but I have to. I tell Christina what she wants to hear. I answer all her prodding questions.

As I sit there, I study the talking room. I hate it, this room. In this small space, there are no windows, no photographs, no design. No color. Just white walls cornering me on all sides. It's suffocating. It reminds me of a mental institution. Maybe it's fitting, though. Maybe—just maybe— I'm losing my mind. I'm making wild accusations without reliable evidence. I'm making decisions based on my intuition, not on facts. I'm close to being evicted from this island. I'm about to be fired from my job for taking advantage of someone under my supervision.

And the worst of it is that a part of me doesn't care. Finding Reese is my main objective now, and I know, I know, in my heart of hearts, that something terrible happened to Reese while she was here. I'll continue to search for her if it kills me.

43:Reese

A couple hours later, Magda knocked on my door. It was time to get ready for the nightly cocktail party, and she was here to do my makeup. I knew I was a mess. I could feel the swelling in my face, the puffiness around my eyes.

The rapping continued, intensifying.

"Reese," she yelled. "Let me in!"

I didn't want her to see me like this, but I also couldn't not let her in.

"One minute," I said. I wiped my cheeks and checked my appearance in the closest mirror. It was just as bad as I had feared, but there was nothing I could do about it in the next thirty seconds. I sucked in my breath and I opened the door. I kept my face turned toward the floor, but Magda didn't miss it.

"Vhat happened to your face?" she shrieked.

"I'm sorry, Magda." I winced. "It's been a rough day."

She screamed and turned on her heel. She muttered various curse words as she padded down the hall. I wasn't sure where she was going, but I was glad to be alone. I shuffled to the bathroom, turned on the faucet, and splashed cool water on my face and neck. I huddled over the sink and took deep breaths, trying to calm myself down.

"Reese?"

I jumped at the nearby voice. It was Christina, hovering over the end of the marble sink. The running water must have muffled her footsteps.

"Christina, hey. I didn't hear you."

"Magda said you were upset. She went to get you some ice."

I pressed on my cheeks in a futile attempt to both hide my face and bring down the swelling. "I'm fine. I'm just tired."

Which was true. I was exhausted. We hardly got any sleep, with the early mornings and late nights. We also didn't eat much, with the odd meal times, so I felt like I was constantly low on energy. Or short-tempered and hangry. I wondered if I would have acted differently—not hitting Nick, not crying so much over Lamb, being more careful with my words—if I was rested and satiated. I didn't even have a distraction at the retreat, so all I could do was focus on the participants, my love life or lack thereof, and the same circular thoughts. Sometimes, it felt like I was going crazy. Like Teddy sobering up and stuffing a check in his pocket. Did I imagine that, or did that really happen?

"Do you want to talk about it?" she asked. "We could go to a talking room."

I sighed. I didn't have the stamina to filter my responses. "I really, really don't." I reached for a hand towel to dry a lingering wet spot on my cheek.

"I think it'll help to talk it out," she prodded.

"What do you want me to say?" I finally snapped. "That you were right? That Lamb was sleeping with someone else? That, no matter what

I do, I seem to end up with the same, shitty guys? That there's something so wrong with me that I can't hold on to someone for even a week?"

I instantly felt bad about my outburst, but I was too embarrassed to apologize. I threw the hand towel onto the marble sink, flopped down onto the vanity stool, and covered my face in my hands. It was quiet, and then I heard Christina's footsteps. I prayed she left the room. Of course, I was wrong. I felt her tap my forearm a minute later.

I glanced up to find her on the other vanity stool. She had moved it from the second sink so we were arm's length apart. Her expression surprised me. There was a sadness there I hadn't recognized before.

"There's nothing wrong with you," she said softly.

My eyes moistened at the unexpected kindness. When I didn't respond, she continued.

"I've been around shitty people my whole life. At first, it was an act of rebellion. I was mad at my family for abandoning me, so to get attention I found the most destructive people I could. And then, it just sort of became a habit." She was speaking to me, but I could tell she wasn't really speaking to me. Her shoulders were hunched, and she was staring off to the side. "Maybe it's a form of masochism. Penance for the wrongs you think you did."

I didn't know what to say. Up until this point, Christina had been so closed off, revealing so few personal details. I was curious about her, of course, but I didn't want to pry if she didn't want to share. And now that she was sharing, I couldn't believe we had something in common. She always seemed so poised, so indestructible.

Christina met my gaze and held it. She opened her mouth, as if she was about to say something. Of course, Magda came rushing in before Christina could vocalize her thought.

"I got ze ice," she cried, waving the pack in front of her. Magda's entrance seemed to bring Christina back to the present. She sat up, crossed her legs, cleared her throat. Whatever she was going to say, she seemed to have changed her mind. She took the ice pack from Magda and handed it to me.

"Thank you, Magda," Christina said. "Why don't you go work on another participant?"

"But she's the last one."

Christina shot her a look, and Magda nodded in understanding. She left, and Christina and I were alone again. When my bedroom door clicked shut, Christina continued: "Anyway, the point is: You're better than that. Don't let other people's opinions define you."

I nodded, scrunched my eyebrows. She was being vague, but I thought I understood what she was saying. I needed to dust myself off, get back out there. This sounded good in theory, but the reality was I was just too tired. Christina seemed to read my mind. In another rare instance of compassion, she rubbed my shoulder.

"Why don't you lie down for a few hours? I'm not supposed to let participants skip the beginning of the cocktail party, but we can make an exception this once."

"Thank you," I sighed. I almost started crying again, but Christina held her palm up.

"No more tears," she said.

I nodded. "Okay."

When she left, there was an eerie silence that filled the void. I crawled to my bed, sank into the mattress, and closed my eyes. I tried to shut out all the thoughts bouncing around in my head. Lamb and Trixie. Teddy's check. Christina's confession of sorts. Right before I drifted off to sleep, Christina's words came back to me: I'm not supposed to let participants skip the beginning of the cocktail party. That seemed like an odd thing to say. I thought she didn't answer to anyone.

44: Reese

I woke to a light *tap, tap, tap* on my forehead. I swatted at it, but the pressure increased.

I opened my eyes enough to see Magda, tapping her forefinger between my brows. The slit in my eyes, combined with her proximity to my face, created a fish-eye lens, making her upturned button nose appear bigger than it was. Her gaze crawled down to meet mine, magnifying her eyes behind her large rose-rimmed glasses.

"Vakey, vakey," Magda said.

I pushed myself up with my elbows. The room was hazy. I felt like someone who had risen from the dead.

"Ve need to do your makeup now," Magda said as she pressed a cool compress to my eyes. "It's been few hours and eyes are vorse."

"Okay, okay," I said, using both arms to create some space between us. "Give me just one minute, and then I'll come sit for you, okay?"

Magda harrumphed and muttered something incoherent under her breath. She shuffled her little legs quickly to the bathroom, not shifting her weight, making her appear more robot than human. I threw my legs over the bed and tried to shake the last vestiges of sleep.

When I arrived downstairs twenty minutes later, my fog still was just starting to lift. It was also pitch-black outside, the sliver of moon hidden behind clouds, and I was used to starting the cocktail party at sunset. Everything felt off. I accidentally bumped into Nick. He was talking to his two female friends, and his face contorted when he saw me. *Awesome,* I thought. *Just awesome.*

"I'm sorry, Nick," I said. "I just woke up, and I guess I'm still feeling a little dizzy." I waved at his lady friends. "Hello girls. Excuse me."

Before I could leave, Nick grabbed my elbow.

"Hey, you sure you're all right?" His brows were furrowed, his lips pursed. His lips seemed so soft—like clouds.

"I'm not sure," I replied. "No. Yes. No, I'm fine."

"Let's get you some water, okay?"

"Um, all right." This was very surprising. When had Nick decided to forgive me? Nothing made sense anymore.

He led me outside. I glanced over my shoulder to offer an apologetic look to his now-unhappy companions.

While Nick ordered an ice water from the bartender by the pool, I glanced around at the other participants. I noticed Trixie, on one of the sofas closest to the patio doors, stroking Lamb's leg. My stomach lurched, and I turned my back on the sight as quickly as I could.

"Here," Nick said as he pushed the glass of water into my hand. "Drink that."

I gulped it down, hoping the cool liquid would shake me out of my funk.

"Thank you," I said. "That was . . . that was nice."

He offered a soft smile as he passed the glass back to the bartender. "Can you refill that?"

I thought of Christina's words: You're better than that. I decided it was now or never to apologize.

"Nick?"

"Yeah?" he responded as he grabbed my refill.

"I'm really sorry, again, about the other night. I feel terrible about what happened."

He studied me, seemingly assessing my sincerity. Then his lip curled up and to the left. I hadn't noticed his lopsided grin before. It was endearing.

"Don't worry about it," he said. "We're all going a little crazy here."

My shoulders fell in relief. I hadn't realized how much that had been weighing on me.

In my periphery, I saw Lamb approach, and my shoulders hunched right back up. I wasn't ready to talk to him yet. I didn't respond when he wrapped his arms around me.

"Hey sweetheart," he said with a quick kiss on my lips. "I missed you."

I stood stock-still. I didn't know what to say. I just wanted him to leave me alone, quit humiliating me.

"Are you okay?" Lamb asked.

I nodded. I was afraid if I spoke, my voice would break. After an uncomfortable pause, Nick came to my rescue.

"We were actually about to go chat."

"Really?" Lamb's eyebrows furrowed. "Why?"

Neither of us responded to his question. Instead, Nick guided me toward the entrance, calling over his shoulder: "She'll catch up with you later."

Lamb looked taken aback, maybe even a bit jealous. A small part of me was happy about that.

The front of the house was quiet, save for the chirps from the forest and the gurgling of water from the fountain. I was starting to feel more lucid. Nick and I sat shoulder to shoulder on the front stoop. He ferreted a pack of cigarettes out of his sport coat.

"You mind if I smoke?"

I shook my head. Truthfully, I thought smoking was gross, but Nick was being kind to me when I didn't deserve it.

"Thank you," I muttered. "For what you did back there."

He shrugged, lit his cigarette. "You saved me earlier, so I was just returning the favor."

He had made a bit of mess with those two girls, but at least they both knew there was another woman involved.

"Do you know which one you'll pick?" I asked.

"No idea." He laughed as he pocketed his pack of smokes. "Maybe neither. There's something missing. That spark, you know?"

I nodded, but I was starting to wonder if the spark was overrated. Or maybe my spark was just broken.

"Do you wanna talk about you and Lamb?"

I rubbed my eyebrow. I really wish people would stop asking me about it. I felt stupid enough already.

"Not really, if that's okay."

"Fair enough. But, between you and me, Lamb's a dumbass. Trixie . . . Trixie's not someone you want long-term."

So I guess everyone knew about Lamb and Trixie besides me. I really was an idiot. I rested my chin on my hand.

"I don't really know her, but she seems fine. She's pretty."

"Pretty isn't everything. And if we're comparing looks, Trixie's got nothing on you." He exhaled, and I couldn't read his expression through the smoke. "I think you should talk to Lamb. If you give him an ultimatum, he'll choose you."

"But he lied to me," I exclaimed. "Multiple times. I won't be able to trust him again."

I had said I didn't want to talk about it, but I guess all it took was some prodding and some compliments from Nick. I was so stinking easy.

"We're supposed to be exploring our options here, and Lamb was doing that. He shouldn't have lied about it, but he didn't want to mess up what you two had. People make mistakes. I'd give him a second chance."

"I give second chances way too easily." I laughed. "And third chances. And fourth chances. I told myself things would be different on this retreat. That I would be different."

He exhaled the last drag of his cigarette and stubbed the remainder out. "Well, then at least talk to him. Tell him how you feel. Or talk to Trixie. Just don't let them walk all over you."

I shrugged.

He patted me on the shoulder, and I turned to face him. With his broad shoulders and deep-set blue eyes, he really was beautiful. I could see why other women fell for him. I could see why Ann would have fallen for him—or his lookalike, anyway.

"At least think about it," he said.

I opened my palms. "I've got nothing else to do here."

He chuckled. "True, true." He stood up then, brushed off his pants. "Well, I guess I'd better get back inside, clean up my own mess."

"Good luck," I replied. "And thank you again."

He offered a corkscrew smile before he opened the front door and disappeared inside.

I sat on the front porch until my backside fell asleep. I still wasn't ready to face Lamb or Trixie, so I wandered over to the luxury SUV parked in the driveway. I noticed the stars were brighter than normal. They punctured the sky like diamonds, tiny pinholes of light in an endless black. I lowered myself onto the pebbled ground, laying supine so I could better admire the stars. They really were beautiful, and I hadn't appreciated the island's beauty enough.

I almost nodded off, despite the small rocks in my back. Even with the nap, I still felt exhausted. Empty. I was in that transition period between wakefulness and sleep when I heard footsteps on the driveway.

"Did you hear Christina's in trouble with the boss?" I recognized the husky voice—it was the handler with the eye tattoo.

"Yeah." Another handler, though I'm not sure which one. "For mishandling a situation with a participant, I hear."

My curiosity was piqued. The boss? I thought Christina was the boss.

The footsteps were getting closer. I wanted to continue eavesdropping, so I did the dumbest thing imaginable: I rolled under the car. Gently, of course, so as not to disturb the gravel too much. The handlers were too busy talking to notice.

"Yes, Reese."

Mishandled me?

"Apparently she saw the check," he added.

I took in a sharp breath. So I didn't imagine that. Was Christina paying him? If so, then for what? I was fully awake now, every nerve in my body in overdrive, and I could feel the rock fragments digging into my skin with a new sharpness.

"Yep. Christina's in for it now."

"She sure is."

They laughed. And then, a click. The car unlocked. The handlers stepped inside, the car buckling beneath their weight. The undercarriage was inches from my nose. The engine started. A rush of hot air and the smell of gasoline enveloped me.

I've heard the primal reactions to fear are fight or flight. From my own experience, I've learned that's not totally true: some people freeze.

And in that moment, I was frozen.

The handlers put the car in drive. The wheels dug into the gravel, rocks sputtering into the air. I closed my eyes, waiting for the inevitable. The blackness. But the wheels stayed straight.

Even after the car was long gone, I remained immobile.

45:Ann

pace back and forth in my room. I count my steps. I count the trees outside. *One, two, three. One, two, three.* I walk from the window to the chest of drawers so many times that my feet seem to leave permanent indentations in the carpet. How am I going to continue to investigate Reese's disappearance if I can't mention her name? I could ask around more discreetly, but what if there are cameras and microphones? And if there are, then who else is in on this production? I can't trust anyone here. Not really.

I remove my phone from its hiding place and go through the usual routine of blocking my door and hiding in the water closet. I have a missed call from Honey, which I ignore. And another from Ned. I shouldn't ring him back—I'm already in hot water—but I can't help myself. I dial his number. When he answers, his voice isn't as chipper as it normally is. It's low and muted.

"Ann, I'm glad I caught you. There's something–"

"I know, Ned. I got an email from the partners this morning."

I hear a sharp intake of breath on the other end of the phone.

"Gosh, Ann. I'm so sorry. I know you told me not to work on Reese's case at the office, but I just got so invested. I got careless. That nosy secretary–the one with a really tight bun and uppity nose–"

"Sherry," I say. It's one of founding partner's secretaries. I've worked with her on a few projects, but I found her work subpar. She always seemed to be more interested in office gossip than actual work. Oh, the irony.

"Yes, Sherry." Ned exhales. "I guess she caught me looking at some news articles about Reese a few times, and then, once she got suspicious, she started following me to the bathroom. She overheard our conversation about Lamb and went straight to the partners."

I wince. I told Ned to never call me about Reese while he was at work. I also advised him to use a personal cell phone and a personal email, so as not to use company resources. It's not that personal affairs are forbidden at the office, but it's frowned upon if it takes up too much time and eats into your billable hours. And it's definitely frowned upon if you ask for extensive help from subordinate employees, and their billable hours slip.

"Ned, it's okay. I was the one who asked you to get involved in this. It's on me. And honestly, it's probably fine. As long as your billable hours haven't slipped, I'll likely just get a slap on the wrist."

"Well . . ."

Shit. I press my forehead against the wall. I should have known. Otherwise, the partners wouldn't have made a big deal of it.

"How bad is it?" I ask with closed eyes.

"My hours dropped by about thirty percent the past week."

Goddamnit, Ned. I want to reprimand him, but I can't. I asked him to do this.

Granted, I asked him to do this in addition to his normal work—not in place of it.

"Okay, it's okay." I say this to Ned as much as to myself. "We just need to cut it off. Do not work on this anymore. I'll work directly with Pat from now on."

I honestly should have done that from the beginning. But Ned was so eager, so helpful. And he had recent experience with criminal law—he knew better than I did what could be prosecuted and what couldn't. Pat has been out of the FBI for fifteen years.

"Fine, but since it's Christmas Eve, can we at least discuss it until the office reopens? There's no work for me to miss. And I do have some news . . ."

I should say no. I should hang up the phone right now. But I'm too far gone.

"What is it?"

"They filed a missing person report for Lamb."

I don't know whether I should be excited or heartbroken.

"How'd that happen?" I stutter.

"After I talked to his parents, his mom called him repeatedly. After twenty-four hours of no response, she called around to his friends, anyone whose phone number she had. She posted the situation on social media, and everyone said the same thing: No one has heard from him since the retreat. So, she filed a report."

I feel like weights are situated on my chest.

"My God, this is terrible."

"I know," he whispers.

After a pause, Ned continues to talk, and my mind drifts. Ned's voice fades. I stare at a dent in the floor—a nick in the otherwise smooth marble—and wonder how it got there. Surely Christina wouldn't allow such a blemish in her perfect bathroom? I reach out to touch it, to feel the sharp edges on my pointer finger. I dig harder, and harder, and harder, until my skin tears. A drop of blood drips onto the white tile.

"Ann?" Ned calls. "Ann, did you hear what I just said?"

I put my index finger in my mouth to stop the bleeding. It tastes like metal, and the texture makes me queasy.

"Sorry, yeah. Repeat that one more time."

"Pat is bringing this to the FBI."

"That's good," I huff. I rub my forehead. There's a pain behind my temple I can't shake. "Surely now they'll look into the retreat, with a double disappearance."

"I hope so. They're idiots if they don't. But . . . it doesn't help that Reese and Lamb are both known to be flighty. I know you don't like to hear that, but I just want you to be prepared."

"I know," I say.

After a beat, Ned calls my name again. "Ann?"

"Yeah?"

"I think you should get out of there."

46: Reese

hen my heart rate slowed enough to stand, I stumbled inside. My mind buzzed from what I had just overheard. Teddy's check. In trouble with the boss. Mishandled Reese. I needed to find Christina.

The noise level had risen several decibels since I'd been outside. The participants were louder, their speech slower, their eyes glazed. I searched in the kitchen, in the living room, and outside on the patio, but Christina was nowhere to be found. I decided she must be in a talking room, so I started checking each one. I had a couple left when I felt a hand on my wrist. Lamb's blond hair was in my periphery, his forehead lined.

"We need to talk," he said.

"Can we talk later? I'm trying to find Christina."

I tried to ignore the increase of my heart rate as I turned the door handle of another talking room. Empty.

"Do you know where she is?" I asked. I didn't glance back at Lamb as I headed for the next room. I heard the patter of his footsteps behind me.

"I assume with a participant," he called. "Reese, can you wait up? I know you know, and I need to explain."

I still didn't know what I was going to say to him. Luckily, I didn't have to deal with him just yet, as the next room contained Christina. She was deep in conversation with Nick, their voices low. They seemed startled, which wasn't surprising given my abrupt entrance. What was surprising was a twinge of fright in Christina's eyes.

"Reese," she said. "Can I help you?"

"Christina, I need to speak with you." When no one responded, I continued: "It's urgent."

Nick and Christina exchanged concerned glances, and then Nick stood up to leave. "No problem," he said "We were wrapping up anyway."

He grabbed Lamb's shoulder and guided him out of the room before closing the door. I lowered myself onto the chair that Nick had occupied. I had to blink a few times before my eyes adjusted to the lights—it was always much brighter in the talking rooms than in the other areas of the house.

"What's going on?" Christina asked.

I had been so focused on finding Christina that I hadn't planned exactly how to approach the topic.

"I . . . well, a few things are bugging me."

"Like what?" She shifted in her seat, crossed her legs.

"Like, I saw Teddy leave here with a check. Why?"

"We offered a partial refund." She said this a beat too quickly, like it had been rehearsed. "Since he left with two weeks remaining, we didn't feel it was fair for him to pay the full amount."

That made sense. But it didn't explain how he sobered up so quickly.

"Who's we? I thought you owned this retreat. I overheard your handlers mention your boss?"

She was calm. "Like most companies, we have a board of directors. Some investors. I founded the retreat, and I run it, but I still have to answer to the board and the investors."

I wasn't the most savvy businesswoman, but that sounded plausible. Maybe I was manufacturing drama where there wasn't any. The handlers referred to the "boss" as a singular person, but perhaps I misheard. Or maybe they meant the board president?

"Who did you overhear?" she asks.

"I didn't see them. Just heard them. They also mentioned you mishandled me. What did they mean by that?"

Christina was still. She blinked rapidly before scanning the room. She brushed her hair behind her ear before answering.

"I'm not supposed to let participants skip activities. I told you that earlier."

"But why? If someone wants to skip an activity, what's the big deal?"

She sighed. "It's not how the journey works. Since you're only here for a limited time, we want participants to make the most of it. No missed opportunities."

"But," I stammered. I was running out of questions. "How did the board know you mishandled me? They're not here, are they?"

"I report to them every day. We had a call after I kicked off the cocktail party. I shouldn't have mentioned letting you get a couple hours' sleep, but they understood, with the circumstances."

"Oh." I slumped into the chair. All of this made sense. Why was I so alarmed? Maybe I really was losing my mind. Christina took advantage of my silence.

"Have you had a chance to talk to Lamb yet?"

"No." I sighed. "I'm not sure what to say yet. I don't think there is much to say. He wanted to have his cake and eat it too, and I'm not interested in being with someone like that."

"I think you should hear him out."

How did everyone seem to know the situation with Lamb better than I did? How was I missing so much?

"I'm going to set up a one-on-one date for you two tomorrow so you can at least clear the air. I'm thinking scuba diving. It's really gorgeous, and it's hard to be in a sour mood during that experience."

"There isn't a lot of talking during scuba diving."

"No, but you'll have a chance to connect before."

I twirled my crimson hair between my fingers. "Could I go with someone else? I'll talk to Lamb, eventually, but I want to gather my thoughts before I do so. I just . . . I don't know. I feel so stupid, still."

Her face pinched together, and she drew a long, slow breath through her nose.

"Okay," she said. "But then, after that, you can't put it off any longer. Remember what we talked about: you're better than that. You need to stand up for yourself."

I agreed, but I wondered how long I could get away with avoiding Lamb if I kept asking nicely. She asked if I had any more questions, if I felt more at ease, and I said I did. She inquired about my talk with Nick, my general disposition, and after a few more unsuccessful attempts, my feelings about Lamb and Trixie. I was honest. I didn't have the energy not to be. After forty-five minutes of conversing, she told me it was time to wind down the cocktail party.

I offered a silent prayer and slipped to my room quickly so Lamb wouldn't have time to grab me. I huddled under the covers of my massive bed. I wished, not for the first time, that I had my phone so I could call Ann. She would have known what to do. Because even long after my conversation with Christina ended, I couldn't shake the feeling that she was lying. There was something, or someone, that frightened her.

47 : Ann

t's been almost twenty-four hours since I talked with Ned, and every minute has felt off. Christmas has never been my favorite holiday, at least since my parents died, but today has been especially disorienting. We had a mandatory group breakfast—a first on the retreat—flowing with Bloody Marys, Irish coffee, and more hot food than is necessary or appetizing in tropical weather. With the earlier start time, I forgot to check in with Ned. I planned to text him after, but there was a group date immediately following the meal. So I told myself I'd message him later, and in the meantime, I needed to keep a low profile, blend in as best I could. I made small talk. I removed Reese from my vocabulary. I let Nick kiss me, hold my hand, run his fingers through my hair. I participated in every single goddamn activity Christina requested.

But the holiday and Lamb's news are like acid in my stomach, slowly eating me from the inside out. By the time the last activity of the day ends, I'm desperate for some fresh air, a small break from the façade. I still need to contact Ned, but I have a little time before I reach the twenty-four mark—the designated time frame before Ned is supposed to call the police.

I head outside, toward the beach. The sun is setting, a red lantern hanging low in the sky, cloaking the world in a bloody veil. Christina is outside too, talking to one of the participants near the patio doors. She has changed into an off-white dress. In normal light, she would have looked—not quite beautiful—but elegant, and certainly bridal. But in the sunset, the dress is on fire.

It's more peaceful near the ocean.

I need something peaceful.

I plop down on the sand and let the waves massage my feet. I put my head between my knees and squeeze my eyes shut.

I don't know what to make of Lamb's disappearance.

Does that mean that he and Reese are both dead? It seems like too big of a coincidence that they are both missing. Did they go off, after the retreat, and run into trouble? Or did they die here? Perhaps by accident? Or maybe they're both hiding. Together? Separately? I've never considered, not really, the possibility that Reese voluntarily went missing, but perhaps if the situation were dire enough, she might think that was her only option.

Reese has always wanted to leave Nashville. She brought up the topic numerous times over the years, but one memory in particular is seared into my brain. We had just finished a hike at Percy Warner Park —that was my go-to when the cravings were bad in the early stage of my recovery—and we sat on the steps overlooking Belle Meade Boulevard. From that vantage point, you can only see two parallel roads in a carpet of trees. The foliage fades into the horizon, and it's as if you're sitting on the throne of nature, the gatekeeper to the end of the world.

"If you could," Reese asked, head in hands, "would you give up a year of your life to sail around the world?"

I don't like to travel much. Spending hours packing and getting from point A to point B, sleeping in a foreign bed, being stripped of your belongings—the experience exhausts me. Plus, I get terrible motion sickness. The last time I was on a boat, I spent my time leaning over the railing, retching. Every time I thought I was finished, the boat would rock, my footing would become unsteady, I would catch a whiff of fish or sulfide, and I would be right back where I started.

"That sounds fucking terrible," I replied.

Reese threw her head back and laughed. She couldn't contain herself—tears streaked her cheeks, and she had to grab hold of my wrist to steady herself. When she could speak again, she nudged my shoulder with hers.

"Oh come on," she pleaded. "The experience would be so amazing. I'd see every wonder of the world: the Egyptian pyramids, the Great Wall of China, the palace of Versailles. Yellowstone. There's so much beauty out there, and I've only seen a sliver of it. I've never even left Tennessee, you know?"

"Really?" I asked. "Not even when you were a kid?"

"No. We couldn't afford it. Even if we could, we weren't the family-vacation type. I always thought I would leave when I got older, but then I had to work on getting sober. And now I'm with the Nashville Dance Company. It's funny—before you know it, life can slip through your fingers."

"Wouldn't you get lonely, though? Not seeing your friends for a whole year?"

"I don't know." She shrugged. "I make friends pretty easily. I could meet people along the way. And besides, some of my loneliest times were in a crowd of people."

I stared out at the road ahead of me, mulling over her words. It was autumn, and the surrounding trees were butter yellow. It was like standing on a pot of gold. How could Reese want to leave this?

"I would miss you, though," Reese said, as if she were inside my brain. "I'd land every few days so I could send you a postcard. That way, it'd be like you were traveling with me."

"You'd better," I said. "I'd be worried sick if you didn't."

48:Reese

"How ya doin', sailor?" Lamb asked as I leaned over the side of the boat, watching the island disappear into the horizon. He grazed my face with his thumb and index finger, brushing away a stray lock of hair that was stuck to my forehead. I flinched at his touch and pushed him away.

I was still fuming that he was here.

"I told Christina I didn't want to spend the day with you," I said.

Lamb's shoulders fell. "I begged her. You kept avoiding me last night, and this was the only way I could think to spend time with you."

I went to the other side of the boat, where Henry and the scuba instructor were whispering. Lamb gripped my arm, a little too tightly.

"Let go," I said through gritted teeth.

"No, you can't keep walking away," he shouted. I saw Henry and the scuba diver glance in our direction. "Why won't you talk to me?"

He had been prodding all morning, ever since he'd sauntered onto the boat. Once he had boarded, my jaw on the floor at the sight of him, the scuba instructor immediately motored away. I was trapped, and I didn't even see it coming.

Lamb had been pleading with me ever since, for the past thirty minutes or so, and I was at my wit's end. The boat was only so big, and there were only so many ways to say no. I finally snapped.

"Because there's nothing to say," I yelled. I could feel three sets of eyes on me, but I was too livid to care anymore. "You lied to me. You told me you weren't seeing Trixie, and then I caught you fucking her in the crew's room."

Lamb looked taken aback. I didn't usually curse.

Or shout.

"How do you think that made me feel?" I continued. "If you had been honest about seeing other people from the beginning, I might have understood, but you didn't. You lied right to my face, over and over again." I started laughing. I felt like a maniac, lost at sea. "And you know what the worst part is? I actually thought you were different from all the other guys I've dated. You seemed responsible, mature, considerate. You fed me all this bullshit about wanting a long-term relationship and feeling something special between us, and it turns out, you're just like all the other losers I've slept with."

Lamb's Adam's apple quivered as he swallowed.

"Well," I shouted with open arms. "Say something. You wanted to talk, so go ahead."

"You're right," he finally said. "I should have been honest about seeing Trixie. I wasn't ready to commit after that first night, but now I am. Please, please give me another chance."

He got down on his knees, put his arms around my waist, and buried his head in my stomach.

"Get up." He didn't move. "Lamb, get up right now before I really lose my temper."

The resolution in my voice must have been convincing, because Lamb slowly got to his feet. He peered at me, desperation in his eyes. I told myself it wasn't going to work. Although I'll admit, it did feel nice to still be wanted.

I could still feel the scuba instructor's eyes on us. After an awkward minute of silence, he cleared his throat.

"Should we get a move on then? We're ready."

During all my yelling, I hadn't realized the boat had stopped.

"I think that would be wise," I said. I walked over to where he was standing. Eventually, Lamb followed, his shoulders hunched in defeat. The tension between us was still palpable, but the scuba instructor continued an attempt to neutralize the situation.

"Okay, just remember: Follow my lead, don't come up too fast, and always, always breathe."

I tried to set aside my feelings about Lamb and recall the scuba diving rules hammered into my brain this morning as I practiced descending, ascending, and keeping a neutral buoyancy in the shallow waters of the lagoon near the mansion. At the time, I had thought it was odd that I was practicing alone, but Henry and the scuba instructor had assured me that my date had already been prepped. Now, I knew the real reason my date had been missing.

Just breathe, I thought.

Now was not the time to be angry; I needed calm. I needed to focus on what the scuba instructor was saying.

"Do you remember what happens if you rise too quickly or don't breathe?" The scuba instructor asked.

"You rupture your lungs or ears. Or both," I answered. Again, I tried to recall his exact words to keep my mind occupied. He had told me that I had to lower and raise myself slowly so my body could adjust to the pressure differences, or my organs would pop like balloons. It made me nervous then, and I was still nervous. Those were some serious repercussions.

The scuba instructor proceeded to demonstrate, again, how to clear our masks and read our gauges, which let us know how much air remained in our tanks. He showed us his scuba-dive computer, which he kept on his wrist, that tracked our time and our depth. He said we wouldn't go deeper than eighteen meters, which meant absolutely nothing to me.

"And don't touch anything," the scuba instructor added.

"There aren't, uh . . . sharks, are there?" Lamb asked. It seemed as if the instructions, the warnings, and the imminent risk had distracted him from our earlier fight as well.

"No dangerous sharks, no. Just blacktips," the instructor responded.

"How do I know if it's a blacktip and not a . . . dangerous one?"

"The blacktip shark has a black tip on its fin." The scuba was kind enough to say this last bit without much condescension.

"And what does a dangerous shark look like?"

"Well . . . there are tiger sharks. Those have stripes on the side, like a tiger," the instructor said as he brushed three fingers in a horizontal position across his left rib cage. "But, the stripes do go away with age."

Oh, great. So no identifying marks for the adult man-eating sharks. The instructor must have sensed our increasing fear. He softened, tried to placate us.

"Don't worry. You'll be fine.

"And you're sure we don't need, like, a suit?" Lamb asked as he pointed to his bare body, clad only in swimming trunks.

"No," the instructor said. "That's only for cold water."

As the instructor exchanged a few words with Henry, Lamb and I strapped on our flippers in silence. When we finished, we got into position, our legs dangling over the side into the ocean. Lamb cleared his throat and straightened his posture.

"It'll be great," Lamb said. "People do this all the time, and we have a pro with us. One of my buddies did it for the first time about a year ago, and he said it was one of the greatest experiences of his life. We'll see some seahorses, coral reef, schools of fish . . ."

"You're right," I replied, with about as much conviction as he had. I was still angry with him, but right then, I needed encouragement more than I needed my pride. "It'll be awesome. People do this all the time."

"They wouldn't let anything happen to us out here," Lamb continued. Despite his words, there was uncertainty in his voice. I had a bad feeling about the date, and I wondered if it was too late to call the whole thing off.

Before that thought could muster speed or strength, the instructor came up behind us and gave us the "go" signal. I took a deep breath, trying to calm the remainder of my nerves, put on my mouthpiece, and went under.

49: Ann

On the beach, eyes still firmly shut, I'm still reminiscing about Reese. Reliving a better time in my life when she was by my side. I contemplate how things could have gone so wrong. And then, the present catches up to me like a slap in the face: An ear-piercing scream pulsates across the beach.

It's so out of the blue, I almost think I imagined it. But the sound is too shrill, too alarming. I jump up and glance toward the cry. I see Sally—Small Sally—in the distance, running toward me. She's in a life vest; it dwarfs her small frame. She's barefoot.

I take off to meet her.

I run faster than I've ever run before. I don't feel my legs or the sand beneath my feet. I just focus on her face—her panicked, wild-eyed face, with tendrils of wet hair flopping in the wind—and I close the distance between us.

"Sally," I cry when I'm within earshot. "What's wrong? What happened?"

"It's Dermot," she screams. Ocean water drips from her hair, her life jacket. Her bathing suit is like a wet rag. "He fell. He said the harness was too loose. He said it, he said it."

"Okay, slow down," I say as I put the pieces together. Dermot is one of the participants—Doctor Dermot. He and Sally went on a one-on-one date together today. "Where did he fall? From parasailing?"

"Yes, yes." She nods. "He hit the water. It was so loud. Like a brick. He won't wake up. He said it was too loose, he said it."

I glance behind her to evaluate the scene. With my eyes closed and my mind occupied, I hadn't noticed the speedboat approaching. I see that it's on the shore now, the lime-green parasail floating lazily in the water. There are several handlers surrounding a stretch of beach near the boat, huddled around something. Dermot, most likely. In their black uniforms, they look like officers at a crime scene. Two handlers are running toward us. I don't have a lot of time.

"They were trying to calm me down," Sally continues. "They said he was going to be fine, but he's not moving, Ann. He's not moving."

"How did you get away?" I ask.

"I told them I just needed some air. They weren't listening. I need someone to listen to me. To believe me." She gazes at me with full-moon eyes.

"I believe you," I say as the handlers approach. "I believe you."

50:Reese

We descended slowly into the water, just like we had practiced that morning. It took a moment for my eyes to adjust, but once they did, I was enveloped by the velvet blue of the ocean. A few fish darted around us, but for the most part, the sea was still and unmoving, creating a soundless void that was eerily peaceful.

I watched our instructor carefully as he studied his wrist computer, and I waited for the hand signals that told us to descend or pause. We continued to lower methodically, but it felt unnatural. I was used to diving into the water headfirst, unbothered by depth or speed, so this snail's pace of a descent felt like a trap—a suspension in time and space.

Once we reached about ten feet below the surface, Lamb touched my wrist and nodded toward the ocean floor, careful not to make any sudden movements. I was nervous to take my eyes off the instructor, but something about Lamb's demeanor told me it was worth it.

It was. Vibrant coral skeletons carpeted the floor. The reef extended as far as the eye could see, no two square inches alike. Finger-like trees of soft pink. Tubes of violet. Shrubs of baby blue. Ribbons of burnt orange. And fish—of every shape, size, and color—slipped in and out of the ocean's garden. There were angelfish with black-and-white zebra stripes. Arrowhead fish the color of daisies. Puffer fish that ballooned to the size of my head. I had never seen so much color; every shade of the rainbow was highlighted in the ecosystem. It didn't even appear real.

I grinned behind my regulator mouthpiece. I forgot about my worries, just like that. The uneasiness I had felt was pushed to a corner of my mind. This was the most beautiful thing I had ever seen, the most beautiful moment I had ever experienced. This was why I had come to the retreat: to witness magic. Beautiful, breathtaking magic.

Closer to the ocean floor, I spotted an enormous sea turtle swimming through the reef. She was my size, between five and six feet. She didn't have a hard shell—more like a leather jacket. Canary-yellow fish nibbled at her head, her shell, her arms, but she didn't seem to mind. She kept sucking on the reef. There were several other turtles nearby; they looked more like the animals I recognized: greenish, hard shell, smaller than my torso. But the life-size turtle was my favorite. I thought I even detected a grin, but that was likely wishful thinking.

At one point, I was engulfed by a school of fish—hundreds and hundreds of cherry-red fish the size of my palm. An underwater poppy field. I was drunk with happiness. I giggled as the fish tickled my arms, legs, cheeks. Bubbles rose above my head. I wasn't supposed to laugh—it used more compressed oxygen than necessary—but I couldn't help it. Lamb seized my hand to pull me out of the field. If he hadn't, I think I would have stayed in that position until my dying day.

We needed to keep up with the instructor, who was approaching a murky object in the distance. The water grew thicker and more turbulent.

I had to strain my eyes to see. Eventually, I realized the object was a ship on its side. It was rife with holes, covered in silt and various marine life. It was a sad picture. I imagined the sailors on board, separated from their home, their families, their friends. Forever lost at sea.

And then I stopped.

I realized why the water was unsettled.

Sharks. Dozens of sharks, circling above the wreck. Taunting us. Taunting me. I held my breath before I remembered that I had to breathe. Inhale. Exhale.

There were so many of them. Their massive bodies glided weightlessly in the water. I tried to inspect their fins, to check if they were blacktip sharks, but it was impossible from that angle. The instructor gave us the "okay" hand signal, although his body language didn't convey the same message. He pointed away from the animals, and we backed away slowly, our eyes never leaving the wreck. The sharks didn't seem to notice us, which helped me stay calm. I reminded myself most shark attacks were accidents; they confused humans with other types of prey.

When we had retreated a safe distance, I exhaled. Almost safe. The instructor pointed upward, indicating it was time to ascend. We started to rise. So far, so good.

But then Lamb's leg caught on a piece of coral. A tear in his calf muscle. I froze as I waited for the inevitable.

Blood escaped from his leg, diffusing into the water and creating small wispy balloons.

The sharks didn't appear bothered. For now.

The instructor gave us the "okay" signal again, and we continued to rise. Despite my rapid heartbeat, I tried to maintain a normal breathing pattern. *If you rise too fast, your lungs will pop, Reese. The sharks are too far away. It'll be fine.* I wondered which death I'd prefer: a ruptured lung or a shark bite.

I promised myself that if I made it out alive, I'd never step foot into the ocean again. Just get me to the top.

About halfway up, with a trail of blood below us, I saw a couple sharks halt their circular pattern around the ship. They swiveled in our direction and started to close the gap between us.

Oh God, I thought. Oh God. This is it. This is how it ends for me.

The sharks descended closer to the ocean floor, where the blood had originated. We were about three-quarters of the way to the top. Time had never seemed so stagnant. The instructor kept giving us the "okay" signal, reminding us that we couldn't ascend too rapidly. But things were not okay.

Not at all.

The sharks reached the ocean floor directly beneath us and reengaged their circular swim pattern, mixing the blood with the rest of the ocean water. And when we were only a few feet from the top, almost an arm's length away, the sharks started to rise.

My hand broke the water's surface. I checked on the sharks' progress. They were approaching rapidly, open mouths and teeth bared. I spat out my mouthpiece. The instructor did the same. He pushed me toward the boat's stern, where Henry was waiting.

"Grab her," the instructor said through gritted teeth. Henry must have picked up on our thinly veiled panic. He reached for my arms, pulling me onboard. Even after my flippers were safely inside the boat, I had the feeling something was gnawing at my feet. I ripped the flippers off. And then I focused on helping to get Lamb and the instructor out of the water.

Henry already had hold of the instructor's right arm. I couldn't see Lamb's head yet, but I had to focus on getting the instructor out. I seized his left wrist, and with a strength I didn't know I possessed, I helped lift a two-hundred-pound man in scuba gear out of the ocean. The instructor toppled into the boat and threw off his buoyancy control device and oxygen tank.

I shifted my attention back to the ocean. Lamb's head was bobbing on top of the water. He dog-paddled our way, careful not to thrash too much. His eyes were as wild as the animals below us. Just as the instructor and Henry reached for his wrists, Lamb was jerked downward. Our small boat nearly toppled over from the momentum. I ran to the other side with our oxygen tanks and weights, trying to even the weight distribution. I couldn't let the boat overturn.

I couldn't see what was happening with Lamb. I felt a wave of nausea, but I held it in. Not now, I thought.

"Hang on," the instructor shouted, his voice primal and panicked. "Lamb!"

I heard a thud, and I felt the boat shift in my direction. I slammed against the side of the boat, my forehead ricocheting off a metal rail.

And then everything went black.

PART 3

51:Ann

At the cocktail party that night, I keep searching for Sally and Dermot. I check my watch. Thirty minutes since the event started, and still no sign. I shouldn't have left Sally and Dermot on that beach. I should have stayed with them. But I thought it was just a scare.

When the handlers finally reached Sally and me, her hands still gripping my arms as if I were a life raft, the handlers were out of breath. The sandy-haired one spoke first.

"Sally," he panted. "Jesus, you're going to scare everyone on the island. Dermot is fine. He opened his eyes. He just had the wind knocked out of him."

All the tension I had been holding in my shoulders released. He was fine. Just a scare.

"Really? He's awake?" Sally stuttered, disbelieving. "Can I see him?"

"Sure," the handler said. "He's asking for you. Ann, why don't you head back to the house? We don't want to overwhelm Dermot right after he wakes up."

Sally exchanged a glance with me. *Do you think he's telling the truth?* Her eyes seemed to say. I shot her a soothing look back. Why would they lie about that? Why would they invite Sally down to the beach to inspect Dermot if he wasn't awake? Then she would just scream again. Make a bigger scene.

"Uh, okay," Sally stammered. She appeared embarrassed. I felt for her. But I would have done the same—if I thought my date was put in danger by the retreat, I would have run from the scene too. Tried to get help.

Before I went inside, I peered at the scene one last time, hoping to catch a glimpse of Dermot. But he was still cordoned off, blocked from view. A raindrop brushed my cheek, and the sky darkened. A storm was coming.

I should have gone down there. I should have stayed with her.

Because now, four hours later, Sally and Dermot are nowhere to be seen.

Stephanie chose a particularly tight dress for me tonight, and I can barely breathe. I search for the nearest crew member. Of course, it's the handler with the eye tattoo. I wonder if he was one of the men surrounding Dermot on the beach. I can't remember if he was there or not.

"Excuse me," I say. He's as still as granite, but I keep going. "Do you know where Sally and Dermot are?"

"Dermot had a scare today. They're having a night to themselves. To recuperate."

"So they're not coming to the cocktail party at all tonight?"

"No."

I need more. Christina told me to stop investigating, but I'm not asking about Reese. I'm asking about Sally, and she was terrified today. It would be downright inhuman if I didn't ask after her. Ah, fuck it. Who cares if Christina gets upset—let her try to kick me off the island.

"Where are they? I noticed they weren't in their rooms."

"In a private space, away from the mansion." He purses his lips. "Leave it alone."

I know the handler won't give me more information, but he doesn't have to. I know where they are.

52:Reese

woke feeling dizzy, disoriented. I felt the soft mattress of the bed beneath my body. I wanted to fall back asleep, but my head was throbbing. I brought my hand to my forehead and felt a knot as big as a baseball. My stomach lurched at the pain. I jumped up, which only made the room spin more. I held onto the bed until my hands went white.

Finally, the nausea passed, and I sat gingerly on the side of the mattress, holding myself up by the bedpost. A drop of sweat trickled down the side of my face, and I wiped it with my sleeve. The texture caught me off guard. For the first time, I noticed my attire: silk pajamas. These weren't mine.

I studied my surroundings. It looked like my room, but off, just slightly. The dresser was a couple feet farther to the right. The armchair, which normally held my pajamas, my actual pajamas, was empty. It was also quiet. Much too quiet. At the mansion, there was always the hum of conversation, the patter of footsteps, the rush of running water. I turned around and looked out the window. The sun, a fiery red mass of light, was peeking over the horizon, casting the water in an angry shade of maroon. I couldn't tell if it was dawn or dusk.

The ocean.

And then it all came crashing back: The scuba diving. The sharks. Lamb.

Oh my God. Did he get back on the boat? I didn't see him. Why didn't I see him?

I stood up quickly, too quickly, and small dots clouded my vision. I rested my hands on my knees, let the second wave of nausea pass. It wasn't as severe as the first.

I pressed my eyes shut. I remembered toppling into the side of the boat, the sharp pain in my forehead. I must have passed out after that. Surely they got Lamb while I was out. Please, God, please.

I left my room in search of Lamb, but despite my prayers, I had a nagging feeling I wouldn't be able to find him.

53:Ann

S ally and Dermot have to be in the other house, the house next to the crops, on the opposite end of the island. That's the only place where Christina can safely hide them, away from others. I need to go there, find them. Tonight.

I'm devising a plan, when someone grabs me.

I'm pulled into a bathroom. It's Nick. The space is tiny. His pelvis is just inches from mine. I can feel the thud of his pulse, his breath on my cheek. He smells of smoke. His eyes are hooded. He's drunk. I really, really can't do this right now.

"Nick, I don't have time—"

He clasps his hand over my mouth. He puts a finger to his.

"What are you doing?" I mutter through his hand, pressed so firmly against my face, I start to panic.

And then, he reaches for my breast with his free hand.

Without a second thought, I knee him in the groin. When he keels over in pain, I slam his head against the wall.

I'm about to shout at him when he puts his hands up in surrender. In his right hand are two small black objects. No bigger than a push pin. The surface of one is glassy, while the other is textured. He puts both in my palm, and I analyze them as he stands. His face is crimson, contorted. He takes a deep breath, looks like he might vomit.

When he regains his composure, he takes the objects from my hand. Then he points to the same place on my body. Above my breast. The dress is thick, like all the dresses here are thick, so there's nothing noticeably visible or tactile. I feel the area, searching for spots in the fabric that are solid. And then I find it. I tear at the dress with my fingernails until I can remove the small items.

I study them under the bathroom light. When I'm sure what they are, I glance at Nick to confirm my suspicion. He nods. My skin prickles.

It's a microphone. And a fucking camera.

54:Reese

made it out into the hallway, relishing the cool touch of the hardwood on my bare feet. I checked each room that I passed on my way to the stairs. All doors were open, all rooms were empty. Where was everyone? Where was I? What time was it?

I padded down the staircase, expecting to see some sort of movement when I reached the second floor, or the first floor, but there was none. Except for the faint lapping of the ocean outside, the house was silent. I wandered into the kitchen, the living room. Just like my room, there were miniscule differences in setting. Same layout, same furniture, but slight variations in arrangement. Or was I imagining it?

"Hello?" I called.

No response.

Maybe everyone was outside. I staggered to the sliding glass doors, tinted red from the sunlight, and stepped outside. There was an infinity pool, and a patio, but most of the outdoor furniture was missing. Did someone move it? How long was I out? And where was everyone?

My chest rose and fell in quicker succession as my panic bubbled.

From inside the house, I heard a crash. A shattering of glass. Shouting.

I hurried toward the noise.

55:Ann

So Ned was right all along: Christina is filming us. This is some bizarre, twisted, ludicrous reality TV show. The signs were all there, and I just didn't want to believe it until the evidence was dropped into the palm of my hand.

Nick takes my trembling fist, uncurls it, and removes the camera from my palm. Then he flushes both devices down the toilet.

"Thanks," I whisper. I close the lid of the toilet, sit down. I imagine my face on some screen, kissing Nick, acting insane, for all the world to see, and I put my head in my hands.

"Who else is in on it?" I ask.

"The filming?"

I nod.

"Christina and the crew, obviously. And then ten of the participants. Me, Teddy, Rhea, Trixie, Dermot . . ." He lists five other participants who, in hindsight, acted suspiciously dramatic. "There always has to be one willing participant on camera—"

"Because Hawaii is a one-party consent state when it comes to recording," I mutter. "I know. As long as the recording doesn't take place in a bedroom or a bathroom, and one of the participants agrees to be recorded, it's fair game."

"Yeah," Nick sighs. "Also helps make it more . . . you know . . . entertaining."

"Awesome," I say. I still can't look at him. This whole situation is a disaster.

He pulls my hands from my face, gets on his knees, and makes me look him in the eye.

"Ann, I'm so sorry. I didn't realize it would cause this much hardship. When Christina approached me about the project, she made it sound fun. I'd play the part of a villain, just like those villains cast on *The Bachelor* and other reality shows. I wouldn't do anything crazy. Just stir the pot while people actually search for love."

I don't watch *The Bachelor*, or any reality shows, so I don't know how that works. It sounds ridiculous, though.

"I was trying to do something different than my parents. Trying to get out of their shadow, and this seemed like an inventive, original concept."

Original? *Big Brother* and *The Bachelor* have been primetime staples for decades. It's a rip-off.

A badly devised rip-off.

"Nick, I don't care about your insecurities."

He winces at my bluntness. "Right. So anyway, the stunts and the ploys became more intense. It was more psychologically damaging than I'd anticipated. I had no idea that I looked like your ex-boyfriend, or that Lamb and Reese would go missing, or that stunt with Sally and Dermot would happen today. I mean, they are brewing some PTSD shit. I didn't sign up for this."

"Wait . . ." My heart freezes in my chest. "Are you saying Lamb and Reese's disappearance is part of the show?"

"I don't know for sure," Nick says. "But I think—"

"Is this," I say, motioning to the space between us, "part of the show as well? Is there a camera in here somewhere?"

I scan the empty walls for a lens. It's illegal to put cameras in bathrooms, but it is private property, and at this point, I don't know what Christina would and wouldn't do.

"No, there isn't. At least I don't think so."

"Then why are you telling me this?" I whisper-shout.

"Because," Nick hisses as he motions for me to lower my voice, "I could tell you're really worried about your friend, and I didn't want to lie to you anymore."

"So what's the truth? Where is Reese?"

"I think maybe Christina is hiding them until the show premieres. To prevent spoilers or some shit."

I search his eyes as if by staring I can read his mind. "Oh." My shoulders fall. The monument of worry that I've been carrying on my back for the past month crumbles.

Reese is safe. She's safe.

But then—

"Why would Reese do this to me?" I plead. "Why would she put me through so much worry? She has to know I've been going out of my mind."

"I don't know, Ann, there's a lot of money involved in these reality TV shows."

"Are you telling me my friend would torture me like this for money?" My skin starts to tingle, and my vision goes hazy. I grab on to the wall to steady myself. He reaches for me, and I swat his hand away. If this is all an act to get closer to me, or stir up more drama, it's not going to work. Based on my impending panic attack, maybe it already has. The line between fiction and reality has become so thin it's practically non-existent.

To his credit, he does look hurt by my rejection.

"No. I'm just saying that this is an explanation for the two of them disappearing. Christina doesn't always think things through, but she's not evil. She wouldn't hurt them."

He stares at the wall and scratches his head. If he wasn't lying before, he's definitely lying now.

"Anyone," I spit, tunneling my vision until all I can see are the whites of his eyes, "and I mean, anyone, who would put another human being through this is a sociopath."

"I know, I know. This has gotten so out of hand. I'm going to get in a lot of trouble for telling you all this, but I—"

A knock at the door interrupts him. One of the handlers.

"Everything okay in there?"

"Yeah, be right out," I say. I can't be in this room any longer. "I'll go out first, and then you follow thirty seconds later."

"Ann, talk to me," he says.

What to say? How do I explain the betrayal, the stupidity, I feel? I'm relieved Reese is okay, of course, but I can't reconcile the Reese I know with someone who disappears without a care for those she left behind. I can't believe that Reese would willingly allow Christina to fake her flight home and cause a police investigation.

But Nick is here, with irrefutable proof, so I guess at least part of what he said must be true. Maybe I don't know Reese as well as I thought I did. How well do you ever know another person? Even Ned had an inkling that she was okay.

Oh my God. Ned. I need to call him. It's been over twenty-four hours, our agreed-upon time of no contact before Ned calls the police. Shit.

I open the door, careful to keep Nick out of view. A handler waits for me, expectant.

"Is your dress ripped?" he asks as he points to the torn fabric above my breast.

"Yeah, I snagged it when I was outside," I say. "I'm going to go upstairs and change."

As I head for the stairs, one of the handlers calls after me.

"Your outfit has to be approved by Stephanie."

I ignore him as I disappear out of his sight.

56:Ann

lock my door behind me when I get to my room. When I pull out my phone, it's lined with several texts from Ned. The most recent, sent six hours ago, is frantic: He's worried, and he doesn't know why he hasn't heard from me. Shit. Shit. Shit. I can't believe I forgot to check in with him all day. I'm about to tell him everything is fine when his first message stops me: *Been digging more into the investors—*

I hear a knock at the door before I can finish reading.

"Ann?" It's Christina. My temperature boils at the thought of talking to her. I can't believe she put me through all this. Just for some entertainment.

"Just a minute," I yell.

I open Ned's full message and read it. Then, I read it again. And again. This doesn't make sense; Ned lists my ex-boyfriend as one of the investors. What are the odds he's involved in this?

Christina rattles the doorknob and knocks again, more loudly. "Ann," she yells. I hear a key go into the lock.

Footsteps approach. I see Christina's heels in the corner of my eye, but I'm in too much shock to hide my phone.

"Ann?" Christina asks.

I lift my head to meet her gaze. Her icy eyes are panicked, and I suddenly realize why Christina looks so familiar. I have met her before. A long time ago. We were children, but in her adult features I finally recognize the eight-year-old girl from the creek.

57:Reese

The commotion sounded like it was coming from the front of the house. I ran as quickly as I could, but my head was still fuzzy, so my movements were slower than normal. The voices transformed to whisper-shouts, and some instinctual part of me told me to approach with caution. I followed the noise until I was standing in front of a closed room at the end of the left hallway.

"She's not going to wake up," a candy-coated voice hissed. I knew that voice, but I couldn't place it. "You sedated her didn't you?"

"That was twelve hours ago." I recognized this voice too: Christina. But there was an unfamiliar edge to it. She was scared. "She could wake up any minute."

"Stop picking that up," the sugary voice continued, laced with venom. "We have employees who clean."

Who was that woman? I knew her. I knew her.

But the voice was out of context, and my brain was still veiled in a thick fog.

"I don't know what else to do." Christina's voice was shaking. "I can't go back to the mansion, and I can't stay here either, just hiding, just waiting, just . . . alone with these awful thoughts."

I glanced around. So we weren't at the mansion. I knew there was something different about this place. But it looked so similar. So Christina built a second, replica mansion? Why?

"You have to go back to the mansion. You have to continue as normal."

The voice finally registered with me. I slapped my hand over my mouth before I could gasp. It was Honey. Why was she here? Was she the boss the handlers referred to? Why wouldn't she have told me that beforehand?

A memory floated to the forefront of my mind.

"You'd be perfect for the retreat," Honey had said when I ran into her at my local grocery store—a grocery store twenty-five miles from where Honey lived. She had explained she was running errands in the neighborhood, and she went out of her way to talk to me. I didn't think too much of it at the time because I *was* perfect for the retreat. I was a hopeless romantic, a woman desperate for a love she hadn't yet managed to grasp.

Now, I wondered if there had been another reason Honey had sought me out.

"And you don't think it'll be odd when no one sees Lamb after the retreat ends?" Christina asked. "You don't think Reese will come forward and say she never saw Lamb again after fucking sharks encircled them?"

I stopped breathing when I realized what Christina was saying. Lamb never got back on the boat. *Oh my God. Lamb never got back on the boat.*

"Why'd you make them go so far out at sea, anyway?" Christina continued. "The scuba instructor told you that area was dangerous. Your need for drama and excitement is outweighing your common sense. And now, if we cover the whole thing up, then . . ."

She didn't have to finish her sentence.

"And then what?" Honey asked, her voice rising. "No one would come within a hundred-foot radius of Last Chance. We've invested everything in this retreat. Everything. There's nothing left in our trust. I've put a second mortgage on my house. We can't afford for this to be a failure."

"Maybe that wouldn't be so bad," Christina whispered. "Starting over, I mean. Don't you ever wonder what it would be like to not have everything handed to you?"

"I like my life just the way it is." Honey's voice dripped with anything but honey.

There was a moment of silence. My breathing was still hitched. And Lamb was dead. He was dead.

"No," Honey said. "Don't you think people will find it odd that you've been around two fatal accidents? One is a coincidence, but two? Two are suspicious."

"Bear was your 'accident,' in case you've forgotten," Christina said in a clipped voice.

"Doesn't matter. You're the one Daddy shipped off to boarding school. You're the one people associate with his death. And if Lamb's accident comes to light, it's on you as well. You're hosting the retreat, after all."

Daddy? Honey and Christina—sisters? That explained their similar appearance—in visage, in attire, even in home furnishings. I thought Honey was an only child. I tried to remember what Ann had told me, but I tended to tune out when Ann discussed her. Wait, was that what

Christina had been talking about when she mentioned her family abandoning her? Boarding school? Why did her family send her away? Who was Bear? And what did she do? I felt lightheaded. I needed to lie down before I passed out again.

"Sometimes, Honey . . ." Christina's voice was barely above a whisper. "Sometimes I don't even recognize you."

"Here's what we're going to do," Honey said. "We're going to tell everyone Lamb left. The only people who know what really happened are you, me, Henry, and the scuba instructor. We're obviously not going to share what happened with anyone, and I already took care of Henry and the instructor. The instructor has even agreed to board a flight in Lamb's name. They have a similar build and similar skin coloring. I think he can pass as Lamb using his ID. Then, when Lamb goes missing, we're not responsible. He left the retreat, and we don't know what happened after that."

Christina didn't respond.

I rested my forehead against the door. In my state, I hadn't noticed it wasn't fully closed. It shifted farther inward at my touch, emitting a heart-stopping screech.

58:Ann

"Where is she?"

Christina's shoulders fall. She knows that I know.

I'm fuming. I can feel the heat, the anger, radiating off me like a sunburn. Do I not know anyone anymore? How could Honey do this? Invest in this charade? My oldest friend. How could she sit by, while I withered away from Reese's disappearance, and not comfort me with the truth? How could she listen to me recount my panic attacks, my sleepless nights, and stay silent? Jesus Christ, how could she put me through this entire production? Honey can be selfish, yes, but so can everyone. I never thought she was capable of this level of torture.

"Downstairs," Christina says. "I'll take you to her."

We don't speak as she leads me down the Cinderella steps and toward the front left hallway. Two guests are lingering there, whispering between soft kisses. Christina tells them to go to the living room, now, and they shoot us questioning looks. I remain a few paces back. My fingers are twitching with fury, and I'm afraid if I get too close to her, I might strangle her. When I look at Kris—Christina's name back when we were kids—all I can see is Bear.

I imagine his limp body, spread across the stones of the creek, rivulets of water washing away his blood. I imagine Kris, with red hands and crocodile tears, lying to the police.

When the guests are out of sight, we head to a crew member's room, the farthest one at the end of the hall. It looks similar to all the other bedrooms in the house, with one exception: Inside, there's another door.

"How'd you get Honey to agree to all this?" I ask as Kris moves toward the exit. It is surprisingly easy to no longer think of her as Christina.

"What?" she asks. Her hand hovers over the door handle.

"How'd you get Honey to agree to this . . . this production?" I wave my arms around the room, as if illuminating the hidden cameras.

"This was Honey's idea," she whispers.

"I don't believe you," I reply. "I didn't believe you back then, and I don't believe you now."

Her hand falls to her side. Her eyes close, her chest expands.

"Oh, you think I killed Bear?" she asks. Her expression is pained.

"Of course I do."

"I didn't—" Kris squeezes the bridge of her nose. "Ann, have you ever done something insane for a person you loved?"

"What?" I spit.

"I just . . . I wanted to protect her that day, keep her safe."

"Protect who?"

"Honey, of course. Everything is always for Honey."

"Oh stop it. Bear's blood was on your hands."

She smiles, but her eyes are dull. "Yes, no one ever believes me. Not now, not back then. But I was stupid enough to believe her when she said this retreat would be my chance to start over. To forge a new path, make a new name for myself. To finally have some control." She laughs, but her heart isn't in it. "I was never in control. Not even when I found Honey in that creek with Bear."

My feet are glued to the floor as my mind processes the information. Honey was the one in the creek with Bear?

Kris opens the door to reveal a dark staircase and lowers herself inside.

"She's down here."

59:Ann

At the bottom of the steps is a stage. The stage of a theater. To my right, two red velvet curtains are drawn. To my left are hundreds of seats. I walk toward the center of the stage, using my hand to block the blinding lights. When my eyes adjust, I see Honey in the center of the empty audience.

She stands, her movements slow and mechanical.

"Ann," Honey says. "I was hoping to surprise you."

"She knows, Honey." Kris sighs.

It's hard to read Honey's expression from this distance. She doesn't blink, she doesn't move. "Kris, can you give us a minute?"

Kris obliges and walks back up the steps. I stare at her backside for far too long; I'm afraid when I look at Honey, the anger and the hurt and the confusion and the thousand things I want to yell at her might combust inside of me, killing me from the inside out.

"Do you want to come sit with me?" Her voice is soft, soothing. As always.

"What is this place?"

"It's where we can monitor guests' activities."

She fiddles with a handheld device—a remote, most likely—and the curtains behind me part. I turn to find an enormous television screen at least two stories high, with hundreds of little boxes. In each box is a different scene: of a participant, of a room, of a spot outside. The quality isn't great, but smaller cameras do tend to have lower resolution. Maybe they're going for an authentic, documentary look. I turn back to Honey, my eyes scanning the hundreds of theater seats.

"And what are all these seats for?" I ask.

"Well, you've seen how many employees we have." She laughs.

My anger bubbles out of me like boiling water; I can't contain it any longer. "Stop lying to me!" I scream, my voice echoing off the walls.

I notice a couple chairs at the edge of the stage. I hurry toward them and drag one to center stage. I lift the chair above my head and hurl it at her. She flinches, but she's too far away for the chair to hit her. I storm offstage to grab the other chair, and I carry it toward the television screen.

"Ann, stop. I'll tell you everything, just wait!"

She screams as I ram the chair's legs into the television screen. The glass fractures in four different places, and four different scenes disappear. I move to another spot, smash out those boxes. I keep moving, the remnants of the television screen collecting at my feet, on my hair, in my eyes.

Shards cut into my skin, but I keep going, and going, and going, until I can no longer reach an undamaged spot on the screen. I throw the second chair toward Honey now that I'm done with it. I notice she's sat down, her hands rubbing her forehead.

"Stop lying to me, Honey," I scream again. "Just stop it."

"Okay," she says after a beat. "What do you want to know?"

"Let's start with what this theater is for."

"The show hasn't found distribution yet," she says evenly. "I'm hoping, when we're done filming and editing, that I'll be able to invite interested networks for a screening. And, if a network picks it up, we hope to premiere the first episode here for the crew and anyone else who wants to watch."

"Why didn't you just have people sign up for the show? Plenty of people want to be on reality television."

"I wanted to bring a level of authenticity to reality TV. These days, everything's scripted. I wanted the emotions to be real."

"But it's not real, is it Honey? Ten of the participants are actors."

She sighs. "Yes, well there are certain laws we couldn't get around. Plus, the actors bring a level of drama that would be hard to manufacture in four weeks with twenty guests who are just getting to know one another. The actors help to . . . speed things up."

"And what sort of drama do they manufacture?" I think I know the answer to this, but I want her to say it. "What sort of drama did you manufacture with me?"

"Come on, Ann."

"Tell me," I hiss.

"Nick . . . You don't react to most dates, but I thought you'd react to him."

"Because he looks like my ex?"

"Like my *husband*." She glowers at me as she emphasizes that word. "Christina stumbled across him at a restaurant in L.A., couldn't believe the resemblance. We thought he'd be perfect for you." She laughs, looks down at her feet. "And then Reese punched him in the face. That was an added bonus. We didn't anticipate that."

I'm vibrating with anger.

Honey's moral compass hasn't always pointed north, but I never thought she'd stoop to such levels.

"What was the drama you manufactured for Reese?"

"We um . . ." She rubs her eyebrow. "We told Lamb to pretend to mess around with Trixie. Since Reese has been—"

"Cheated on by almost every boyfriend she's ever had," I finished for her, as I processed that Lamb was in on it too. "So you tried to make her feel worthless? To humiliate her?"

"You're making it sound worse than it is. It's just some harmless drama for entertainment purposes."

"Bringing Luca here. Was that harmless?"

"He wouldn't have hurt her again; we have the handlers here—"

"And that stunt with Dermot this afternoon?" I interrupt her. "Was that harmless?"

"He's fine," she says with big hand gestures. "We just had him pretend to pass out for a while."

I pull at my hair. I want to rip it out of my skull. "Oh my God, Honey! That's not harmless. Sally was terrified. I was terrified."

"He's fine," she repeats. "Now they're enjoying some nice one-on-one time. I think Dermot really likes her. They might actually have a shot after all this."

"You're delusional." I can feel my voice starting to get hoarse from all the screaming. "Once Sally finds out this shit is all made up, she's not going to stay with Dermot."

"You'd be surprised what people do for love."

I rub at the skin on my forehead, my cheeks, my neck. How does Honey not see the flaws here? She's not stupid. She should be able to see her plan is punctured with holes.

"How'd you decide who to invite to the retreat?"

Honey brushes the velvet seat next to her, seemingly mesmerized. Finally:"We had to do a lot of research. We needed people who were attractive, obviously. People who would look good on camera."

I huff, but she seems unbothered by the interruption.

"They had to be articulate and interesting. Generally likeable, so viewers would keep watching. Fairly gullible. And more than anything, they had to be desperate to settle down. Between all the actors and employees we hired, we found enough people who fit the criteria. And then we sent out the ads in the mail, like the one Reese got. I figured that would be harder to trace back to me. We also sent out brochures to surrounding apartments and houses of the people we targeted, so it wouldn't look suspicious. Not everyone we wanted responded, but enough did."

Attractive. Interesting. Likeable. Naïve. Reese was perfect for the retreat.

I don't realize I've said this aloud until Honey nods.

"So perfect. So obsessed with finding her miracle man. So we said we would let her come free of charge in return for promotion after the retreat ended. We knew she couldn't afford it, so we had to make up something so the complimentary spot seemed legitimate."

My shoulders slump. "Was any of it real?"

"Yes," she says without hesitation. Like she actually believes it. "The participants' emotions were real. Even the actors' backstories were real. Mostly. We fudged a few details for dramatic emphasis, but creative license, you know?"

"And Teddy's drinking?" I ask.

She winces. "Yes and no. At first, yes. We had him leave early when Reese was here. We thought that would get to her, since she's so into AA and all that shit. But then, she caught him when he was leaving, a check for his acting in hand, and he was too shocked to act drunk. So when we had him come back during your stay, we thought it might be more realistic if we slipped him something."

"You roofied him," I say evenly.

Honey stands and starts to pace up and down an aisle.

"Who'd you get to impersonate Reese on the airplane? An actress with a wig?"

Honey nods.

"And the text from her phone about getting away? Did you send that?"

She nods. "Yeah. We didn't want anyone to go looking for her. We had to make it look like she really ran away."

"You don't think there were better ways to handle that? You really don't seem the harm in any of this?"

"I know!" She stops to scream. "I know, okay? God, everything has just gotten so out of hand. It wasn't supposed to go this way. We weren't even supposed to have a second round of this before we found distribution, but the story lines from Reese's stay got fucked up, so we had to get more guests to shoot additional film."

"Why'd you do it, Honey?" I ask, finally vocalizing the question that's been nagging at me for the past hour. Why?

She stops pacing, sits on the edge of a seat, head in hand.

She sighs. "Money. Isn't that why everyone works?"

"You have money," I reply. "Lots of it."

She shakes her head. "Power, then. I thought having a kid, playing housewife was what I wanted, but I got bored. I felt like I didn't have any agency in my own life. Everything was about the baby, or about the marriage, or about the family. I wanted to do something meaningful. I wanted real power, like my dad had. Sure, I have his money, but everyone knows it's inherited. I wanted people to respect me for me."

She slumps into the seat. "So Kris and I decided to put our trust funds to use. She knew things about television from her time in Hollywood, and I've always wanted to work in an industry that has real impact. So we invested everything in this retreat and then some. We had to borrow money, a lot of money, and if this doesn't go well . . ."

"You did all this to protect your investment?" Now that some of my anger has worn off, I can feel a sob building in my chest. I swallow, in an attempt to keep it down. "You don't care about me at all, do you? You never have."

Honey sits up. "Oh, Ann. Of course I care about you. You're my closest friend."

She starts to stand, to come down to my level, and I hold up my palm. "How could you do this to me? I know you never really liked Reese, but how could you do this to me? After everything we've been through?"

Honey looks like she wants to continue moving in my direction, but she respects my gesture to stay where she is.

"I know you won't believe me, but when this whole thing started and I found Nick . . ." She stares at the seat beside her, crossing her arms. "That's why we accepted you when Reese sent in your application. We hadn't anticipated that, hadn't even thought about you as a possible participant. But then I thought: Maybe this'll be a good thing. Maybe you'll actually like Nick or someone else. Maybe I could give you what you lost."

She turns back to face me, and her voice changes from contemplative to cross. "After the first round of guests and everything that happened with Reese, I changed my mind, of course. I tried to convince you not to come here, but you're so goddamn hardheaded. I thought about rescinding your spot, but I didn't want to raise any more flags than we already had. And, on some level, I thought you might still be interested in Nick. God, you don't know how badly I want you to move on."

She emphasizes the last two words with her hands. My skin feels tight. So tight it'll crush my insides.

My next words are softer, almost too quiet to hear.

"I wouldn't need to move on if you hadn't slept with my boyfriend."

I don't know if that's actually true. I've always suspected he cheated on me, but Honey's always insisted her romance started after my relationship ended. This time, though, she doesn't try to deny it.

"Come on, Ann," she pleads. "The relationship was over in everything but name."

My chest gets even tighter.

"And it's not like he was just some one-night stand," she continues with flailing arms. "We're married now. We have a child together. I love him, and he loves me. Plus, we work together, better than you ever did. Our backgrounds are more similar, our personalities more compatible. I mean, look what happened when you two got together: You became a fucking drunk! You need someone less laid-back, less understanding. You're fragile, and you need someone who will keep you in check."

I look at my feet so Honey can't see the tears that well in my eyes. For so many years, I've thought I deserved my best friend marrying my ex-boyfriend. If it weren't for my drinking, if it weren't for me, my parents would be alive. I accepted my punishment, karma's cruel form of retribution. But now I see the truth: I didn't deserve Honey's betrayal. Reese knew this, but I was blind.

I really don't know Honey at all. And, as it turns out, she doesn't know me either. I will my eyes to dry, pull my shoulders back, and look Honey dead in the eye.

"Reese is still here, isn't she?"

Honey studies her feet before nodding.

"I need to see her."

"Ann, what—"

"Honey." My voice is stern, controlled. "You owe me that much."

After what seems like an hour, she moves toward the exit.

"Come with me," she calls behind her.

60:Reese

hen the door opened, Christina and Honey were motionless. Honey stood, gripping the door handle with an intensity that could have snapped a weaker piece of wood, while Christina was on the floor. She appeared to have been picking up shards of porcelain. They were in a room similar to all the other bedrooms in the mansion. Blindingly white walls, furniture, carpet.

"How long have you been standing there?" Honey asked, no inflection in her voice. Christina covered her face in her hands.

I didn't know how to respond. I was furious with them, for putting Lamb and me in that situation, for considering hiding his death, and for the grief that would ensue from a cover-up. But I was also terrified. Supremely, unapologetically terrified. They were ready to cover up an accident to ensure there were no consequences to them. My spine tingled at the thought of what they would do to me. I wanted them to pay for what they did to me, and Lamb, and God knows who else, but I had to be smart. I had to get off the island first.

"I–I just got here," I stuttered. "I heard a crash."

Honey's eyes narrowed. I had to be more convincing.

"Are you here visiting, Honey?"

A vein in Honey's forehead twitched, even in spite of the Botox. I glanced in Christina's direction.

"Where's Lamb?"

"Cut the shit, Reese," Honey snapped. "What do you want?"

I should have known my acting wouldn't fool them. I was a terrible liar. I could feel my eyes cloud—at the thought of Lamb lost at sea, at the hopelessness of my situation, and at the realization that people are capable of such unspeakable acts.

"I want to go home," I said. It was the truth.

Honey studied me, her eyes boring into mine like her life depended on it. Then she strode to the edge of the bed, sat down onto the mattress, and pulled at the skin on her neck.

Christina lifted her head, glancing back and forth between Honey and me. No one spoke for what felt like forever. Finally, without meeting my gaze, Honey said:

"Could you speak to another guest before you go? We'll make something up for why you're leaving early."

I nodded. "I'll say whatever you want me to say."

Honey was eerily still. And then, in a monotone, she muttered: "It's decided then."

We rode back to the mansion in silence. Christina came with me to my room while I changed and she prepped me for what I'd tell the guests that night. Somewhere between my eavesdropping and the preparation, Christina had decided to follow Honey's lead. We would pretend that Lamb had left the retreat voluntarily, and I was too heartbroken to stay. My heart sank at Christina's choice. She wouldn't look me in the eye as we rehearsed my lines. Our true thoughts and emotions hung in the air like an invisible cloak, weighing us down until we could no longer see the light at the end of the tunnel. We were both broken in our own ways, but I think Christina must have been damaged beyond repair. It filled me with an unparalleled sadness to realize this.

I'll never know if I could have left if I recited my lines to the other guests. As Magda put on my makeup, and Christina marched back into my room, I couldn't help but think that I was providing Honey with an alibi, that I was preparing my own cover-up. Maybe I should have gone downstairs and shouted from the depths of my lungs that Lamb was dead, and that it was Honey's fault. But those handlers carried guns, and somehow I knew Honey wouldn't be afraid to order them to use them. So my mind, like a broken record, became stuck on one single, solitary idea:

Run.

61: Ann

Honey leads me outside through a back entrance, where Kris and one of the handlers are whispering. At our arrival, they freeze like deer in headlights.

"We're taking Ann to Reese," Honey says. "Go get the car keys."

"But, Ho—" Kris tries to interject.

"Go." Honey repeats. "Ann already knows."

Kris glances at each of us and then heads inside to do as her sister asks. It's hard to remember their relationship when we were children, but I could have sworn that Kris was the one who took charge. Perhaps I'm misremembering. What happened with Bear was so long ago. Memory is tricky—it's like trying to create a motion picture from a few still images. It's impossible, so we fill in the gaps with informed imagination.

The rain has abated, and the air feels sticky. I glance up at the sky to see dark clouds still huddled together like an angry mob just waiting for the opportunity to strike. When Kris reappears, unlocks the car with a quick click, and hands the keys to Honey, I feel a raindrop graze my shoulder. A storm is coming.

"Ann, you can sit in the front with me," Honey says.

"Do you want me to come?" the handler asks.

"Yes, get in the back."

The handler walks around to the other side of the car, the gun in his back pocket gleaming in the moonlight, while Honey and Kris expertly traverse the pebbled ground in high heels. I take my own off; I can't walk in these things.

Once inside the car, I buckle my seat belt, ensure it's firmly in place, and then hold on to the center console and the door with a cat-like grip. Honey doesn't offer her normal reassurances. She heads off on a winding path through the dark woods.

The only conversation in the car is between the tires and the gravel. I try to focus on what I'll say to Reese when I see her. I'm elated that she's alive and safe, but I can't quite forgive her for putting me through this. I keep secrets for a living; surely Honey and Reese know I could have kept quiet until the premiere. I didn't have anything to gain from spreading the news, and everything to lose from their silence. I thought they would know that I'd be out of my mind with worry, that they cared more for my well-being. Honey's actions sting, but Reese's betrayal severs my heart in two. In one night, in the span of just a couple hours, I've lost the two people who meant the most to me.

We exit the woods, and the second mansion looms in the distance like a gallows. Without the protection of the trees, the rain has open access to the car, hitting with a thousand tiny pitter-patters. Honey turns on the wipers, and through the windshield I notice a larger-than-normal star. It burns bright through the sky's tears, and for a second, I could swear it's moving toward us.

The car slows to a stop, and my breathing evens. Then I notice that we've stopped in the middle of the marigold field. We're about a quarter mile from the second mansion.

"What are you doing?" I ask Honey.

Honey keeps her eyes on the road. "We're here," she says.

Honey removes her seat belt and exits the car with heavy footsteps. The rest of us follow her lead. I forget to shut the door, so the car dings in uniform succession. The open-door light illuminates the dark field. I glance around for another house or a small shelter that I've missed, but it's just an open field. Why would Reese be here?

And then it hits me like a freight train, Lily Marigold's words ringing in my ear: Reese loved the marigolds. She would get lost in them. There's an unbearable pressure in my chest, worse than any pain I can remember. Is this what a heart attack feels like?

"I can't breathe," I wheeze. "I can't breathe."

I fall to my knees and gasp for air. My vision tunnels, and I can barely hear Kris's exclamations over the blood pounding in my ears. I hold myself up with my hands. I feel someone reach for my arm, brush my hair back, but somehow I can't fully register the touch.

I know why Reese is in the open field. If I'm being honest with myself, I think I've known for quite some time. I just haven't wanted to face it.

62:Reese

After Honey's handler broke my finger, I screamed and thrashed as he and his colleague dragged me from the woods to the SUV. Honey was in the driver's seat, waiting. Christina sat to her right, head bowed. After I was thrown in the car, Christina repeated what she had said earlier.

"Reese," she cooed. "It doesn't have to be like this."

"You're right," I cried. "It doesn't. You can still do the right thing. Tell everyone what happened to Lamb. Don't cover it up. Please. Please. Let me go. Two deaths don't cancel out one."

I knew my words were futile, but a part of me couldn't give up hope.

Honey put the car in drive, and the adrenaline convinced me to make one more run for it. Because the handlers had made one mistake— one fatal mistake—when they propped me in the car. They sat me next to the window.

If they wanted me contained, they should have placed me in the middle seat, one handler on each side of me.

Whether this mistake was an accident, a discreet attempt to help me get away, or something more calculated, I'm not sure. All I knew was, I had one last chance.

I waited until we were moving thirty or forty miles an hour, at least. And then I unlocked my door, rammed it open, and threw myself into the night. I felt something inside me snap as I tumbled onto the paved road in the middle of the forest. Honey slammed on the brakes and threw the car in reverse. But she backed up quickly, went too far. As the wheels approached my neck, I couldn't help but wonder if she knew what she was doing.

63:Ann

ventually the pain in my chest subsides enough for me to take in my surroundings. Kris and the handler sit on the pavement with me. We're soaked, and I have to blink rapidly to see through the raindrops.

"I thought she knew?" Kris yells at Honey.

Honey is still.

"How did it happen?" I rasp. Kris starts to answer, and I stop her. "I need Honey to tell me."

"It was an accident." Honey's tone is somber, serious.

"How did it happen?" I have to scream over the impending storm.

"She jumped out of a moving car. It happened too fast for me to stop."

Saliva pools in my mouth. "Why would she jump out of a moving car?"

Honey puts her hands on her hips, stares at the ground.

"Honey!" I'm screaming again. "Why would she jump out of a moving car?"

"Because she thought we were going to hurt her. There was a scuba-diving accident with Lamb. It was an accident, honestly, Ann, and nothing good would have come from announcing his death. We wanted to keep it under wraps for the sake of the show and our livelihoods, and that didn't sit well with Reese. We were trying to reason with her, and she just wasn't listening."

My stomach inches up my throat.

"So you killed her?"

"It wasn't my fault. She jumped out of the car. It was an accident."

"And what about Bear, Honey? Was he an accident, too?"

It's hard to tell with the weather, but I think I spot tears. I don't know if I've ever seen her cry before. The sight makes my own eyes water.

"Please, Ann."

"It was you in the creek with him that day, wasn't it?" I cry. "Kris found you, and she took the fall, and you were too much of a coward to come forward."

Honey wipes her eyes, smudging her makeup. A trail of black mascara now cuts across her cheek.

"We were just playing. He wouldn't kiss me, and I pushed him. Playfully, teasingly. His head fell back and hit a rock. It happened so fast. I was just a kid, Ann. I didn't know what to do, and Kris took care of me."

I crawl to the edge of the road and vomit. All the while, I wonder how I never saw Honey for what she really was: deeply insecure and deeply unhappy. Did she like Bear before he showed interest in Kris? Did she like my ex-boyfriend before we started dating? Maybe a part of her did, but I think a bigger part believed the grass was always greener on the other side.

And when Kris took the fall for Bear, Honey learned she could get away with anything.

When I have nothing left in my stomach, I stagger to my feet and wipe my mouth with the back of my hand. "You covered up three accidents to save your ass?"

The rain is falling harder, and I have to get even closer to hear Honey. "The truth won't bring them back, Ann. It'll only cause more damage. Kris and I will be ruined. My family will be abandoned. They'll have nothing."

Honey pulls herself together again, her words even and calm. Her cool demeanor sends me over the edge, and before I know it, I'm on top of her, screaming.

The handler pulls me off before I can do any real damage, and I thrash and kick in his grasp. Honey manages to remove the gun from the handler's back pocket and slams it down on my head. My vision goes white, and I think I'm about to pass out from the pain. The handler lets me fall to the ground, and I hold my head in an attempt to calm the agony, to turn my surroundings right side up.

When the world stops spinning, I realize Kris is screaming.

"Honey, what are you doing?" Her eyes are wild, her arm outstretched. My gaze follows her arm, and that's when I notice Honey above me, a cocked gun pointed at my face. She's close enough that I can feel her breath.

"You're going to kill me, too?"

"You hit me first," she replies. "You're not thinking clearly. You're not thinking about how this situation will affect me if it gets out."

I burst into a deep belly laugh. "You're holding a gun to my head, and all you can think about is how this affects you? You really are a terrible person, aren't you?"

Honey's grip starts to tremble.

"Honey, just calm down." Kris's voice quivers. "Ann is your friend. She's not going to tell anyone."

I laugh again. I feel like a maniac. "If I get off this island, I'm telling anyone who'll listen. I'll tattoo it on my forehead, run an ad in the newspaper."

Kris turns to me, her face panicked. "You're not helping."

"You know what?" I say, keeping my eyes on Honey. "Go ahead and do it. I want you to live with this for the rest of your life. I want you to remember this moment."

Honey is right: I'm not thinking clearly. I should be trying to negotiate with her, save myself. But the truth is, once Honey brought me to this field, I never stood a chance.

I wait for the sound of the gun, but it doesn't come. Honey remains immobile, the gun in her hand shaking.

In her moment of hesitation, I kick her in the chest, sending her backward. The gun flies out of her hand, skidding across the pavement. The handler lunges for it, but I'm closer, and I get to it first. Before the handler or anyone else can touch me, I point the gun at them. I stand. And my hand doesn't shake—my dad taught me better than that.

Honey is lying on the pavement, coughing. Kris and the handler look at me, their eyes wild. I don't actually have the heart to kill someone in cold blood, but I need a little time to figure out what to do. How to get out of here.

"Ann," Kris says with her hands in the air. "Just put the gun down. You're not going to kill anyone."

"You don't know me, Kris," I lie.

No one moves.

"Move back, now," I say through gritted teeth. My mind is buzzing, and I can't get it to slow down. I need a plan. What am I going to do?

A phone. I need a phone to call the Hawaiian police.

But can I stall Honey, Kris, and her handler until the police get here? How long would it take if they have to travel by boat or plane? Fuck it. I don't have another option.

"I need a phone," I yell. Kris and the handler exchange glances.

"We don't have one," Kris stammers.

I aim just to the left of Kris's foot and pull the trigger. Even through the rain, the bullet sounds like a bomb. My ears ring. Kris screams and tumbles backward. For the first time, the handler looks genuinely frightened. Truth be told, I'm also frightened of what I might have to do.

"Okay, okay," Kris screams. She nods to the handler, who rummages in his back pocket and tosses me his phone.

I catch it with my free hand. It's an iPhone. I press and hold the side and volume buttons until the emergency screen pops up, allowing me to sidestep the lock screen. I try to drag the Emergency SOS slider, but it's too slick from the rain. I drag once, twice, three times, but it's not working. Fuck, fuck, fuck.

With the gun in my right hand still firmly on Honey, I lift up the bottom of my gown with my other hand so I can wipe the screen with my semi-dry leg. The screen clears, and I'm able to swipe. I let out a small cry as the call goes through, connecting me to the nearest Hawaiian precinct. Just as the words *Phaux Island* escape my mouth, I'm tackled to the ground. I feel my brain knock against my skull as my back meets the pavement.

My hand tightens, and the gun goes off.

I can't hear anything over the ringing in my ears. I can't breathe. I can't move. Someone is on top of me. Motionless. When I force my eyes to focus, I see Honey's head on my chest, her blonde hair dark and syrupy from the rain.

"Honey," I whisper. Kris comes to her side and helps to lift her torso off of mine. And that's when I notice the blood. In the middle of Honey's chest. Dark and angry, spreading quickly. Honey reaches for the wound before meeting my gaze. Her eyes bulge, and her lip trembles.

"Honey," I say again. "It's okay, the police are coming. You're gonna be okay."

Kris lays her on her back, and I tear off the end of my gown to stanch the blood. But I know it's useless. Blood starts to trickle from Honey's mouth.

"Oh my God," Kris says as she backs away, her hands over her face.

The handler is by my side now. He takes off his shirt. "Use this too," he says.

I place it against Honey's wound, trying not to look at her face. But she reaches for my hand, now greased with blood, and I'm forced to meet her gaze once more. Her eyes are streaming, and despite everything, I feel mine fill too.

"Hang on, Honey."

And just when I hear the sound of another car approaching–it could have been minutes, or it could have been hours–I watch the life fade from Honey's eyes for good.

64:Reese

Before you die, they say your life flashes before your eyes. That's not true. It's more like snippets. Stills from a moving picture.

I saw myself when I was six or seven, locked in my mom's trailer. The first time I ran away, spending the night in a shabby apartment with the first willing guy I met at a bar. Sleeping in a run-down, abandoned house with a crowd of people in sleeping bags, high as a kite. My first morning sober, when the shakes were so bad I couldn't hold a glass of water.

And then some happy memories too. My first AA meeting. Trying on a pair of ballet slippers. The moment I was accepted into the Nashville Dance Company. The sight of marigolds. My endless string of lovers—intimate kisses, fumbling in a parked car, my relentless search for a miracle.

And Ann.

And in those last few moments, before the world went black, I realized I had witnessed a miracle.

It just wasn't the type of miracle I had expected.

Epilogue

Ann—Six Months Later

climb the steps to the brick house at 5925 O'Brien Avenue. The wooden steps are rotting, derelict. They creak with the tiniest bit of pressure. Before I open the door, I hear the murmur of voices. Laughter. I catch a whiff of cigarette smoke and cheap coffee. The sun is warm on my back today, the most beautiful of summer days, and my hand hovers above the doorknob.

Reese is gone, but a part of her will always be with me. In certain places, at certain times, her presence is stronger. And on the steps to the O'Brien Avenue meeting house, it's almost as if she's standing beside me. After another deep breath, I step inside.

The house has changed a bit over the years—different posters on the bulletin board, a new coat of paint on the walls—but it's mostly the same.

A humble foyer with a white linoleum floor that leads to two meeting rooms, one on the left and one on the right. A table in the middle of the foyer with coffee and Styrofoam cups. A dark-haired man sits at the table. His face is worn, but with his sharp jawline and high cheekbones, he still makes your head turn.

"Am I too late?" I ask.

"Nah, it's just getting started," he replies. "Go on in."

When I open the door to the meeting aptly named the "Back Room" group, about fifty heads swivel in my direction. Before I stopped going to AA, this group was always my favorite. Partially for sentimental reasons— it was my first—but also because it was bigger than your average meeting. It's easier to be anonymous among fifty than ten.

But not if you're late, like I am now.

I mouth the word *sorry* to the woman running the meeting and take a seat near the door.

While we recite the Twelve Steps, I take an inventory of the room. At one side are a dozen teenagers, rolling their eyes, looking bored. They've been ordered here by a judge, no doubt. In the middle of the room is a larger group of men in their forties and fifties, wearing a mixture of golf shirts and casual tees. Scattered among the men are several women in their Sunday best, AA's *Big Book* squarely in their laps. I recognize a couple old-timers at the front—hippies with tie-dye shirts and white beards that have been growing since I met them ten years ago.

And there are probably a few people like me—young professionals in blazers and tailored pants, even though it's a Sunday. And like me, they are probably going to the office after the meeting, just trying to get ahead.

Despite my help in the arrest of Kris Harris, and the very public takedown of Last Chance, I'm still on thin ice with the other partners at my firm; I have a way to go before I earn back their trust. Ned, on the other hand, is a few months away from a promotion. He handled my clients well while I was gone, and he has a real knack for the position—although after recent events, Ned is thinking about returning to criminal law.

"It draws you back in," he told me on the flight back to Nashville in his antique plane, his new watch displayed proudly on his wrist.

About an hour before the Hawaiian police arrived, Ned had turned up with the FBI. The large star I'd seen in the sky on the way to the marigold field wasn't a star at all; it was Ned. After Lamb's parents reported him missing, the FBI had been convinced something criminal was occurring. When Ned didn't hear from me, he got Pat to alert the FBI and speed things up. They obtained a warrant to collect all video and audio footage from Last Chance and loaded a plane as quickly as they could. Ned was to join them, as he could point the FBI in the right direction for evidence.

Once they landed on the island, one of the handlers at the mansion drove Ned and the FBI to the marigold field, where they arrested Kris. After that, it wasn't difficult to collect evidence. The video and audio footage contained several condemning conversations about Reese and Lamb's death. And those who knew what had happened to Reese and Lamb—even Henry and the handlers—corroborated what was on the tapes. Lamb's body was never found, but Reese was recovered from beneath the marigolds. A coroner's report confirmed her injuries were consistent with vehicular death.

Kris hasn't once spoken publicly about the case. Due to flight risk and financial resources, she wasn't granted bail. She spends her days—silently, keeping entirely to herself, from what I hear—in the Tennessee Prison for Women. With the constant national headlines on the case, as well as Nick's attempts to sell the story to Hollywood, it's probably better she's not out in public. I haven't visited, and I don't plan to.

I don't plan to communicate with anyone from Last Chance ever again. In an attempt to move forward with my life, I told myself I wouldn't obsess about Honey either. I would attend her funeral, say good-bye one last time, and then put that chapter to bed. I considered skipping the funeral altogether, but even in spite of her colossal betrayal, she had been my friend for almost thirty years. She was the last person on Earth who knew me in every stage of my life, who watched me overcome all my hurdles. She knew my parents. She knew Reese.

So wearing large sunglasses and an oversized hat, and from a considerable distance, I watched her casket descend into the Earth. I listened to her husband—my ex—profess Honey's innocence in the whole matter and lay the blame on Kris. With the news cameras in the background, I listened as he described Honey's loyalty, her generosity, her larger-than-life personality. I listened to so many lies, reminding myself that I too once believed the same. And then, shoulders back and eyes ahead, I walked away.

I focused instead on giving Reese a memorial. A proper memorial, as a funeral has to wait until the trial is over. I selected a location that matched her grace and her legacy: Nashville's most prestigious dance auditorium. Over five hundred people came to pay their respects. Attendees were elbow-to-elbow, literally spilling out of the doorways. Some were prurient followers of the case. Some were longtime ballet fans. Many, though, were people Reese knew in the AA program. Dozens and dozens of men and women whom Reese helped along the way in recovery.

The theme of today's meeting—faith—is announced after we finish reciting the Twelve Steps. The first speaker shares his story. I try to focus my attention on the narrative, but I can't help scanning the room once more. My eyes land upon a young girl—early twenties, by the looks of her—I didn't notice before. She's in a corner, alone, her head of red hair propped against the wall. Her skin is sallow, a sheen of sweat shimmering to the surface. By the shake of her hands, I can tell this is her first meeting.

"To me, faith is like skating on a frozen lake," the man continues. "You can either skate with the constant fear of falling, or you can skate with the belief that you'll make it to the other side."

The girl glances up at me then. Her eyes are rimmed with black liner. The whites are crisscrossed with red. But the irises—the irises are the color of the ocean. A breeze blows through the open window, and I catch the faintest scent of salt air. An image of the field on the island comes to me then, the flowers swaying in the breeze, wild and overrun.

"Your attitude won't affect your chances of falling, but isn't life so much better when you believe you'll make it through?"

I rethink my plan to go to the office after the meeting. Maybe I'd have time for a cup of coffee. To introduce myself. Nothing too intimidating, just a casual conversation. To give back what I've received so many years ago. From another woman with eyes the color of the sea, eyes that still watch over me from somewhere beneath the marigolds.

THE END

For Further Discussion

1. How do you feel about the fact that neither Ann nor Reese end up with a partner, given the goal of reality dating shows like *The Bachelor* is to walk away with a marriage proposal? How do these types of shows and Last Chance reflect or amplify certain social pressures?

2. The story references physical watches and time—or lack of it—frequently. What does time symbolize?

3. The deaths in the book—Bear's, Lamb's, and Reese's—have reverberating effects on Ann, Kris, and Honey. How does each character react to these events, and how do these reactions reflect the characters' moral compass? How do the characters change—or not—after each death?

4. Why do you think the author chose to open the book with Magda putting makeup on Reese? What does makeup represent in this novel, and how does it parallel with reality television and constructed societal roles?

5. Although he plays an important role in Ann's history, Ann's ex-boyfriend from college is never named. Why do you think that is?

6. Both Ann and Reese are in recovery from alcohol and drug addiction. Why do you think the author chose to portray characters in recovery as opposed to characters in the midst of addiction? How are addicts normally portrayed in fiction and popular culture?

7. The relationship between Honey and Ann is complicated. Do you think Honey genuinely cared for Ann, or was Ann merely a means to an end?

8. Marigolds are known as "companion plants." In other words, they help adjacent plants and flowers grow by repelling bugs and insects. With this in mind, discuss the meaning of the title of the book, *Beneath the Marigolds*.

9. What role does Bear's death play in the book? How does it mirror Reese's fate?

10. What's the significance of the red-haired woman in the AA meeting in the epilogue? What do you think happens to her, and to Ann, after the novel concludes?

Acknowledgments

must start with my brilliant editor, Helga Schier. Thank you for your expert guidance, creative vision, and steadfast support. You are every author's dream.

Many thanks to the rest of the CamCat team, including Maryann Appel, Bill Lehto, Meredith Lyons, Laura Wooffitt, and Sue Arroyo. Sue, thank you for believing in this story, encouraging me to submit my manuscript to your fabulous team of storytellers, and being an all-around fantastic friend and role model.

Thanks to everyone who read early drafts of my novel: Nina Fortmeyer, Cheryl Rieger, Meredith Lyons, Arl Farris, Sue Arroyo, Lily Wilson, and Kathleen Cosgrove. Melissa Collings, I'm giving you a special shoutout, since you read at least three iterations of this book and spent countless hours on the phone with me. Thank you for always telling me to keep going.

I am so grateful for the support of my amazing writing group: Cheryl Rieger, Meredith Lyons, Sue Arroyo, and Melissa Collings. Thank you for spending your Sundays with me, discussing writing, good books, and the vicissitudes of life. I'm not sure how I got so lucky.

My thanks go to Arl Farris, who answered all of my questions about police and legal procedure. To Jessi Tremayne, who answered all questions regarding criminal law. And to my sweet father, who ensured that Ann was a believable corporate attorney. I'd also like to thank his clients, as they will be receiving this book as holiday gifts for years to come.

To Chelsea Sells, for the invaluable advice about literary agents and the daunting publishing world.

To Manjari Singh and Allison Isaacs, who lent me their expert ear for voice actor selection.

To Kathy, for being the first person with whom I shared my dreams of writing. Thank you for always believing in that dream.

To everyone who has read, bought, or shared this story. Thank you, from the very bottom of my heart.

And finally, to my family. Thank you for traveling to fictional islands and back for me.

About the Author

mily Whitson received a B.A. in journalism from the University of North Carolina at Chapel Hill. She worked as a marketing copywriter for six years before pursuing a career in fiction and education. She is currently getting her Master of Education at Vanderbilt University, where she writes between classes.

She is particularly passionate about women's education and female stories. This interest stems from her time at Harpeth Hall, an all-girls college preparatory school in Nashville, Tennessee. When she isn't writing or in the classroom, Emily can usually be found with her dog, Hoss. *Beneath the Marigolds* is her debut novel.

If you've enjoyed Emily Whitson's

Beneath the Marigolds,

you'll enjoy

Dead Air by Michael Bradley.

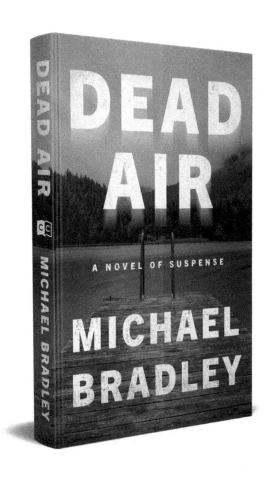

1

She'd been found out. There was no other explanation.

On any other night, Kaitlyn Ashe would relish the breathtaking view of the Philadelphia cityscape. The twinkle of white streetlights, red, yellow, and green traffic lights, and the white and red hues from car lights on the streets below looked like a swirling star field, constantly changing as if at the whim of a fickle god. From the twentieth-floor broadcast studio, she could look down upon Center City, could see as far east as the Walt Whitman Bridge and across the Delaware River to the distant lights of Camden, New Jersey. Yes, every other night, this view was mesmerizing. But not tonight. Tonight, Kaitlyn Ashe trembled at the thought that someone out there knew her, knew her secret, and was making damn sure she didn't forget it. The past had come a step closer each time another letter arrived. Her fingers tightened their grasp on the latest, a crumpled paper creased with crisscrossed lines and folds. It was a cliché. The mysterious correspondences consisted of letters and phrases torn from newspapers and magazines, crudely pasted onto plain paper. Always the same message, always the same signature.

Behind her, music played softly. She turned away from the window and moved around the L-shaped counter in the middle of the room to slide onto the tall stool behind the control console. Kaitlyn leaned forward, glancing at the needles on the VU meters that jumped and pulsed to the music's beat. She touched one of the ten slider controls and adjusted the volume to remove some mild distortion.

Kaitlyn watched the onscreen clock count down to the end of the current song. Fifteen seconds to go. She slid the headphones over her ears and drew the broadcast microphone to her mouth. She tapped the green button on the console and pushed the leftmost slider upward.

Kaitlyn leaned into the microphone. "Taking things back to 2005 with Lifehouse on WPLX. That was 'You and Me,' going out to Jamie from Kristin, Tiffany from Steve, and to Tommy—Jackie still loves you." She glanced again at the clock in the upper corner of the computer screen. "It's ten past ten. I'm Kaitlyn Ashe with Love Songs at Ten. 888-555-WPLX is the number to get your dedication in tonight. I've got Adele lined up, as well as John Legend on the way next."

Her fingers darted over the control console, tapping buttons and moving sliders. Kaitlyn took the headphones off. As a commercial for Ambrosia—her favorite seafood restaurant in downtown Philadelphia—played, she stared at the crinkled letter that rested beside the console. She read it once again beneath the dim studio lights. Her eyes focused on the name at the bottom. The Shallows. She shivered. Who knew? And how much did they know?

Kaitlyn slipped a green Bic lighter from her pocket, lit the edge of the letter, and pinched the corner as the flames swept up the paper. She'd stolen the lighter from Kevin O'Neill's desk. She knew the midday

DJ would never miss it. He had half a dozen more where that one came from.

She dropped the paper into the empty wastebasket, and watched the fire dwindle into nothingness, leaving behind blackened flakes. A faint trace of smoke hung in the air, then dissipated quickly. She wrung her hands and sighed. There'd be another waiting in her station mailbox tomorrow, just like the four others that she'd received, one each day this week. She was certain of it.

The flash of green lights caught her eye, and she looked down at the studio telephone. All four lines were lit up. She hesitated for a moment, then tapped the first line. "WPLX, do you have a dedication?"

"Yeah, I'd like to dedicate my weekend to kissing your body from head to toe." The smoky voice echoed through the darkened studio.

Kaitlyn laughed, and felt her face become warm with embarrassment. "Brad!"

"How goes it, babe? Having a good night?"

She forced a smile, trying to sound upbeat, just as she'd learned in her voice-over classes. "It's not too bad."

"What's wrong?"

She cursed under her breath. She never could hide things from Brad. "I got another letter today."

The line was silent for a moment. "Same message?"

She glanced at the computer, then back at the phone. "Yeah. Exactly the same."

"You should call the police."

It was the same suggestion he had made a month ago, when the letters started arriving on a weekly basis. With this week's sudden volley of letters, he had taken to repeating his advice nightly. Kaitlyn had shrugged it off as just some crank. "You get those in this business," she'd told him.

"Still no idea who sends these letters? Or what they are about?"

She hesitated for a second before replying. "No idea," she lied.

"You need to tell someone. If not the police, at least tell Scott."

Kaitlyn frowned at his remark. The last thing she wanted to do was tell her program director Scott Mackay about the letters. His overly protective nature would mean police involvement for certain. "I can't tell Scott. He'd place an armed guard on the studio door."

Brad laughed. "Would that be so bad?"

"There's no point. It's probably some infatuated teenager." She knew how ridiculous the words sounded even as they escaped her lips. No teenage listener would know about the Shallows.

"Do me a favor—watch yourself tonight when you go home."

CamCat Books

VISIT US ONLINE FOR
MORE BOOKS TO LIVE IN:
CAMCATBOOKS.COM

FOLLOW US

CamCatBooks   @CamCatBooks   @CamCat_Books

CPSIA information can be obtained
at www.ICGtesting.com
Printed in the USA
LVHW101911160522
718835LV00026B/123/J